The Flores Cartel
Goes to Maine
(Big Mistake)

By
Randall Probert

The Flores Cartel Goes to Maine
by Randall Probert

www.randallprobertbooks.net

email: randentr@megalink.net

Cover sketch by Sarah Lane of
Bethel Bait and Tackle Shop

Disclaimer:
This book is a work of fiction and not to be associated with any known cartel or individuals.

ISBN: 978-1542430333

Printed in the United States of America

Published by
Randall Enterprises
P.O. Box 862
Bethel, Maine 04217

Acknowledgements

I would like to thank retired game warden pilot Gary Dumond for letting me use his name as a character in this book. I would like to thank Sarah Lane for the cover sketch and Amy Henley for your help in typing this and the many revisions. I would also like to thank Laura Ashton of Woodland, Georgia, for her help formatting this book for printing.

More Books by Randall Probert

The Flores Cartel Goes to Maine
(Big Mistake)

Chapter 1

Varina Grubber gave birth to Hans Grubber on the eve of the Ides of March. Her husband Wilhelm had to support her as they walked through the blistering snowstorm and wind to the hospital. Varina was exhausted and Wilhelm had to carry her up the steps to the front doors. He was not a large man, but he was unusually strong.

It was a difficult birth for baby Hans, but he and his mother had both survived, as he would always find a way to survive in this struggling time of German history. Hans was small and fragile and his mother would coddle and protect him. Always making excuses why he was so small and weak. His father Wilhelm would say he was *schwachlick*. Puny, no good. Wilhelm was ashamed of his son.

Varina understanding that her son would never be able to do heavy manual work like his father at the shipyard, knew his only chance for survival was if Hans learned at an early age to use his mind and not a strong back. At age two Varina noticed how Hans was more mentally advanced than other children older than he. So she began to school him at home. And by the time he was three years old he could speak German, French and English fluently.

Varina's father was English and her mother was French, and she studied German in school and became very fluent with it. After college she had taken a vacation to visit Berlin's museums and the university. She had met Wilhelm one evening and they were soon married and moved to Kiel, near the shipyard where Wilhelm worked.

Varina taught French and English to the students in the local school in Kiel. But no student ever progressed as fast or spoke either language as easily as Hans. But this did little to impress his father.

"What is speaking French or English ever going to do him any good when he has to work for a living?"

Growing up, boys his own age would bully him and tease him, because he was so small. So he would walk on the sidewalks or in the park with his mother. At home he found an exciting life in books. He would lay awake in his bed long after his father had said to go to bed, reading books by the light of a single candle.

He knew more about cultures in foreign countries than his teachers. Mathematics was as easy for him as welding sheets of iron plating was for his father at the shipyard. He learned to play chess at age five and when he was eight he was Germany's chess master. Academically, there was nothing Hans couldn't do or find a solution to a problem and find a way to work around it. He was a brilliant child and Varina hoped he might become a professor at Berlin's University after he graduated from school and college.

At the beginning of the First World War when the Arch Duke Franz Ferdinand of Austria was assassinated, Wilhelm was too old to be dragged into service. Besides, he had a too favorable job welding at the Kiel shipyard to leave. But the Grubber family along with many other families were struggling to get by. Over night prices on everything sky-rocketed and then came rationing. There was no money to pay teachers, but Varina kept teaching for awhile without pay; always hoping things would get better. As did many other teachers. But the day came when Wilhelm insisted she get a job at the shipyard. "We can no longer survive without you having an income, Varina."

"What will I do at the yard, Wilhelm? I can not weld."

"You will carry supplies from the sheds to the workers. If Hans was not so puny he could work at the yard also. But I have found him a job cleaning streets and sidewalks. That job does not pay much, but what little he will earn will help."

So on the day before his seventh birthday Hans started cleaning streets.

Hans didn't mind the work. At least he was helping out his family and every day he was so tired that he would often go to sleep after supper. And with the constant exercise Hans began to grow taller and put on some weight. He was still smaller than other boys of his age, but he was changing and this alone made him happy and looking forward to work the next day.

By March of 1916 prices in Germany were still rising, but the wages were not and every family was finding it exceedingly more difficult to survive. The war—Germany was fighting on two fronts—was not going well at all and when the United States joined the Allies against Germany every German knew what the final outcome would be. Many were anticipating it and hoping for better days, not *if* Germany surrendered, but *when*.

* * *

After the armistice on November 11, 1918 people all over Germany wanted to rejoice, but they were too afraid. It would be another two years before things began to improve.

A year after the armistice Hans went to work for a local diamond cutter Karl Hermon. At first all Hans was allowed to do was clean up and menial jobs. But as Herr Hermon noticed Han's interest he started to instruct Hans how to cut and polish the diamonds. He would stay at the shop long after working hours to learn the trade. For Hans this was a fascinating job and he wanted to learn all there was to becoming an accomplished cutter and finisher.

One of Hans' duties was to collect the diamond dust daily which was sold to industries. Herr Hermon was pleased how easily Hans was learning the trade and how interested he seemed to be.

"Hans, come here."

"Yes, Herr Hermon, what is it?"

"I have come to a decision, Hans."

"Yes, Herr Hermon."

"Hans, you can no longer work here." When Karl saw the happy expression leave Hans' face he continued. "Hans, I think it is time for you to go somewhere, where you can learn more than I can teach you. There is so much more you will need to know that I do not have the time to teach to you.

"I have written to a friend in Barcelona, Spain who can teach you what you will need to know." Hans had at first a strange expression on his face. Almost as if he had suddenly been abandoned. Then slowly his expression started to change with great interest. He had yet to say anything. He waited for Kerr Hermon to finish talking.

"Just this morning I received my answer from Antonio Luis. Because of my recommendation he will expect you at his place of business Monday June 8th. That will give you three weeks," and Karl gave the letter with the address to Hans.

"I do not know what to say, Herr Hermon. I am so happy that you thought enough of me to do this for me. And I am already excited about going."

That evening when Hans told his parents about going to Barcelona to study diamond cutting his father only grunted. His mother was so happy she began to cry.

"What's the problem with continuing to work for Herr Hermon? Why do you have to go to Barcelona?"

"Because, Father, Herr Hermon said he has taught me just about all he can. He says there is much more to the industry than simply be able to cut and polish diamonds."

"How long will you be gone, Hans?" his mother asked.

"It is a study and work program for two years. I will be working for the Luis Company when I am not studying. Then after the course is completed I must work for another three years for the Luis Company before I am certified and able to go out on my own. This is a great opportunity," Hans said.

* * *

Hans asked his father to borrow enough money to buy clothes, toilet articles and a suitcase and Wilhelm said, "No! I don't have that kind of money."

"Father—for twelve years I have been working to help you support this family and I have never asked you for much. This is a great opportunity for me and you cannot expect me to go in these clothes."

"No," his father said again and slammed the door as he left the house.

"I have enough money, Hans, to buy you a suitcase, but that is all. I am sorry," Varina said.

Hans had no choice but to ask Karl Hermon if he could borrow enough money to purchase the things he would need. "I do not enjoy asking this of you, Herr Herman, but I have no recourse. My mother only has enough money to buy me a suitcase."

"You have worked well here for me, Hans. I would be happy to give you what you need. The diamond business has improved since the end of the war and I can afford it. Let's say this is a bonus."

"Thank you, Herr Hermon. I appreciate all you have done for me."

The next day Hans had to obtain a passport. And he was surprised how easily he was able to get one. Afterwards he purchased what he would need, including note paper and pens.

The day came when he had to say goodbye to Karl Hermon and then his mother walked with him to the train station. "I am so happy for you, Hans. You have a chance to leave this life behind and create one for yourself. Write when you are settled."

* * *

It was an exciting trip by train from Kiel, Germany to Barcelona, Spain. There was still much war-torn damage in both Germany and France. There were places when the train had to stop and wait for the track crews to replace some of the damaged rails.

Once the train was in France, Hans decided to leave his German speech behind and he shifted to French, that his mother had taught him. He figured there would be fewer glaring stares toward him.

Hans saw more war-torn damage in northern France and began wondering how these people could put their lives back together. There was so much damage that still needed repairing.

It was a slow trip across France. The train had to stop, it seemed, at every village to let passengers get off and others to board. He wasn't sure if the French passengers knew he was from Germany or not, but they did not seem all that friendly. Perhaps they had a good reason, after all it was his country that invaded theirs.

Hans found the Spanish people more friendly and it became obvious they didn't care if he was from Germany or not.

The train arrived in Barcelona, Spain one morning just as the sun was coming up. Not wanting to speak German, Hans tried asking for directions to the Luis Company in French; without much success. So he tried English and was surprised how many people could speak some English.

The company was on the north end of the city on Main Street. Not wanting to use his money, he decided to walk. He could use the exercise after that long train ride.

He found the address without any difficulty. There was a nice store in front facing the sidewalk and Main Street, with a huge glass window showcase, that was displaying many expensive looking diamonds and settings. There was someone inside already and when he noticed Hans looking through the window he motioned for him to come in.

The man—Hans guessed was Antonio Luis—spoke first

in Spanish and when he realized Hans did not understand, he tried in English. "Good morning, I am Antonio Luis and it would be my guess you are Hans Grubber."

Hans replied in perfect English, "Yes Sir, I am Hans Grubber."

"Come in, come in. You are two days early, but that is not a problem. I have not yet had my breakfast, would you care to join me?"

"Yes Sir. I am hungry."

"Good, follow me. After we eat and before I start the day I will show you around."

Antonio and his wife had a beautiful apartment above the store. There was another smaller apartment to one side. "This is where you and three others will live as long as you are here. You can leave your suitcase here."

A dark haired woman, maybe in her mid-fifties, met them in the kitchen. Antonio spoke to his wife first in Spanish and then in English for Hans' benefit.

"Hans this is my wife, Señora Ilucia Luis. Ilucia, this is Hans Grubber from Kiel, Germany."

"It is my pleasure, Mrs. Luis," Hans said.

"When you address my wife you are never to address her by her first name Ilucia. It must be Señora Ilucia, Señora Luis or Mrs. Luis."

"Yes Sir, I understand."

"Good, let's eat breakfast. I'm hungry," Antonio said.
While they ate Antonio wanted Hans to tell him all about himself. This way he could develop a fuller understanding of the young man.

"According to Herr Hermon he has already instructed you much of the diamond cutting industry. He explained in his letter that after the raw diamond has been cut you already know how to polish and finish the stones. That you have done some facet cutting. If you are as good as Herr Hermon says you are, it may not take the two years to fully teach you the business."

After breakfast Luis put Hans to work in the shop area behind the show room. "I have some stones that I have already cut facets in them; they will all need to be polished."

Hans was eager to show Mr. Luis what he could do. He worked until 8 o'clock that evening, until he had finished. Luis inspected each stone and was pleased with Hans' work.

"Mr. Luis, do you suppose Señora Ilucia could teach me to speak Spanish?"

"She has worked with some of the students in the past so, yes, I think she would be happy to do so."

While Hans was busy the next day helping Luis in the shop the other three students arrived: David Pablio from Barcelona, Aaron Gervias from Le Harve, France and Felipe Bruno from Madrid, Sprain, all three the same age as Hans.

"Hans you will have to work alone for a while, while I tend to these new students."

Hans worked late into the evening again. He was enjoying the trust that Luis was showing in him.

The next morning after breakfast Luis had the four apprentice students gather in the classroom section of the shop.

"In two years I will teach you how to cut, facet and polish diamonds. I will teach you how to identify a raw diamond from a piece of glass or clear quartz. I will teach you to recognize blemishes and defects within some diamonds. I will teach the difference in value of raw diamonds to a finished polished stone and one in a beautiful gold setting.

"You each will receive a weekly allowance, then as you begin to produce some salable work you'll receive more in the form of wages. Four hours each morning will be class room studies, and four hours of work in the afternoon. Until you start to produce salable work, like polishing diamonds and settings, you'll do menial work around the shop and run errands.

"Hans Grubber has a start on the three of you. He has been polishing and finishing diamonds and settings before coming here. So Hans, you'll receive a bit more each week than the allowance. Any questions?"

* * *

Each evening after Hans finished work for the day he would study all about the diamond cutting industry. How and where to purchase quality raw stones and what to look for in real quality diamonds. He wanted to learn all about the diamond industry and not just how to cut facets and polish the stones. He wanted to become an expert.

Each week he was producing more finished stones and being paid more for his diligence. While the other students were still only receiving their allowances.

Working for Herr Hermon in Kiel, Hans had never realized how much there was to learn and understand about the diamond business. He found his studies challenging and he applied himself totally to his new studies and his job of polishing the cut stones. The other three lacked his enthusiasm and were slower to learn. For them it was only a job. But for Hans it was another challenge he knew he would be able to master.

Aaron Gervais from Le Harve was always trying to cause problems for Hans and at night when Antonio was not around Aaron would bully Hans. At first Hans thought his bullying was because even as a young man Hans was still of small statue. But as the taunting continued Hans began to understand it was because he was from Germany. An enemy of the French during the war. And also because he was more knowledgeable about the diamond industry and applied himself.

After a month of Señora Luis helping him to speak Spanish, Hans would use his new ability and speak in Spanish with Luis. This seemed to increase Aaron's bullying against him.

Hans was making enough extra money now and he bought some new clothes and a bouquet of flowers for Señora Ilucia Luis. "For you, Señora Ilucia, for teaching me to speak the language."

"You are progressing well, Herr Grubber. Soon you will talk like one of us, without an accent."

There were days when Antonio was busy and he would ask Hans to help the other students learn to polish. Only Aaron resented this.

One afternoon while Hans was busy polishing and Aaron was cleaning, he noticed Aaron very sheepishly put his hand in his pants pocket. When Aaron turned and noticed Hans was looking at him, he abruptly turned away. Hans thought this was strange, but he understood. Aaron's behavior could be only his resentment towards him. So he forgot about it.

Whenever Hans had some free time which was usually only on Sundays, he would walk about the city. He was able now to converse with people he met on his walks and he decided to create a Spanish name for himself. Because of the war and the fact he was German with a so obvious German name, he often felt embarrassed and ashamed.

He decided on Juan Esteban and whenever he met anyone on one of his walks he was now Juan Esteban, and the more he used his new name the more he liked it.

After six months of study Hans had progressed so much more than the other three students. Partly because of working with Karl Hermon. "Hans, today I will instruct you how to cut raw diamonds." The others were busy polishing.

"Making facets on the stones is very slow and delicate work. With nice even facets you can make an ugly diamond sparkle."

"More often a karat diamond can be more valuable if you can cut it appropriately into four quarter-karat stones with beautiful facets.

"Then of course if you come across a large stone with no imperfections you can, depending on your skill of facets, make that one stone many times more valuable than several smaller stones. You see, Hans, it all depends on your eye, how you see the raw stone and can imagine what you can do with it. It's a real art, and one that takes time to create."

"I hope I am as good as you, Señor Luis," Hans said.

"It is my honest opinion, Hans, that some day you will be better than me."

One day Antonio was sick so Hans filled in for him. Teaching polishing to the others and helping them at the wheel. He also noticed Aaron putting something in his pocket and then looking away as if nothing had happened.

Hans decided to keep a closer watch on Aaron. He may be trying to steal some diamonds or chips from the grinding wheel. Which a few grams of diamond dust and chips would be worth money to a steel manufacturing company.

Antonio was back in the shop the next day and Hans decided to wait and see if Aaron would steal anything more before telling Antonio.

A week later Hans saw Aaron putting something into his pocket and then look around to see if anyone had seen him. That night as Hans was helping Antonio close up the shop for the day he said, "Señor Luis."

"Yes, Hans, what is it?"

"Señor Luis, I think Aaron is stealing diamonds, chips, or dust. I have seen him now on four separate occasions while working at the polishing wheel or cleaning up at the grinding wheel, put something into his pocket. Once he noticed me looking at him and he seemed to be very uncomfortable."

"Do you know where he is keeping what he is taking?"

"No, but it has to be in our room somewhere."

"Tomorrow morning while he is eating breakfast I will search through his belongings."

Antonio was absent from the breakfast table the next morning. Hans knew where he was and he kept glancing at Aaron and wondering how much he had actually taken.

Antonio came walking into the kitchen with something in his hand while everyone was still eating. "Aaron Gervais, you are through here. Get your belongings and get out," and he held out the little cloth pouch of diamond dust and chips and a few tiny diamonds.

Hans stood up away from the table and looked at Aaron. Aaron stood up glaring at Hans, "You are a no good snitch." As he walked by Hans he swung at Hans' head with his fist. And much to even Hans' surprise he dodged the blow and stuck out his foot and tripped Aaron and he fell on his face.

"You are a thief and a bully, Aaron. I won't be sorry to see you leave."

Antonio followed Aaron up stairs while he gathered together his few belongings and then followed him outside to the street and stood there watching Aaron as he walked out of sight.

Once back in the shop he said to all three of the students, "I will not tolerate any dishonesty. Aaron had taken the equivalent value of a small diamond."

Now that Aaron was no longer there the mood around the shop and in their bedroom had improved. Before, everyone was always walking around trying not to upset Aaron. Antonio and Ilucia also noticed the improvement.

* * *

By the end of the first year Felipe Bruno and David Pablio were now cutting fine facets on the diamonds and Hans was cutting the raw stones. "All you need now, Hans, is more experience cutting the raw stones and I'll give you a free hand in doing that. You need to know more about the business end of the industry and soon I will take you with me to an auction in Antwerp, Belgium."

Because Hans was doing more work now than studying, Antonio was paying him much more than either David or Felipe. Almost as much as a certified diamond cutter. And Hans began sending money to Herr Hermon to repay his generosity for lending him the money to come to Barcelona. He was also sending some each month to his mother; the rest he was saving.

During the year while in Barcelona studying under the guidance of Señor Antonio Luis, France had been able to repair most of the damaged rail lines since the end of the war and when Antonio and Hans boarded the train for Antwerp, Belgium they both were surprised at the speed they were travelling and the absence of the destroyed rails.

Hans had never been beyond the borders of Germany until Barcelona and was as interested in seeing everything along the rails as the city of Antwerp itself. A whole new and exciting life had opened for him since leaving Kiel. He had become more self-assured and confident in just about everything he did. Even though he was not yet a certified diamond cutter, he was a professional and he knew now that he would be able to make his world wherever he would go.

Antonio saw this change with Hans and was very pleased. He had never had a student who was so eager to learn. Failure was just not possible for young Hans Grubber.

On the morning of the auction they walked around the many tables; when they came to one at the very end, Antonio said, "What do you think of these, Hans? You mentally grade them and what you could get for finished stones."

Hans examined each diamond with his loupe. He was not as fast as perhaps Antonio might have been." Most of the small stones are of nice quality. Some we would not have to cut, only grind the facets and polish them. One of the medium sized stones has a definite flaw, but I think we could cut it making three smaller stones. The larger stones—well only one is flawless, one perfect oval shaped stone has a milky defect, but still, if we cut it right, we should be able to make three very beautiful finished diamonds. This lot is probably the lowest grade of any lot here, but I think we should bid on it. Because I believe there is money to be made here."

"That was very well done, Hans. And you are correct. These probably have the lowest grade of any and I think we could make a lot of money if we cut them correctly."

This was the only lot Antonio wanted to bid on and he was able to purchase the lot at a much lower price than he had budgeted for and was prepared to spend. "This has been a good day, Hans. I am very pleased with the lot we purchased."

"This has been an interesting trip, Antonio. I thank you for inviting me along."

"You're welcome. But this was only part of your education. I do not take every student to an auction. Only those who show some promise. And you, Hans Grubber, have excelled more than any student I have ever had."

"Thank you, Antonio. I have enjoyed this trip and I have learned much about buying raw diamonds. And I find this profession very interesting."

"I am happy to hear that, Hans."

* * *

Even though during the second year Hans was actually working full time now cutting and finishing diamonds, he was still learning a great deal about the business.

One day shortly after their return from the auction at Antwerp Hans said, "Antonio, do you trust me? Do you trust me as a cutter of diamonds?"

"Why yes, Hans, why do you ask?"

"Do you trust me enough to let me work with the large oval diamond? The one with the cloudy flaw?"

"Yes of course. But why are you asking?"

"I have an idea, Antonio, about that large oval stone and if I'm correct, I can make you much more money for it than you first anticipated."

"Okay."

"And I don't want you watching over my shoulder Antonio. I want to surprise you."

"Okay," and Antonio handed Hans the large oval stone.

Hans sat at his work desk and examined the diamond

20

with his loupe for more than an hour. Looking for the best way to split the stone in half along its long axis. The cloudy flaw didn't go all the way through the stone and he decided to split it so the entire flaw would be in one piece. He would have to cleave it precisely with the right amount of force.

Antonio wanted to watch. But he had given his word to Hans. After all, it was a large stone.

Hans positioned the stone on the plate exactly, and without a second thought he cleaved it. When the stone broke perfectly as Hans hoped it would, he jumped up and hollered, "Yes!" Everyone stopped to look at him, even Antonio.

"Sorry about that," Hans said.

The larger piece had the entire flaw and the other piece was now a high grade raw diamond.

Hans was a week working on the piece with the flaw. He was very precise about the placing of the facets. Some were large while others were small. The flat back side he polished off flat and smooth.

When he was finished the cloudy flaw was in the middle of the stone surrounded with facets, so the flaw looked like an eye. Then he secured a thin band of gold around the outer edge of the piece. It was beautiful. This piece was now finished.

The other piece he made facets over the entire rounded surface and again polished the flat back side and secured a thin gold band around it like he had done on the first piece. He was ten days finishing both stones, but he figured the time had been well spent.

He walked over to Antonio and held out his hand and gave the two stones to Antonio. Antonio was speechless for a long time examining both pieces. "I am really impressed, Hans. They both are so beautiful. You were correct, these two will be worth more than the entire lot we purchased."

David and Felipe looked at them and agreed with Antonio. And there was no jealousy in their voices. Actually they both were quite impressed with Hans' ability.

Antonio went upstairs to show his wife. She was more impressed than anyone.

Hans had made up his mind whether to return to Germany or not after the three years. He still had to work for Antonio Luis once he was certified. He liked Spain and he liked the Spanish people. But he decided if he was going to call this home he would have to change his name. He had been thinking for a long time now about this and he would rather have his new name on his certificate.

"Antonio, may I speak with you for a moment?"

"Surely, what is it Hans?"

"I am going to change my name to Juan Esteban. I want to be able to fit in with society here and with a German name I have found that very difficult."

"I think that is a good idea. You speak the language like a natural born Spaniard. I'll see your certificate has your proper name. Do you wish we start now—calling you Juan Esteban?"

"Yes."

Antonio and his wife Ilucia, David and Felipe had no problem with Hans changing his name to Juan Esteban. In fact they all thought the new name was more appropriate.

Soon after Hans, now Juan, went looking for an apartment and he found a nice one-bedroom apartment on the second floor with a balcony overlooking a park. It came sparsely furnished. He would have to have a few things. Next he went to the postal service and applied for an address.

He would not move in until after the certification test. In the meantime he thoroughly cleaned it and bought furnishings that he liked. At the edge of the city he found a used furniture store. They also sold old antique furniture.

As he was throwing an armload of trash in the bin out back he found a passport book laying on top of the trash in the bin. He looked at it and put it in his pocket. Back upstairs in his own apartment he looked at the name and it wasn't anyone he knew and no one in this complex. He put that away in a drawer and walked over to the store and purchased paper similar to that in the passport. He bought pens and a straight edge. He found a place to have his photo taken.

He was spending as much time now as he could in his new apartment and he'd work long into the morning hours painstakingly reproducing a passport in his name that looked authentic. It probably would have been easier to apply for one once he had a certificate in his new name. But there was something in the back recess of his mind that he didn't yet want to break all ties with Germany. He never said a word to anyone about him forging himself a passport. When he had finished it was difficult to tell that it had been forged. Even the signatures looked authentic.

* * *

The final day finally arrived, "Today, gentlemen, I will test you. You make more than two mistakes—well, I won't certify you. But I have watched all three of you for two years now and I do not think you'll have any trouble."

The first part of the testing was a written test. The questions really made you think before answering. There was a section on nomenclature. The last phase of the day long test was accurately identifying real raw diamonds mixed in with exceptionally authentic looking fakes.

Even Juan was taking his time. There were two pieces that he set aside to look at after he was sure about the others. He finally came back to the last two stones and looked and looked. His loupe was making grooves around his eye, he was straining so hard.

"This one is real, although of not very high quality and this one is a clever piece of clear quartz."

Antonio crossed his arms and smiled and nodded his head yes. David and Felipe both were wrong on that one. Although that was their only mistake.

"Congratulations, you all three have passed. I'll finish and date your certificates."

That evening Señora Luis had a celebration supper for them, of roast chicken and stuffing. Later the three went out together, which they had seldom done, to celebrate. They were not going separate ways yet. They each had a three year obligation to Antonio. For now David and Felipe would share an apartment.

Juan had already paid all the money back to Herr Hermon and when his parents had learned that he would not be coming back to Germany and had chosen a Spanish name his father had refused the money he sent and returned it with a short note, *I do not know anyone by the name of Juan Esteban.*

Because Juan had perfected his abilities sooner than either David or Felipe, Juan was left in charge of the shop whenever Antonio had to be away. And David and Felipe didn't seem to mind. They knew Juan's skills were far beyond their own.

* * *

With three more diamond cutters working full time now Antonio closed the shop doors at 6 o'clock in the evening. Juan had always stayed late to work and now he had more time of his own than he knew what to do with it. Much of that time he would spend in the park or walking about the city. On Sundays he would walk or occasionally take a bus to the beach area just up the shore from Barcelona.

He had never learned to swim so he would roll his pant legs up and wade in the surf. He would eat a seafood lunch and then lay down in some shade listening to the gentle sound of the surf breaking on the sandy shore. He was always by himself and he didn't find this loneliness strange at all; even though he would watch couples enjoying each other or families on Sunday afternoon outings.

His life had always been too busy for him to form any

friendships. He had always found comfort in his work. And all this free time now for him was boring. He needed something to keep his mind busy.

He wasn't interested about having a permanent relationship with a woman. There was that restlessness that kept him from a quiet and peaceful life. Sometimes he would go out and find a prostitute to spend the night. But never the same one. He didn't want any attachments.

What he found most troubling, he had no idea why there was this restlessness inside of him. Often times his mind was like a piece of automated machinery that he had no control of. So he whiled away his free time with walks around the city, the parks and beach and an occasional prostitute.

He had become very friendly with many business owners. And he could list each of them mentally by name, address and what business they were engaged in. He had a fabulous mind for details and he remembered pretty much everything he saw and heard. Just not a photographic mind, but close.

* * *

At the end of their three year agreement to work for Antonio Luis, David Pablio and Felipe Bruno decided to leave. Pablio wanted his own business and Bruno wanted to go to Sevilla. He had met a young woman from there that had stolen his heart.

Juan would miss Felipe and David when they left.

"And what about you, Juan?" Antonio asked. "What will you do?"

"I would like to stay, Antonio," he replied.

"I was hoping you would, Juan. I am not going to teach diamond cutting to any more students, I have decided you and I, Juan, will run the business and Ilucia will keep the accounting. I am getting too old to teach young people anymore. I will also increase your wages with a year's end bonus.

"And I think with you here permanently, someone I can depend on, maybe my wife and I can take a little vacation. We have never had one. Not even a honeymoon."

After David and Felipe left, Antonio and Ilucia Luis took that honeymoon/vacation trip to Rome, Italy for two weeks.

"I trust you will have no problems, Juan, that you cannot solve while we are gone," Antonio said.

"Have a good trip, Antonio, and don't worry about the shop," Juan assured him.

Juan had decided to live in the Luis' apartment while they were away so he would be close to the business. Each evening after eating his supper, he would clean the shop and prepare things for the next day. There were cash customers and they found Juan very pleasant to deal with. He was making quite a name and reputation for himself in Barcelona. He and his ability for cutting and finishing diamonds was growing. As were the ideas he had for expensive settings. These were bringing in more money than Antonio would ever have imagined.

Antonio was proud of Juan's trustworthiness, his abilities as a diamond cutter, as well as a facet and setting designer. The shop's profits at the end of that year were the best since Antonio Luis had first started his business and as he promised he gave Juan a bonus of one third of his yearly wages. Juan was speechless. He had never imagined anything like this.

* * *

The roaring twenties were bringing prosperity to much of Europe as well as in the United States. Except for Germany. They were reeling with dismay, unemployment and suffering from war reparations to the allies.

Occasionally Juan would buy a newspaper and look for articles about his homeland. Although he had broken all ties with Germany, he still had strong concerns about the people's welfare.

These prosperous good times were about to come to an end when the London stock market crashed on September 20, 1929. All of Europe felt the ripple effect and everyone was worried. Then when the New York market crashed on October 24, 1929, Europe once again felt the disrupting ripple. Only this time it was more serious.

Antonio was only opening his shop doors for three days a week. Those with money were buying diamonds; thinking their value would be safer than currency or gold. But the market was soft. Juan was doing all the cutting and finishing while Antonio looked for other markets and better buys for raw stones.

Juan's wages were cut, but because he had never wasted his money he could get by with only working three days a week. By the end of 1930 Antonio Luis was still in business, but his customers were mostly at the large auctions. He still had a few industries that bought his grindings and dust, but the walk-ins were no longer coming. Juan had to stop making the expensive pendants and settings. There was no market for the expensive settings. Some investors were looking for low priced deals and Antonio had to reduce some of his earlier prices.

"At least, Juan, we are staying in business," Antonio said one morning as he was opening the shop.

Every day there were articles in the paper about a new movement in Germany called the National Socialist German Worker's Party, and someone named Adolf Hitler was promising sweeping changes for the country.

Because of the depression that was being felt across the world and the reparations Germany was having to pay the allies for the war, this was an opportune time for someone who was promising reforms and sweeping changes within the Reichstag, promising to end unemployment and return prosperity to business and the citizens.

It was a long article and Juan read every word. *This is just what Germany has needed since the war. Someone who isn't afraid to stand up and voice the opinion of millions of citizens.*

27

Juan took that day's newspaper with him to the shop the next day and asked Antonio, "Antonio, have you been reading any of the articles about what's happening in Germany?"

"Some, but not all of them."

"Did you read yesterday's paper?"

"No, I do not get the newspaper every day now."

"Here, you can have mine. This Hitler sounds like he may have some answers for bringing the economy back to all of Europe," Juan said as he gave the paper to Antonio.

"I'll read it tonight after we close up. Something needs to happen to bring the economy back or we all will starve," Antonio said.

When Juan wasn't working he would walk around the city. There were so many people out of work and little money to buy food. He was thankful for the three days a week when he did work.

As he strolled through the park he kept thinking what this Hitler was promising to do. He sat down on a park bench watching squirrels gathering acorns for the winter, and thinking about what he had read in the paper about this Hitler fellow and the National Socialist German Worker's Party and wondering if he could really do all he was saying he could do. *If he could, the whole world would benefit from it,* he was thinking.

The next day back in the shop Antonio said, "I read that article with great interest. I have to agree with you, Juan, this Hitler fellow sounds impressive. But I don't know if he can do everything he is promising. It all seems a bit too much idealistic. It would be good to see people back at work and smiles on their faces instead of sadness. I've noticed also how the suicides are on the rise. That isn't good.

"I have to agree with you, Juan, the entire world needs someone like this Hitler, if he is true to his word."

In the days that the shop was closed Juan would buy a newspaper and then have coffee with Antonio as they discussed the current articles. Spain and Europe's economy was so bad by now, "Juan, I don't know how much longer we can stay open. I was hoping that as word of Hitler's ideas would spread and inspire industries and businesses, people would go back to work. If this Hitler can do what he says he will do, then I wish he would start fulfilling his promises and soon."

* * *

1931 wasn't proving to be any better than the last two years. The soup kitchens and lines for the hungry were getting longer with less sustenance in the soup. "Something has to change soon, Juan. I'm afraid for all of Spain. We cannot continue for much longer like this."

It seemed to Juan that he and Antonio were the only ones who were following the newspaper articles about this Hitler guy and his new ideas. No one else was talking about Hitler's promises to turn the economy around.

On the days Juan wasn't working for Antonio he tried to pick up an odd job. Some days he did, and more days that he couldn't find an odd job. He joined the soup kitchen lines to listen to what others were saying. Everyone seemed to be blaming London's and New York's stock exchanges for putting the entire world into a turmoil. And to Juan's thinking, the only person trying to do something to help his country was Hitler.

* * *

The economy had started to improve some, but by the spring of 1932 the soup lines were even longer with less food to feed the hungry. There were men on the streets and in the park every day. People were at the extent of their patience. They were angry and wanted to work. Gangs formed trying to rob passers-by. It was not safe now to be out on the streets or the park after dark. The police tried to quiet the unrest but things had simply gotten too rough for most people.

One day as Antonio and Juan were having their morning coffee, Juan said, "Antonio,"—a long pause before he continued. "Antonio, I think it is time for me to leave. Business is so slow here now and the shop can no longer support us both." He wanted to see what Antonio would say.

"I have been thinking about that also, Juan. I just couldn't bring myself to say anything. You have always been such a trusted worker and friend.

"What will you do Juan? Where will you go?"

"I have thought a lot about that. I read the newspaper every day what it has to say about this new idea and movement in Germany. If this guy is for real and doesn't back away from his promises I think he can turn the economy around in Germany, Europe and maybe across the globe. I have been thinking I would like to be a part of that."

"I cannot blame you Juan. In fact if I was younger I'd go with you. You have been a good friend, Juan Esteban."

Chapter 2

All that Juan was taking with him was a valise with his papers and his clothes. The rest of his possessions he gave to Antonio.

He used his Juan Esteban passport to travel to Germany and then he filed that away in the valise with the rest of his papers. He had been able to save a lot of money while in Barcelona and he knew he would be alright for a while. Once he crossed the border into Germany he boarded a train for Berlin.

After resting after the long trip from Barcelona, now once again Hans Grubber, he went to the Ministry of Defense. He had been thinking for a long time how he could best serve and decided on the Intelligence Organization (Abwehr). And by chance he met Admiral Canaris, the head of Abwehr.

Canaris noticed a young man dressed in civilian clothes and asked, "Excuse me, but civilians are not usually allowed on this floor. Are you lost? Might I help you?"

"Yes Sir, I suppose you can. My name is Hans Grubber and I would like to join the intelligence organization. Who would I have to see, Sir?"

Canaris began to laugh. "I'm sorry, I did not mean to demean you. I am the head of this organization. I am Admiral Wilhelm Canaris. Follow me please. I am going to my office. We will talk there."

Hans followed behind him and not abreast of the Admiral. He knew that much about the military. There was a Captain and a Major in his office and he asked them, "Would you gentlemen excuse us. I have an appointment with this man," and he nodded his head towards Hans.

"Sit down, Hans Grubber, and tell me why you want to join the Abwebr."

"For the last twelve years I have been living and working in Barcelona, Spain. I went there to study diamond cutting and ended up learning the industry. I learned to speak Spanish fluently the first year I was there. I also speak English and French fluently. I would read newspapers every day to hear what Herr Hitler had to say. I believe he can save this country and I would like to help and I think I could serve best in this organization. I enjoy learning and I pretty much remember what I see, read and hear.

"While working and classes, I changed my name and made or forged my Spanish passport."

"Do you have that passport with you now?"

"Yes Sir," and Hans handed it to the Admiral.

Canaris looked it over and over, page by page then he pushed a button on his desk and an aid stepped into the room. "Yes, Herr Admiral."

"Sergeant, find someone from the document level and ask him to come here."

"Yes, Herr Admiral."

While they waited Canaris poured a cup of coffee for Hans and then one for himself. Before Hans could finish his coffee a knock came at the door. "Come in," Canaris said.

"Herr Admiral, you wanted to see me?"

"Yes, Lieutenant, here," and he handed the forged passport to the Lt.

The Lt. looked it over and over and as did Canaris, page by page. "Yes, a Spanish passport for one Juan Esteban. There are a few entries."

"Do you notice anything strange?" Lieutenant.

"No, Herr Admiral, I do not."

"Let me introduce you to Hans Grubber. He made this

passport himself several years ago and has been using it ever since. He even crossed Germany's border using it."

"You made this passport?" The lieutenant asked.

"Yes Sir."

"Remarkable."

"That's all, Lieutenant."

"Yes, Herr Admiral."

"You have me puzzled, Mr. Grubber. As talented as you seem to be, you may be a cover operative able to speak fluent German."

"I grew up in Kiel and my father worked in the shipyard and my mother a teacher," Hans said.

"Why did you come here to the Ministry of Defense? And not simply enlist as thousands of young men are doing?"

"I believed I would be wasting my time in the rank and file of the Reich. I feel I could better serve in intelligence, so I decided to come to the Ministry, the head of Abwehr, Sir."

"I like your tenacity and what I have seen of you so far I think you would make a lousy soldier. But I tell you what I'll do, I'll give you some books to look over and when you think you're ready to talk with me again, come back, stop at the front desk on the first level this time and ask for me and give the aid your name."

"Thank you for talking with me, Herr Admiral."

After Hans left his office, Canaris sat back thinking about his meeting with Hans Grubber. A young man who knows what he wants and not afraid to go after it. He could tell Hans was not any ordinary person looking simply for a position within the ranks of Abwehr, but someone who would honestly believe in what he was doing.

That morning on his way to the Ministry of Defense he had walked by a public library and now decided that would be an ideal place to review the two books Herr Admiral had given him.

The first book was about military rank and file procedures.

The different ministries and departments within those ministries and who was the head of each ministry and department. The use of proper chain of command and Hans figured this would be very important to know, not just remember. There was a difference.

It had taken the rest of that day to finish the first book. And that evening in his room he reviewed some key points.

After eating breakfast the next morning he returned to the library to study the second book. This one pertained to operations of the Intelligence Ministry (Abwehr) and the covert operations within each department. And how these operations were to be performed and handled. Some of the operations were quite involved. Between the danger the agent would be in and the information to gather. He supposed this is why the ministry was called Intelligence. One would have to have a high degree of intelligence to complete these assignments.

By the time the library closed for the day Hans figured he had a good overview of Abwehr. He would go see Herr Admiral Canaris in the morning.

After eating supper he spent some time walking about the city. Sitting in the library for two days had cramped his legs and he needed to walk off some restlessness. There was something very obvious as he walked along the streets of Berlin. The people here did not seem to be as oppressed about the economy or their future as the Spaniards were. And he couldn't help but think that this new party, the National Socialist German Worker's Party and Hitler had given these people some hope.

Later back in his room he reviewed many key points in the second book about the Ministry of Defense and its information gathering procedures. He had a problem with some of that last procedural part.

He stayed up late studying. Something he enjoyed. The next morning after breakfast he walked over to the Ministry of Defense and stopped at the front desk this time. "Can I help you?"

"Yes, I am here to see Herr Admiral Canaris."

"Your name?"

"Hans Grubber."

"I have written instructions to send you up as soon as you arrive. Second floor."

"Thank you."

Hans met the Admiral in the corridor. "You can go right into my office Hans. I'll only be a minute."

"Thank you, Herr Admiral."

According to military protocol Hans knew a subordinate should remain standing until told to sit down. So he stood. Ten minutes later Canaris reentered his office and closed the door. "Be seated, Hans."

Hans sat in a straight back chair and not one of the more comfortable chairs. "Have you finished reading both of these books so soon, Hans?"

"Yes Sir," and he put them on the Admiral's desk. "I didn't read them, Herr Admiral, I studied them."

In that one statement Canaris knew Hans was a rare individual.

Canaris questioned Hans for hours about proper military protocol and how much he understood about the function of Abwehr.

At noon Canaris asked, "Are you hungry?"

"Yes Sir, I am."

"Good, let's continue this after we have had something to eat."

In the mess hall they were joined by Major Hammell and Captain Jelman.

"Major Hammell, Captain Jelman let me introduce you to Hans Grubber." They all shook hands and Canaris continued. "I am thinking about Herr Grubber joining Abwehr."

After they had finished eating Canaris said, "You may return to my office, I'll only be a few minutes."

"Yes, Herr Admiral."

"Gentlemen, I think we have found our golden nugget for getting information from neighboring countries."

Back in his office Canaris said, "It is extremely unusual for anyone to join Abwehr that has not come through military ranks. But exceptions are made and I am the one who determines those exceptions.

"Your knowledge of our military chain of command and our operational procedures and protocol is no less than one would expect from a graduate of the academy. I cannot afford to let someone of your caliber slip through my fingers. So if you agree, I will give you the oath of allegiance and I'll bestow you with the rank of Lieutenant."

After the oath of allegiance, Canaris said, "Because of the nature of your work you will not be issued a uniform nor expected to wear one. You will carry your credentials with you at all times except when you are on assignment in foreign lands. You will start receiving Lieutenant's pay as of this day. And now you should take these papers downstairs to payroll. They will take care of you from here. I am not sure who you will be assigned to, but my guess would be Major Hammell. He is a good man."

"Thank you, Herr Admiral."

"You're dismissed."

As Lt. Grubber was leaving, Canaris sat back in his chair laughing. He had already made up his mind about Hans Grubber two days earlier when he had first spoken with him.

From payroll, after they had all of Hans' personnel information, he was directed next door to the document department. He was issued a new German passport and lieutenant's credentials with his department title and his commandant's name.

Then he was told to report to Major Hammell's office on the same floor, but at the end of the corridor.

"Come in, Lieutenant. My congratulations."

"Thank you Sir," Hans knew from his studying just how to respond and act when confronted by a superior officer.

"Relax Lieutenant."

"You come with very favorable recommendations from Admiral Canaris. He told me a little about you and how you made your own Spanish passport. Do you have that with you?"

"Yes Sir, I do."

"I'd like to see it," and Hans handed it to the Major. "Very impressive. It certainly looks authentic. Have you forged many documents?"

"No Sir, only this."

"Why? It would have been just as easy to have obtained one from customs."

"Yes Sir, but I wanted to see if I could do it."

Major Hammell laughed at that response. "You are not very big, Lieutenant. But sometimes a small dog is more ferocious than a larger dog. Have you ever been afraid of anything in your life?"

"Yes Sir. My father when I was growing up."

"And how do you feel towards him now?"

"He is my father."

Enough said. "It is late. We'll continue this at 0800 tomorrow. My aid Sergeant Wilbur will drive you to the base and show you to your quarters."

"Is it alright, Sir, if I go by my rent and pick up my belongings?"

"Certainly. Just tell the Sergeant where you need to go."

* * *

Because he was now an officer and a member of Abwehr he was held in higher esteem than he was accustomed to. He had a room to himself in a separate barracks for officers of the Abwehr.

Even though it had been a busy tiring day, after supper he went for a walk around the base, so he could acquaint himself with everything.

The next day Major Hammell discussed with Hans what

his duties would be. "You will need to purchase an appropriate wardrobe, Lieutenant. At lunch you can draw money from payroll. I have already filed a voucher for you. On the base you'll be expected to wear at least a sport coat. And you must have this emblem pinned on your left lapel. Otherwise you may be denied access to certain areas. When you are not on assignment you'll be working in this building, most of the time. And you'll be assisting Lieutenant Schwantes with accessing information. Once you are squared around—well, I am already working on assignments for you via Admiral Canaris directly."

Two weeks of training and working with Lt. Schwantes, Major Hammell one morning said to Hans, "Lieutenant Grubber when you have finished eating the Admiral wants to see you and me in his office."

"Yes, Herr Major."

In Canaris' office, "Sit down gentlemen. Major Hammell tells me, Lieutenant, that you have been doing excellent work assisting Lieutenant Schwantes."

"Thank you, Sir."

"We are going to send you on a trial run to see how well you work in the field. You have said you speak fluent French, so I want you to go to France and gather information on France's military stabilities, and their economy. You will have a month to do this and when you return, you will report to Major Hammell. Can you do this, Lieutenant?"

"Yes, Herr Admiral."

"Good. Major, take the Lieutenant down to documents. You know what he will need."

"Yes, Herr Admiral."

"Dismissed," Canaris said and opened a folder on his desk.

Down in the document section Sergeant Klidal asked, "What name will you be using while in France, Lieutenant?"

"Sean French."

"That will do. We have never had a Sean French in the

ranks before," the Sergeant said. "If you come back at 1500 hours everything will be ready for you."

From there they went to the payroll office and Hans was given fresh new French currency and more than enough, Hans figured, to last him a month.

While Hans waited for 3 o'clock he decided to work out a code by which he could make notes of what he found and be the only one who would be able to decipher what he had written. Major Hammell went back to his office.

He was absorbed in making this code, he wasn't much aware of anything else. At lunch he had a ham and cheese on rye with black coffee. He stopped chewing to think. As far as he knew most French people didn't drink much coffee. They preferred tea. So he dumped out the coffee and refilled it with tea. It was a taste he would have to get used to.

While he ate he kept thinking about this code. When he returned to his work station he started writing, substituting every third word with one coded letter. He knew it would take time to write a detailed report this way, so he would keep it short.

At 3 o'clock he was back in the documentation section. "Lieutenant, I have all the documentation you'll need. Everything is in Sean French's name and a birth date March 11, 1908. Here is your new passport, a French driver's license, ticket stubs to the cinema in Paris and a library card. There probably won't be any reason to check anything besides your passport. But these other documents will provide credence if you should need it."

"I will need your German passport. That'll be kept here for your return."

"Thank you, Sergeant."

From there Hans went to Major Hammell's office. "There is a list of things we are particularly interested with, Lieutenant. Memorize the list and then throw it away."

"What about my wardrobe, Major. I think I should have one nice casual outfit and the others should be more in the line of clean work clothes."

"Good point, Lieutenant. Go down to supply and get what you'll need. Here is a requisition form. If you have everything you need by this evening you can leave in the morning."

"Yes, Herr Major, that shouldn't be a problem."

Once in his quarters, he went over in his mind what he would need and then checked everything that was laid out on his bed. He was excited about this operation and he slept very little that night. Sleep didn't come at all that night. He had decided on an itinerary of going directly to Paris then to Toulon, France's major military base, on the Mediterranean Coast and work his way up along the Atlantic Coast and back through farmland to Germany. He hoped he could do it all in only a month. But as Canaris had said, "This is a trial run."

* * *

It was obvious that no one was supposed to know where he was going, so on the evening when he boarded the train there were no goodbyes. He was wearing his casual worker's clothes so he would not be noticed. There were many stops along the way and the train didn't reach the French border until daylight the next morning. There was a two hour delay as passports had to be checked by French customs and a different engine was coupled to the train.

There were only a few going on to France from Germany and by the manner in which they were dressed they seemed like business people. Listening to the conversations some were looking for work in the farmland in France. No one was talking about the war that ended fifteen years earlier or chastising Germany for the war and destruction.

As the train was making more and more stops in small French villages more people were boarding, heading for the cities, looking for work. No one was talking about Hitler's ideas for ending the depression and hardships. And he found this difficult to understand. Even in Spain people were well aware of this new movement.

It had been a long trying trip from Berlin to Paris and he needed a place to sleep. As he walked from the train station there were signs up everywhere advertising rooms to rent. He found one that was suitable for his needs on a quiet side street.

"How long will you be wanting the room Monsieur?"

"Two days and then day by day."

The room was anything but luxurious, but it was clean and a place to rest. After washing up he lay down for a nap. The rent included breakfast and dinner and he set his mental clock to be sure he was awake in time for dinner.

His landlords, Mr. and Mrs. Hemaur, were both in their late fifties and very nice people. There was one other tenant, a Maurice Halbert who had been there for a month.

After eating, while they sat around the table drinking tea, Mr. Hemaur said, "This Hitler guy seems to be doing a lot for the German people getting them back to work. France could use someone with his ideas and the way he gets things done."

This surprised Hans, especially after the results of the last war.

When his tea was gone he excused himself and said, "I think I'll go for a walk and stretch my legs." Mrs. Hemaur gave him a key to the side door and told him, "You be quiet when you come in."

Hans found his way to the central hub of the city and sat close to a group of young people talking about the state of affairs. They were blaming New York and London. It didn't sound as if any in the group had any fondness for the English or the Americans.

After a while he wandered off in search of another group. They were not difficult to find. When people aren't happy, it was easy to find someone willing to voice his opinion.

In the next group there was some animosity towards Germany for the destruction of the last war, but there seemed to be more animosity against the Americans for not helping sooner.

As he walked along listening to the conversations here and there it seemed as though most of what he was hearing were complaints. Everyone it seemed was complaining about something. And when people on a whole like this are only complaining, it usually meant the people were not happy.

Eventually he turned around and walked back to his room. He was up late making notes about what he had learned from listening to conversations on the train and here in Paris. People living in the country where there was still an abundance of farming, people were better off economically and happier than those in the city. He wrote everything in French to be decoded later to Spanish, so if anyone were to find his notes, they would not know what he was writing.

The next day he walked around the business section of the city and was surprised to see that many businesses were open with very few closed doors and boarded up windows. Apparently the economy was not as bad as he was led to believe listening to the groups the night before.

But one thing he did notice was that people were not spending their money on frivolous things, but towards work clothes and food. These shops seemed to be much busier.

That night he went to several bars to listen to conversations and most of them centered around the state of affairs and low wages. He had a draft beer so to fit in with the group. It seemed that the more beer that was drunk the more boisterous they became. Some even challenging Germany to start another war. 'They would show them.'

Hans joined in the conversation in one bar and asked what they all thought of this Hitler guy's promise to make life and the economy better for Germany.

"That sounds good, but how can he do it? No other country has been able to."

"If you listen to his ideas he sounds sincere," Hans said.

"Yeah, well maybe, but if no other country can turn things around I don't see how he is going to," the same man said.

Hans was quiet there. He didn't want it to seem as if he was trying to convince them.

He stayed out later that night listening to people and gathering information. It was after midnight before he returned to his room. And then he had notes to make of what he had learned that day.

* * *

After breakfast the next morning he left Paris and decided to take a bus this time, to Le Havre. A major French port at the mouth of the Seine River. The bus was crowded, full of tobacco smoke and everyone talking. There was only one mention about Hitler's new ideas to reform Germany. Much of the conversations were about low wages and complaining about England.

Le Havre was a busy petroleum port and the water was foul smelling. Even with a bad economy, the petroleum industries were able to continue production, they all needed fuel. There were two tankers offloading and both ships looked old and needing repair. Perhaps if the economy had been better then the repairs would have been made.

Hans found a restaurant near the docks and had lunch. As he ate he was thinking it might be a good place to find some dock workers after having a mug of beer.

After lunch he walked back to the center of the business district and checked out the shops. He found a jewelry shop that did a little cutting. There were no customers and he asked the man standing behind the showcase, "Hello, my name is Sean French. Business seems to be slow."

"Some days are better than others. Is there something I can do for you?"

"No, not really. I just wanted to talk. I am a diamond cutter. An out of work cutter, that is. I was working in the south of Spain. When the business was only open two days a week, I was asked to leave."

"The times are hard and only the wealthy are buying jewelry these days. I'm selling just enough to stay open and provide food for my family. We lost our house and now live in the upstairs apartment. I cannot complain too much. There are so many who do not have what I have ," the shopkeeper said.

"While I was in Spain I'd read the newspaper every day. The articles about this guy Hitler and his ideas of ending the oppression for Germany. What do you think about that?"

"It sounds good. Maybe a little too good. I think politicians will say anything to get elected. If his ideas work for Germany maybe France will adopt some of them."

"Well, I have taken up much of your time. Thank you for talking with me. Have a good day," and Hans went back outside.

He found a park and a bench to sit on. He had intended to stay in Le Havre another day, but it was easy to understand the state of affairs here. Even though the docks were busy, people in general were not happy. It seemed everyone was aware of Hitler's new ideas and no one believed he could improve their economy or well being.

He found a shady spot and laid down on the grass for a nap. When he awoke an hour later he went for another walk to stretch his muscles. He figured to be back at the restaurant lounge about the time the dock workers would be arriving. He'd eat supper and listen to their conversations.

Clouds had blown and it was looking like rain so he hailed a taxi, to take him to the Waterfront Restaurant Lounge. He ordered a meal and wine and sat in the corner where he could watch everyone.

A few men came in before he had finished eating. They looked like a rough bunch. So far their conversation was centered around their work. Apparently there were some hard feelings about another crew that these men were complaining about.

After a while more men came in, and seemed to only have a few beers, and no food. When everyone had had a bit to drink it seemed to have loosened their tongues. Now they were complaining loudly about their employers at the docks. At one point Hans was even asked for his opinion when things would get better, "I've been away for a while in Spain but, while I was there the newspapers were all printing articles about this Hitler guy and his ideas for improving things."

"Yeah, we have all heard about what he is promising to do for Germany. But in my opinion he will be only another loud spoken politician without a backbone," one of them said.

Then another added, "If these new ideas work for Germany then maybe we should try them here in France."

Conversations like this went on for most of the evening until the workers had to leave. Hans had switched from drinking wine to Budweiser. It was a much lighter beer than German beer and he was developing a taste for it.

* * *

Le Havre was a busy port, but if not for the petroleum industry then it would probably be another fishing community. He decided to move on to Cherbourg. He couldn't see any advantage to be learned by staying any longer. Besides he was tired of the smell of oil and the stink that permeated the docks.

He would go next to Cherbourg. Cherbourg was a Navy Base for the English Channel operations, but Hans was more interested about the fishing industry and the attitudes of the fishermen and their families.

It was almost dark when the bus arrived in Cherbourg. Before eating he went to find a room he could rent. There was one available on a high knoll overlooking the coastline and fishing piers. The room came with two meals, but he was not in time for the evening meal. I will pay you extra for a bowl of soup and a sandwich," he said.

"Sit down then. I'll pour you a cup of tea while your soup warms.

"There are two other boarders here so I have to get up

early to start breakfast, which is six sharp in the morning," Mrs. Chartier said.

"This is a large house, Mrs. Chartier," Hans said.

"Yes. At one time it was full of children's laughter. We had two sons and a daughter. My sons were both killed in the war and my daughter is in Paris now."

"Where does your husband work Mrs. Chartier?"

"He worked in the local cannery until they closed their doors last year. Now he is a night watchman at the fish piers. And he is too old to be doing such work, but he won't stop. Says if he stopped working he wouldn't last a month before I'd be putting him in the ground."

"The people who lost their jobs when the cannery closed, what are they doing for work now?" Hans asked.

"A few went to Paris, some of the men are working on fishing boats and some of the younger boys went into the military.

"People adjust, Mr. French. As a community we are doing okay, compared to some. What do you do for work, Mr. French?"

"I am an out of work diamond cutter. I was working in Spain and my employer cut my work to two days a week. We were able to keep working like that for two years. Then he had no choice but to close his doors."

"Your soup and sandwich is ready, Mr. French."

It had been a tiring day and after eating Hans went to bed. But he stayed up for a while writing in code what he had learned that day.

The next morning after eating he left the house and walked to the village where he found an open sidewalk café and decided on a cup of coffee today. He watched other people with particular interest. People were actually cheery and talking happily with others. And this cheeriness he found throughout the village.

He found no soup lines or kitchens and no unemployment lines, seeking work. The village was a busy bustle. There were no boarded up doors or windows or empty businesses. Things were different here in Cherbourg and he wanted to understand what the difference was.

People were busy working everywhere. Maybe that was the difference, but people in Paris were not as unemployed as elsewhere and they were not as happy as there in Cherbourg.

He found a park on a hillside overlooking the coast and children were running around playing, laughing and screaming.

From the park he walked down to the fish piers and found a small clean restaurant not far from the piers.

While in Barcelona he had eaten a lot of fish, but nothing like what was on this menu list. There was a seafood platter that was sounding appetizing: haddock, scallops and shrimp. He had never eaten any of these. The order was fairly expensive, but he had brought some of his own money for just such an occasion. When his order came, he wasn't sure if he'd be able to finish it or not. There was also rice and a salad. Everything looked and smelled so good.

By now a few locals had come in and sat down and ordered. He was so enjoying his first taste of haddock, scallops and shrimp, he found it difficult to listen to what the others were talking about. But one thing was clear, whatever they were talking about they were not grumbling and complaining about how bad things were. These people actually seemed happy. Even after the closure of probably the area's biggest employer. He doubted very much if these people would be open to Hitler's new ideas. Why should they. Their lives seemed to be very good.

He had difficulty eating the whole platter, but as good as it was he had no intention of leaving any. When he left the restaurant he was full and he needed to walk it off.

He walked out along the fish piers. The air held a strong odor of fish and rotting bait. Towards the end of one pier he found an older fisherman trying to carry a crate laden heavy with fish, "Would you like me to help you?" Hans asked.

"Yes, it would be greatly appreciated."

Hans stepped into the boat with the fisherman and together they lifted the full crate of cod onto the wharf. There were three other crates that Hans helped him with.

"You are new around here aren't you? I have never seen you around the fish piers before."

"That's correct, Sir. This is the first that I have ever been to Cherbourg. I am on my way to Brest and decided to stop over for a few days."

"You looking for work, young fellow?"

"In a manner of speaking. I am an out of work diamond cutter."

The old man laughed, "Huh, huh, huh, you won't find many diamonds around Cherbourg—or people with enough money to buy one."

"I am actually just out looking," Hans replied.

"My nephew works with me on the boat—except he pulled his back two days ago and I haven't been able to find anyone to help me out." Hans knew what was coming next. "I could use a good strong fellow like you. I'll give you my nephew's wages plus fresh fish to take home with you. What do you say?"

"Do you want me to start now or in the morning?"

"Well if you are that anxious, right now would be good. I need to get this catch inside out of the sun and clean the boat and get it ready for tomorrow.

"I should know your name. I am called Burl LaComb."

"My name is Sean French, Mr. LaComb."

"There is no Mister. Just Burl will do fine."

When Hans saw the tables inside, he knew what was to come next. "These fish must be cleaned before they go soft. Leave the head on and the guts go into these buckets. We'll use those tomorrow for chum."

Burl showed Hans how to slit the bellies and clean the innards out. Hans only needed to watch once.

Before they had finished Hans better understood why the

smell of rotting fish hung over the fish piers. But he was happy to be helping Burl.

By the end of the afternoon he was smelling like fish. "Be sure and take one of those haddock with you, Sean."

"Yes, Burl."

"I'll see you in the morning?" a question and not a statement.

"I'll be here."

At the boarding house he had to shower and rinse his clothes out and hang 'em out to dry before he could eat. Mrs. Chartier was happy for the haddock. "I'll bake this tomorrow for supper, Sean."

There was a lot of happy conversation around the table that evening. Afterwards Hans went to bed. It had been a long time since he had done any physical work.

The next morning as Hans was walking down the stairs he was surprised how well he was feeling. Not only physically after back-breaking work the day before, but also mentally. The attitude of the people in this fishing village was rubbing off on him.

He was on Burl's fishing boat before Burl. "Good morning, young fella. I see you are ready for another day."

"Yes, I have loaded the buckets of fish chum and the crates to put the fish in," Hans said.

They were still in sight of land when Burl said, "You can dump the chum out over the back now. Not all at once, more like a steady stream. Dump all the buckets then we'll circle back and throw out the nets."

While they waited for the nets to work Hans asked, "What do you think of this guy Hitler promising to improve the economy and life for the German people?"

"I do not know who this Hitler guy is nor what he is promising to do. I have enough to worry about here in Cherbourg to waste my time thinking about this Hitler guy."

By noon they had filled all eight crates with fish and

were on their way back. "You pretty good fisherman for first time," Burl said.

Hans grinned and said, "Thank you."

That evening after all the fish were cleaned and everything picked up and taken care of Burl gave Hans two big haddocks. "Thank you, Burl. Mrs. Chartier will really like these."

And she was ecstatic when Hans opened the kitchen door and held up the haddock. "Oh my word, Sean. These are beautiful fish. Thank you. Supper is almost ready."

The next day was a repeat of the previous day and Hans brought back two more haddock for Mrs. Chartier. The next morning Burl's nephew was at the pier when Hans arrived. When Burl arrived he paid Hans more than they had agreed to and thanked him.

"Thank you, Burl."

He spent the rest of that morning walking around the fish piers and talking with people. Not one had any idea about Hitler's new ideas, or even who he was.

Before leaving Cherbourg he went back to the restaurant and ordered the seafood platter again. This time he was hungry and the haddock, scallops and shrimp tasted even better.

Afterwards he walked to the park and found some shade to lie down in. He was soon asleep.

He awoke an hour later when he lost the shade and the warm sunshine was on his face. He stood up, stretched and walked along the shoreline. Everyone he saw was busy. What a contrast Cherbourg was to the other cities he had been to. Here it seemed everyone was oblivious to the outside world and its problems. To these people it seemed as though their entire world, their existence was here in Cherbourg. Not one person he had talked with knew anything about Hitler or his new improvements he was promising.

Mrs. Chartier was disappointed when Hans said, "I'll be leaving in the morning."

"Where will you go, Mr. French?"

"I am going to work my way to Brest," he replied.

"I'll be sorry to see you go. You have been a good boarder."

Hans went to his room after eating to write in code about what he had found here in Cherbourg.

* * *

He said his goodbyes at the breakfast table the next morning. "If you come back to Cherbourg, Mr. French, I hope you will stay with us."

"That is a promise, Mrs. Chartier. I have enjoyed my stay here—and your cooking."

He walked to the bus station and boarded a bus for Brest. As an arrow would fly the distance to Brest wasn't far, but the bus had to travel south almost a full day before turning northerly to Roadstead of Brest (a bay). The trip was a day and a half and Hans was exhausted.

The first thing he did was look for a rooming house near the Salou Docks. He found many places advertising for rooms to let. He soon found what he wanted and paid for two days, and left it from there day to day. It was noon but he was so tired he took a nap without eating.

When he awoke he walked down to the fabrication docks and there was a security gate and officers. "I cannot let you in, Monsieur. But if you return tomorrow at 2pm there is a guided tour," the officer said.

"Thank you."

There was much to see here and he had to look through the security fencing. The biggest ships he saw were four destroyer class ships. He also saw three submarines that were being overhauled. And he also noticed a lot of workers on the docks. But at the same time he had walked by two soup kitchens. Albeit the lines were much shorter than he had found in Paris. *With this much work going on at the Salou Docks why are people unemployed?* This puzzled him.

51

His legs were getting tired of all the walking and he found a bench to rest overlooking the docks, until it was time to find a place to eat. He looked for a restaurant lounge. Figuring maybe a few workers would stop in for a drink after work. And after a drink or two, they might start talking a little louder and about ship building.

A block back away from the main security gate there was a corner lounge. This looked perfect. A loud whistle blew from the docks signaling a shift change.

He found a seat in the corner and ordered a beef stew with new bread. Surprisingly he noticed the price of the beef stew was more expensive than the seafood platter he had had in Cherbourg. He made a mental note about the price of beef.

A few workers stopped in for a drink and they were already loud. Talking mostly about their work and complaining about bosses.

He was able to understand that this crew had actually recently laid the keel for a new ship. And from the conversations he understood that it would be a large ship, but he didn't know what kind.

These men, after a couple of beers each they left. There was no point for Hans to stay any longer, so he left too and returned to his room.

* * *

He ate breakfast in the boarding house the next morning. There were three other men at the table who all worked at the shipyard. "And what do you do for work, Mr. French?" one of them asked.

"I'm an unemployed diamond cutter. I came here from Cherbourg where I did some work on a fishing boat for a while until the fisherman's regular help came back to work."

"The shipyard is busy but I do not believe there are any job openings," another said.

"I'm taking the 2 o'clock tour of the docks this afternoon."

"Well, good luck to you." And the three left for work.

Hans left the boarding house and walked towards the business section of Brest. There were no boarded up windows and doors, but this early in the day there were not many shoppers. He decided to talk with some of the business owners.

It was pretty much the same at each business. People were buying necessities, but few extras. But with no empty shops, he decided the economy was better here than in a few places he had visited.

For lunch he had only a cup of tea at a sidewalk café. He had been eating too much on this assignment.

At 2pm Hans was waiting in line outside the main gate for the tour guide. There were twenty people wanting to take the tour. When the guide arrived he welcomed them to the Salou Docks and escorted the group to a dry dock where workers were working on the keel of a large ship. "This ship will be the pride and joy of Salou Docks. This is the beginning stages of the battleship Richelieu. It will be the largest ship ever built here. When it is finished it will be over 35,000 tons and top speed will be 30 knots powered by 6 boilers turning 4 propellers. It will be a marvelous ship. This ship will have 8, 15 inch guns and a secondary artillery system of 5 quadruple turrets. The overall length will be over 800 feet with a 110 foot beam and the armored belt will be 12.9 inches thick. This ship when finished will be France's largest battleship ever built."

Hans wished there had been a picture of the ship available. It certainly sounded impressive.

From there they took a tour bus down along other docks where there were submarines tied up. "These boats are here for refitting and are scheduled to leave tomorrow.

"We are also refitting some large fish trollers and a ferry boat is scheduled to arrive this week. Salou currently employs almost two thousand workers, and hopes to employ more by the end of next year."

The next day Hans took a ferry across the bay to Ecole Navale, a navy academy. Again he was stopped at a security gate and told civilians were not allowed unless by appointment. "Is this institute an officer's college?" Hans asked.

"It is a Naval Academy," the guard said.

"How many students are there?"

"One hundred and fifty. Who are you, Monsieur?"

"Sean French. I'm an out of work diamond cutter and I am only looking around."

"Well Mr. French there aren't any diamonds here. I must insist you leave."

Hans left and walked around some until it was time to board the ferry back across the bay.

The next day he was working his way along the coast. Stopping at Nantes, LaRochelle, Bordeaux; fishing communities and commercial centers. And again the people and the economy appeared to be better where there was a fishing industry. In the commercial centers he found soup kitchens and some with long lines. Only an occasional person knew anything at all about Hitler and how he planned to improve peoples' lives in Germany. He left the west coast and took a train to Marseille, a resort on the Mediterranean Coast. There were no soup kitchens here as this was a resort for the politicians and the wealthy. He listened to their conversations and most of it was about how much money they could make and waiting for the New York Stock Exchange to get back on its feet. Even the politicians were more concerned about how much money they could make rather than finding a solution out of the depression. There was some mention about Hitler's new movement, but they were not too worried or concerned.

Hans concluded it was a rich place indeed, and indeed for the richest. He left Marseille angry and took a bus to the military port of Toulon. A submarine construction site and France's principal Navy Base.

Here Hans learned the submarine yard was currently

building France's newest, largest and most advanced attack submarine. The Toulon shipyard was expansive and was the biggest employer in the area. And here he found a completely different attitude, maybe perhaps because of the Naval Base. But most people were still feeling resentment towards Germany for the last war and were willing to fight them again. The people here were more aggressive than he had earlier found in France. It was quite a contrast.

He had been two and a half weeks on his assignment and decided to board a train for Paris and then work his way back to Germany through France's farmland.

After leaving Paris by bus he found it more difficult finding boarding houses and rooms to let, so he'd often make arrangements with a farmer to work two days on the farm for food and bed. This agreement benefited the farmer, so he was always assured of food and a place to sleep. At one farm the only place for him to sleep was in the barn on a bed of straw.

Here, like the fishing industry, he did not find any soup kitchens or lines and there was work for everybody, if one wanted to work. Sometimes the pay wasn't great, but it would provide for food and shelter. And like the people in and around Cherbourg, they were not too aware of the new movement taking place in Germany.

He traveled east from Paris and his last stop was a farm near Metz. He worked two days on that last farm. Talking subtly with the farmer and his wife and two of their part time helpers, living that close to Germany they still were not aware of Hitler's new movements. They only knew that worldwide there was a depression. But on the farm they more or less experienced bad times and low wages most of the time. So this depression was really nothing new for them.

From Metz Hans took a bus to the border. He crossed over and boarded a train for Berlin.

Chapter 3

As soon as Hans returned to base in Berlin he reported immediately to Major Hammell. "How was your assignment, Lieutenant?"

"Surprising is the only word I can find to describe it."

"Oh, and why is that?"

"I thought I would discover different information. That's the only way I can describe it, Herr Major."

"I will need a written report as soon as possible to present to the Admiral."

"Yes Sir. It will take some time, Herr Major. I have everything written in code."

"What code are you referring to, Lieutenant?"

"My code, Sir. One I created." Then he showed Hammell his notebook and continued. "I have written everything in French to a fictitious friend. But before it can be decoded it must first be translated into Spanish. Even if someone found this they would think I was only keeping a travel itinerary to a friend and if it was translated into Spanish they first would have to have my key."

"When did you think all this up, Lieutenant?"

"The evening before I left."

"Very well. Do you think you could have it type written for the Admiral by 1200 hours tomorrow?"

"Yes, Herr Major. That will not be a problem."

"Good, when you have finished it, bring it to my office."

"Yes, Herr Major."

"Dismissed. And good work."

Hans decided not to wait for morning to start decoding his report. He'd stay late and have it finished tonight. Besides what else was there to do.

First he translated his report line for line into Spanish and then he used his key to write a report for Admiral Canaris.

Before he had completed his report he was glad he didn't wait until the next day. It was midnight before he walked over to his quarters and showered and went to bed.

The next morning after breakfast he walked into Major Hammell's office with his report. "That was fast, Lieutenant."

"I stayed last night, Sir, and I'm glad I did. It took longer than I thought it would"

"I'm going to skim through this first before I take it up to the Admiral. You may return to your duty section. Just in case the Admiral might want to see you, make yourself available."

"Yes, Herr Major."

As Hammell read through Hans' report, he was impressed with his details and conclusions. He had certainly been thorough. When he finished reading the report he took it upstairs to the Admiral's office. "Excuse me, Herr Admiral."

"Yes what is it, Major?"

"Lieutenant Grubber is back from his assignment and here is his report. I've skimmed through it, Sir, and was quite impressed."

"Thank you, Major. I'll review it. But I have a telephone call to make first."

"Yes, Herr Admiral," and Hammell went back to his office.

While Hans was eating lunch in the cafeteria Major Hammell said, "Lieutenant Grubber, you and I are to report to the Admiral at 1300 hours."

"Yes, Herr Major."

Hans was already waiting outside the Admiral's office when Hammell arrived. Canaris' aid opened the door and said, "Come in gentlemen, the Admiral is expecting you."

"Come in, Major, Lieutenant, sit down," Canaris stood up and walked around to the front of his desk and partially rested on the edge.

"I have studied your report, Lieutenant, and I am happily surprised with its completeness and thoroughness. When Major Hammell suggested he send you on a trial assignment to see how well you would perform, neither of us expected so much information and detail.

"I understand what you wrote about the contrast between the fishing and farming communities with more industrial communities. And it seems that while France is reeling in a bad economy and wanting changes, that they are only vaguely aware of the direction Germany is going. You reported that those who were somewhat aware were not opposed to them, but only doubted if Hitler could make good his promises.

"You also reported about the construction of France's battleship, the Richelieu. While we were aware of the new attack submarine being built, we did not know anything about the Richelieu. When had the Richelieu's construction started, Lieutenant?"

"The keel had only recently been laid, Herr Admiral."

"This is good information. For a battleship of this size and tonnage it obviously violates the Treaty of Versailles agreement.

"How were you able to keep so accurate information—I mean for a month?"

"I wrote everything in code each evening of that day's travel."

"Tell me about this code, Lieutenant."

"I would write in French. But in order to decode it, it would first have to be translated to Spanish and then my code key would apply. If anyone found my notes it would only appear to him as an itinerary to a fictitious friend."

"Ingenious, Lieutenant. Simply ingenious.

"Were you in any danger at any time?"

"No, Herr Admiral."

"Were any of the people you encountered in any way suspicious of you?"

"No, Herr Admiral. I fit in very well with the communities wherever I went."

"That's all, Lieutenant. You are dismissed. Major, I'd like you to stay."

Canaris waited until Hans had left and closed the door before speaking. "Well, Major, this was his first assignment, how well do you think he did?"

"It is as if he has had many years of experience of gathering information and not his first run."

"What I am working on for the Fuher's staff, this information will certainly help. And how ingenious of him to create a way to code his information. I would never have thought of that," Canaris said.

"I see the Lieutenant rising rapidly in the ranks."

"I have another assignment for him, Major. Here is an outline of the intelligence I need. Maybe give the Lieutenant two days off and then the two of you make this happen," and Canaris gave the outline to Hammell.

Hammell closed Canaris' door and returned to his office to read over the outline. Hammell sent his aid to find Hans, "And ask him to come to my office."

A few minutes later, "Come in, Lieutenant, and close the door."

"Both the Admiral and myself, we were pleased with the thoroughness of your assignment. I have another one for you. But first you need to take two days off. Relax and have some fun."

"Major, this is fun. And I do not need two days off."

"Okay, here is an outline of information that intelligence needs. As you can see it will involve much traveling. Your time table is short. In spite of the traveling the Admiral would like you to return by mid-September. That gives you five weeks to complete this.

"Now, you brought us intelligence that France has violated the Treaty of Versailles tonnage restrictions and we have information that the United States has also exceeded the tonnage limits on their battleships. We need to know if England is also exceeding the tonnage limits. We have no intelligence on this.

"To expedite your travel, you'll be flown to Paris on Germany's civil airline. You'll have to make your own flight arrangements from Paris, wherever you want to start, whether it is in England or Scotland. I'll leave that up to you. And perhaps you should have a British passport this time and I am assuming you will use your expertise as a diamond cutter for a cover."

"Major, I will need more money this time with all the air travel. Last time if not for working on the fishing boat and on the farms there would not have been enough."

"I'll see to that, Lieutenant. Study that outline and then destroy it. I assume you will have no problems remembering the information."

"No Sir, not at all."

"Good, now go down to documents and tell them what you'll need. Then to supply and pick out the appropriate attire and traveling bag for your British cover."

"Yes Sir."

At the documents division Hans asked for the same identity, Sean French, and not a British passport. He was also given additional identification and railway ticket stubs and a movie ticket stub from London.

And instead of a British style carry bag he asked for the same one he had used in France. Major Hammell had already signed a voucher, so Hans could draw more money this time. The payroll Sergeant asked him how much he would need. Airline ticket from Berlin to Paris had already been obtained.

The next morning Hans went to talk with Major Hammell, "Sir, I decided it would be more authentic if I was a French tourist and not posturing as a British citizen. I believe there will be fewer questions this way."

"Okay, I'll have your identity changed."

"I already did, Major."

"When are you planning to leave, Lieutenant?"

"This afternoon would be good. I already have everything I need." He had that morning put his loupe in his pocket.

* * *

He had never been in an airplane before, let alone fly and this was proving to be an exciting assignment.

Circling over Paris waiting for a slot to land was fascinating for Hans. He would never in all his life expect to see something like this. He had a two hour wait for a flight to London. While he waited, he found a snack bar and ate a ham and cheese sandwich with tea. There were hundreds of people here and all were talking. He listened intently and he never heard any conversation involving Hitler or Germany. And the poor economy surely was evident here.

The city was bigger than he had thought. As much as he would enjoy walking around he boarded his plane for Glasgow.

* * *

It had started to rain as his plane went airborne and he didn't get to see much of the island. The air was rough and he wasn't able to sleep at all. So when they landed in Glasgow he was exhausted and it was 2 am.

He found an empty quiet corner at the terminal and slept pitifully on a bench style seat until the airport came alive at 6 o'clock.

A cafeteria was opening inside the terminal and he ordered breakfast—with an English tea.

After breakfast the next thing he needed was a room. He took a taxi out toward the Clyde River. The two ship builders; Fairfield Shipbuilding and Engineering Company and The John

Brown Company were both on the Clyde Bank River. He got out at the waterfront to walk about to see what there was for rooms. Two blocks away from the waterfront he found a nice Mom and Pop restaurant and they were advertising rooms to let overhead. Thelma and Clyde MacIntosh were in their seventies and probably were having to still work because of the slow economy.

"I would like a room please. I'll pay two days in advance and then by day. I'm not sure how long I'll be in Glasgow."

"Surely, and your name please," Thelma asked.

"Oh pardon me. Sean French."

"The rent only provides you lodging, but you won't find any finer cooking than right here," Clyde said.

"Fair enough. When do you close in the evening?"

"7 pm and we start serving at 6 am."

It was a small room, but he wouldn't be in Glasgow long. He lay down to sleep and a whistle at one of the shipyards blew and he awoke. He went down stairs for a sandwich.

There were only two other people eating besides himself. "Mr. French," the old man said, "when you have finished your sandwich and tea, perhaps you would join me for a walk in the hills. The Mrs. won't let me go by myself any more—afraid I might not come back."

"Sure, I'd enjoy a walk." He figured Mr. MacIntosh would be a good source of information.

"I used to come out here in the hills every morning before work and again on Saturday and Sunday providing it was not raining so much. Out here one can get above the smell of iron and rust from the yards. Sometimes the noise from the yard is so loud I can hear it in my dreams."

"Did you work at the yard, Mr. MacIntosh?"

"I much prefer if you'd call me Clyde and drop the Mr. Yes. I worked at the yard. It kept me from being taken to the war—even at my age. I worked with the turbines. They have gotten so huge in today's ships."

"Tell me, Monsieur French, what is it that brings a healthy young man to Scotland in these hard times?"

"I am an out of work diamond cutter. Before the depression I was actually working in Spain. I was only working two days a week at the last of it and then the shop owner announced he was closing the shop. I was able to save much of my income, but now I'm looking for a place to start up again."

"There are many well-to-do people in Glasgow."

They walked on to the top of the hill in silence. Then Clyde said, "Turn around, Sean, you can see both yards from up here. They're both busy now. In fact they need more welders and fabricators. Too bad you aren't a welder. They are paid pretty good."

"What are the yards working on, Clyde?"

"Two of these biggest battleships Great Britain has ever built."

"I have never seen a big ship before," Hans said hoping Clyde would take the bait.

He did. "Well, young fella, if you aren't busy tomorrow after breakfast I will give you a tour. Because I worked so many years there they let me come and go as I wish."

Years ago Clyde had built a bench to sit on, on top, and now he said, "I find I need to sit down and rest before we start down."

It was nice out there in the hills and as Clyde had said, they were above the noise of the yards.

Hans walked with Clyde back to the restaurant and then he went for a walk around the city. Everything was so clean here. Even the city streets and sidewalks had been swept clean.

After supper Hans returned to a bar he had seen earlier, hoping he might listen in on some conversations. Here no one drank wine. It was ale or beer. Here the yard workers seemed to be excited about the two new ships they had recently started building and no one was complaining about the economy. In fact no one was bad mouthing their bosses either.

The shops were all open also, so Hans decided that the economy was good. People were not complaining.

* * *

After breakfast the next day Clyde guided Hans through the Fairfield shipyard. "I worked in that building over there.

"No one is allowed through this fence that's not working on the boat. They started work on the keel since early May."

"It sure looks like it'll be a long ship," Hans baited Clyde again.

"Yes Sir, no half way for old King George."

"King George?" Hans asked.

"Yes, this will be crowned the *HMS Duke of York* and the one being built in the John Brown Yard will be the *HMS Howe.* Both ships will be of the King George V-class battleships."

"How big will it be, Clyde?"

"Both ships will be around 40,000 tons. And both ships will be equipped with 10, 14 inch guns. Can you imagine that? A dam missile being shot out the end of a cannon 14 inches in diameter?

"The armament on these two beasts will be almost 15 inches of iron. It is no wonder they will be so heavy, carrying armament like that. They each will have quite an assortment of secondary guns and antiaircraft guns, too.

"They both will be able to produce over 75,000 shaft horsepower. In my days in the yard we never heard of such a thing. I surely wouldn't want to be on the receiving end of one of these battleships.

"I hope I live long enough to see these two set sail. It'll be a magnificent sight," Clyde said.

"Is Scotland more industrialized than agriculture?" Hans asked.

"There is some fine farming soil, but I'd have to say there is probably more industry. Industry is keeping us Scots from standing in soup lines. Myself, I always wished I could have afforded a small farm. I think I would have liked that.

"I think we should return now. If we hurry we might be in time for tea and crumpets."

* * *

As he lay awake in bed that night he decided to leave in the morning. He had the information here that the Admiral was wanting.

The next morning he said goodbye and then boarded a bus for Newcastle upon Tyne. There wasn't a direct route from Glasgow, instead it went first to Edinburgh and then down along the coast to Newcastle, making many stops along the way.

At Newcastle the air was thick with coal smoke and smoke from the iron industries. The ground between Newcastle was thick with coal seams dipping toward the east.

Before leaving he discovered two more battleships being recently laid down. One at Swan Hunter and Wigham Richardson shipyard; the *HMS Anson* and the other ship, the *HMS King George,* was recently laid down at Vickers-Armstrong Naval Yard.

Both battleships were of the King George V-class battleship and both displacing 43,000 tons. Both were equipped with 10, 14 inch guns and an array of secondary guns. And an armor belt of nearly 15 inches.

As soon as he had the information he wanted he boarded the train for Liverpool which would first take him west to Carlisle and then along the Atlantic coast south. As the train was slowing on the approach to Barrow-in-Furness, Hans was looking out the window and saw several submarines tied up in a shipyard.

There was a cold drizzle starting and it was time to eat and then look for a room and sleep. He'd check out the submarines tomorrow.

People here were not as happy and friendly as he had

found in Glasgow. Everyone walked around with a sullen look about their face.

After breakfast he walked down to the submarine pens. Some were tied up while two were being worked on. He could only see five. The docks were enclosed with strong security fencing and guards at the main entrance gate. There was no way he was going to be given permission to enter.

There was no need to stay any longer so the next morning he boarded the train and continued on to Liverpool. The train made a brief stop at the beaches in Southport and then it continued on. The terminal was almost in downtown Liverpool and this isn't where he wanted to be. The Cammell Laird Shipyard was across the bay in Birkenhead.

He stopped at an information desk inside the terminal. "Excuse me, Ma'am, could you tell me how to get over to Birkenhead?" He asked in perfect English.

"The easiest way is to take the ferry from the waterfront. Let's see, she is due to leave at 10:30. It is now 9:30. You have an hour, governor, to get there."

"Thank you." He wasn't quite sure why she had called him 'governor'. He had never heard that before. He would have to remember it.

He hailed a taxi which drove him to the ferry terminal. Only about a ten minute walk. But he had no idea in which direction.

He bought his ticket and waited next to a group of young women. They were doing a lot of conversing, but nothing about the economy or ship building. People here were busy, but they didn't seem to be very happy.

Two blocks back away from the water front in Birkenhead he found a similar setup as he had in Glasgow. A small restaurant on street level with vacant rooms on the second level.

Hans unpacked his few things and went downstairs for lunch. While he waited for soup and sandwich he talked with one of the owners. "If you're looking for work at the yard, young fella, you won't find none. Three months ago now they started hiring and in four days all the slots were filled. Men, they came from all over to help build the *Prince*.

"Oh, by the way, my name is Earl Hereford. My Mrs. does the cooking, she does. I'll give you a little advice, when you talk to the Mrs. you'd be better off if you didn't call her by her given name Bethesda. She likes to be called Mrs. Hereford."

"Actually I was hoping to find something at Cammell Laird. Maybe I'll go over tomorrow morning and inquire.

"You said earlier something around the *Prince*—"

Earl interrupted him and said, "That I did, The *Prince of Wales*. Going to be the best battleship in the Royal Navy."

"How near finished is she?" Hans asked.

"Oh, they only laid her down in January. Won't be christened until spring of '41. Takes time, it does, to build something like the *Prince*.

"She'll be a heavy girl too. I hear she'll displace more'n 43,000 tons. Never could understand how something that big and heavy can float. I mean, her hull will be more'n 14 inches thick. No torpedo will ever be able to penetrate her side."

"How big are the guns, Earl?" This was easier than he thought it would be.

"She'll have 10 of those 14 inch guns. I'd like to see the shell that goes in her breach. Must take a crane to load her.

"Not to change the subject, but you never told me your name."

"Sean French. And before you ask, yes I am from France."

"Then what are you doing in Birkenhead? And exactly what is it you do?"

"Actually I'm an out of work diamond cutter. I've been working in Spain until the company had to close its doors because of the economy. I didn't know but what I might find work in the shipyard as a tool maker. I have had some experience in that field," Hans said.

67

"My, for a Frenchman, you surely do speak nice English."

"Well my mother is English and she insisted that I learn to speak English fluently."

"Well you do a right good job of it, Sean French."

* * *

Hans couldn't see staying in Birkenhead any longer. He had the information he had wanted. So the next morning he boarded a train for London.

There were so many stops along the way he was actually two days getting there and completely exhausted. There was only one other passenger who boarded in Liverpool that went all the way to London.

All of his life his mother had told him stories about the grandeur of London. She had said, "London is to the world as Paris is to Europe."

Standing on the platform he had no idea where to go. So he looked for an information desk inside. "Pardon me, can you help me?"

"Why I hope so," a cute blue eyed blonde said, "What do you need to know?"

"I'm new here and I don't know where to go to look for a room to rent."

"There are many flats throughout the city advertising rooms to let, but I suppose if you don't know where to look that can be sort of a problem. How long will you be in London?"

"Three—four days."

"There are some rooms to let near Piccadilly Circus and Trafalgar Square, but you might have to pay a little extra. That's where I would look. There is much to see and the Palace is just a short walk from Trafalgar Square."

"Could you give me an address I can give a taxi driver?"

"Sure can," and she wrote out two addresses. "Just tell the cabbie what you are looking for and he'll know right where to go."

"Thank you."

"Where you going mate?" The cab driver asked.

"I'm looking for a room to rent for three or four days near either Piccadilly Circus or Trafalgar Square. The information lady gave me these two addresses," and he handed them to the driver. "She also said you would know exactly where to go."

"I do at that, mate. Ever been to London before?"

"No Sir. My mother is from here and she has told me so much about London."

"If you're looking for night life, I'd suggest near Piccadilly. There are some nice bars and lounges, theaters and if you like to dance there are several clubs. And if you are looking for a girl, then this is where you will want to go."

"What about Trafalgar Square?"

"Trafalgar is a more historical place. There are museums, statues and monuments and a public meeting place for the public. And it is only a short distance to Buckingham Palace. You really should see the changing of the guard."

"There is another place you will want to visit."

"What is that?" Hans asked.

"Hyde Park. It is the world's largest park. You'll want to walk about the park in the daylight in order to enjoy its beauty. Then the real excitement is early evening at the Speaker's Corner close to Kensington Way. People gather there to discuss almost anything. The police patrol through there in the evenings to break up the fights. Too many have a few mugs of beer before going to the Corner."

"I'll keep that in mind."

The taxi driver pulled over to the curb and said, "This is the address the woman gave you for a room near Piccadilly Circus. You see that rooms to rent sign on the building across the street? That's a beer pub and restaurant and they are advertising rooms. This will be your best chance. There are cheaper rents, but they will not be so close to this area."

"I think this will be fine. Thank you."

He had to pay in advance for a week at a time and it was twice as expensive as any other of his rents. The restaurant food was more expensive also.

After eating lunch he went for a walk about Piccadilly Circus and Trafalgar Square. They both were intersections where several roads joined.

He walked the circle around Piccadilly and indeed it appeared to be a fun place to spend an evening. Then he walked on to Trafalgar Square. And it was a square. It was a place of old history mixed with the new. He found a place to sit down and he watched with interest as people passed him by and through the Square. Not many had any interest in the history that was probably here.

He decided to wait for the next day to visit Buckingham Palace. He went back to his room and worked on his coded report for the Admiral.

Afterwards he laid down for a quick nap before eating supper. He stopped his thinking right there. He had to think like he was English and the English call it dinner and not supper.

There were so many thoughts running through his mind he couldn't relax enough to sleep so he got up and went downstairs. It was time for dinner anyhow.

"And what would you like for dinner, Mr. French?"

"This boiled dinner sounds good. It has been a long time since I have eaten one."

While he waited for his dinner he chose a table in the corner where he could watch others, and sipping his English Tea. He'd much prefer a cup of coffee, but he had to play the part.

The boiled dinner was delicious and when he had finished he asked the owner, "Can you give me directions to Hyde Park?"

"Certainly. You turn left on this street for six blocks, turn right and that street will take you right to the park. Sometimes there is a rough group of young people there looking for any chance to fight. But the police do quite a good job patrolling."

"Thank you."

After that dinner Hans (Sean) figured he could use the walk. It was a nice evening and many residents were still eating dinner. He found the park with no difficulty.

After sitting on a park bench for a while he started walking on one of the many trails. There were a few people in the park but not many. He strolled over to the pond and sat down watching ducks in the water.

As the sun began to set more people started to come. Probably having just finished eating and wanting to enjoy the cool air.

He remembered being told to find the Speaker's Corner. There he would find the most conversations and arguments. He also noticed two policemen on foot.

He joined in with a group of men who were talking about how Germany would have been defeated sooner if the United States had joined the Allies sooner.

Then one older man said, "I think Winston Churchill was correct when he introduced a bill into Parliament in 1919 to attack the United States."

"Why on Earth did he introduce that?" another asked.

"Why, it should be obvious, I say," the older gentleman said, "Winni and many of the older Parliament members were afraid of the United States. Great Britain had lost their naval superiority in the war to the United States."

Another said, "Well I for one am glad that bill never was approved. What a mistake that would have been."

Hans couldn't stay out of it, he said, "I would declare that Britain is regaining her hold with these four new battleships being built."

No one there knew anything about the four war ships and Hans found himself engaging in the conversation more than he would have liked. But it did show him that much of the population had no idea what was happening in their shipyards.

When the conversation switched to the economy and

then Hitler's new ideas, Hans thought it best to stay out of this one and just listen. Some thought the ideas had merit, but where did this Hitler come from? And could they trust him?

Eventually the conversations changed to more local issues and how much the royal family was spending.

By midnight he had had enough and returned to his room. The only thing he wanted to do the next day was watch the changing of the guard. Then he decided to return to Germany.

After breakfast the next morning he returned to his room and wrote coded reports until it was time to leave for the Palace. It was a bright sunny day but off to the west were dark clouds moving in.

There was already a crowd gathered to watch the changing. He wondered how many people here had seen this before and how many times.

He watched with interest. He couldn't imagine if he was one of the guards having to go through this pomp and dress every day. And he really couldn't see the significance of it all, unless it was only tradition. 'But every day?'

He ate lunch at the restaurant and explained he had decided to move on. "I cannot refund the days you have paid in advance."

"That is okay. No problem."

He took a taxi to the airport and booked a flight to Paris. He had two hours to wait.

Chapter 4

Thunder storms blew in off the Atlantic and shut down the airport. His two hours turned into twelve. Then his flight was put on hold over Paris as another airliner had had a slight accident, that had to be cleaned up before Hans' flight could land.

Then from Paris to the German border the train had pulled into a side rail to let another train pass. By the time Hans reached Berlin he was tired of traveling. He reported first to Major Hammell and then he went to his own quarters for sleep.

He returned to base the next day and in the morning, decoding his report and typing it.

"This is very interesting, Lieutenant, and I see you visited one facility at Barrow that we knew nothing about. Let's go up and see the Admiral." Hans walked with Hammell up the stairs to Canaris' office.

"Come in. You are back early, Lieutenant."

"Yes, Herr Admiral, I couldn't see any point in dragging the assignment out any longer. I had the information you wanted," Hans replied.

Canaris read through his report briefly. "Congratulations, Lieutenant. Now I have something that requires my attention. I will thoroughly examine your report, Lieutenant, as soon as I can. Dismissed."

The Admiral's telephone rang as Hans was closing his door. As Canaris listened he started to break out in a sweat. He was busy trying to take notes and listen. Finally he said. "Yes, Mein Führer."

He wiped his forehead with his handkerchief and picked Hans' report up. As he read through it, he kept thinking how precise and thorough Lt. Grubber was. His report contained much more valuable information than he had been sent to gather. He was particularly interested in the statement the man in Hyde Park had said about Churchill introducing a bill into Parliament in 1919 to attack the United States. *Maybe Churchill was not the friend to the Americans that he proposed to be.* This was the first he had ever heard about this bill.

England and Scotland both seemed to be heavily industrialized. The Scots according to this report were doing just fine as they were. But Canaris knew that in battle the Scotsman have always proven to be gallant warriors. And the English, although heavily employed in ship building, their economy had not improved as much. And according to the Lt.'s report he found the English a grumbling lot, but at the same time willing to fight for England's cause.

France was building a battleship, the *Richelieu,* against the agreements in the Treaty of Versailles, and England was currently building four battleships in violation of the Treaty of Versailles. Plus they were each building attack submarines.

Canaris concluded that the Führer's staff needed to know about these facts, and soon. He wrote up his own report to Hitler summarizing both of the Lt.'s reports. Then he had his aide take them to the Führer's staff headquarters.

When his aide returned he had him go downstairs and "...find Lieutenant Grubber and Major Hammell and tell them I wish to speak with them immediately."

Ten minutes later in Canaris' office. "Sit down, gentlemen. First Lieutenant, I took a more thorough look at your report and the information was so important I had my aide take it over to the Führer's staff headquarters. You had accumulated some very important information that we did not have.

"Now to the point why I asked you two here now. As you were leaving earlier I received a telephone call from the Führer.

He is sending me and an aide as a special envoy to Spain to talk with El Caudille Francisco Franco, and since I do not speak or understand Spanish, Lieutenant, you will accompany me. You will be my interpreter, since you are fluent with Spanish and Spanish customs.

"We will travel in civilian attire and we must leave tomorrow morning. What I have to talk with El Caudille about is time sensitive and the Führer directed me personally to go. We will fly to Paris and then change airlines for Madrid.

"And Major, I would like you to follow up on that Argentina business while I am away."

"Yes, Herr Admiral."

"Lieutenant, make arrangements for us to depart Berlin at the earliest possible tomorrow."

"Yes, Herr Admiral."

"Dismissed."

On their way downstairs Hammell said, "Lieutenant, I believe you are on the fast track for advancement. When you rise above me, I hope you will not forget me."

* * *

At 0600 hours the next morning Canaris and Hans boarded a plane for Paris. It was a smooth flight. They boarded a Spanish airliner immediately and they had to stop for fuel in Bilbao, northern Spain.

It had been a day and a half of travel and they went to a hotel for the night. After eating Canaris suggested, "You and I need to go for a walk, Lieutenant. There is much I must tell you, but I couldn't until we were alone." That's all that was said until they found a secluded spot in the park and a park bench. "There are some things that I must tell you before we talk with Franco tomorrow. I am bringing you into the intelligence loop, Lieutenant. That's how much I trust you and the work you have done."

Hans didn't say anything. He waited for the Admiral to continue. "The Führer has run into too much opposition to his new ideas for Germany. He wanted to unite and control all of Europe. He seems to think this is the best way to improve the lives of German people and all of Europe. He is prepared to go to war to accomplish these goals. I wanted you to know before we talk with Franco. I didn't want Franco to see any hint of surprise on your face. He will be reading us, as we will be reading his reactions.

"After the election in 1936 Franco and other generals tried a military coup which failed. Franco soon became the group's leader. The Civil War has recently ended and Francisco Franco has declared himself El Caudillo (the chief). Franco and Hitler have much in common and I think that's why Der Führer thinks our meeting tomorrow will be of a great value to Germany."

"It seems I left Spain just in time or I would probably have been inscripted into Franco's army," Hans said.

* * *

The next morning when Canaris and Hans arrived at Franco's headquarters they had to wait outside in the hall for an hour. Maybe this was to show the German Admiral who was in charge here.

The delay was because Franco had sent his aide to find someone who could speak German. He wanted to know what the Admiral and his translator were saying in German. He was not a trusting sort.

In perfect Spanish, Hans introduced the Admiral and himself. Franco was surprised with the Admiral's aides perfect usage of his language even the proper dialect.

For an hour their conversation was mostly niceties and small talk. Then the Admiral said. "El Caudillo, I am sure you must be aware of the Führer's progression to improve the economy and the lives of not just Germans, but for the people of all of Europe." Hans translated word for word and Canaris continued. "Der Führer has two questions for you, El Caudillo. He feels it may become necessary to use military force to convince some countries of his true goal of uniting all of Europe. It appears that some countries are dedicated to their old ways of doing things. They cannot see the value of Germany's new movement. Already the German people are feeling relief from the Great Depression and full industrialization. Der Führer would like Spain's—your support, El Caudillo—helping Germany to achieve these goals. And Der Führer would like your support and allow Germany, the Riech's Marine, to use the port of Gibraltar as a tactical attack base in the Mediterranean and the Atlantic Ocean."

As Hans was translating this Canaris was watching Franco for any change with his facial expressions. There were none.

There it was, everything had been put on the table. And Hans was only a little surprised when he heard the Führer would use force if he had to.

"I appreciate your sincerity, Señor Admiral. This is a big decision. I must first talk with my advisers. If you could possibly return tomorrow morning I am sure I will have an answer for you."

As they were leaving the building Canaris said, "Do not say anything until we are far away from here."

They walked to the same park and sat down on the same park bench overlooking the pond. "How do you think El Caudillo received our request?"

"I was under the impression you certainly took him by surprise, which set him at a disadvantage. I think he is worried that Germany may try to take Spain by force. It wasn't exactly what he said but he stumbled over his words some, I think trying not to offend you. My personal opinion, Admiral, I don't think he wants to involve his country," Hans said.

"I think you may be correct on all accounts. Spain just

ended a civil war, they will not be too anxious to fight in another.

"Lieutenant, what you have heard here today, the populace of Germany know nothing about. You must'nt ever repeat what you learn here."

"No, Herr Admiral, you have my trust."

* * *

Canaris was a bundle of nervous energy as he waited to talk with Franco again. In part he was worried how Hitler would react if he failed to gain Franco's alliance or use Gibraltar as a tactical attack base.

The waiting was over as Franco's aide escorted them to the inner office. "Sit down, gentlemen. I have given your request, Admiral, much thought. But I am afraid my people might react if I involve them in another war."

What Canaris had to say next took Hans by total surprise. "El Caudillo, it is my considered opinion that Der Führer is going to declare war on any country that does not voluntarily join Germany with their support. Der Führer, I think, is going to start a war that he cannot win. Therefore my suggestion to you, El Caudillo, is to stay out of it. And do not give aid or support to the Allies either, for if you should, I believe Germany would come down on Spain with vengeance."

When Hans had finished translating all three men sat in silence. In one way the Admiral had said to Franco not to join Germany in a war in which it cannot win and telling him at the same time of the consequences if he should join the Allies.

Finally it was Franco who broke the silence. "I will take your suggestion under advisement and consideration. But in all fairness I cannot allow Germany to use the Port of Gibraltar as an attack base. I think you can understand that, Señor Admiral."

* * *

Canaris and Hans left Spain and returned to Germany. Admiral Canaris was unusually quiet during the two day trip. Hans wasn't sure if the Admiral had failed or not and if he did fail what would Hitler do? Punish him for failure?

"I want to thank you, Lieutenant, for your help. I suppose now we both go back to doing what we were."

The next day Major Hammell went to see Canaris, "Come in, Major. What can I do for you?"

"I have an idea, Admiral."

"What is it?"

"We already have an agent working at the Naval Air Station in San Diego, California. What if we had a way to get shipments of guns across the border to this agent. As a precaution if the United States joins the Allies. We would have a means to attack the U.S. from within."

"Put someone on it to work out the logistics, Major, then get back to me."

"Yes, Herr Admiral."

Hammell went downstairs to Hans' work area. "Lieutenant."

"Yes, Herr Major?"

"Come with me."

"Yes Sir," and Hans followed the Major outside where he told him about the agent that was stationed in San Diego and working at the Naval Air Station.

"I need a viable plan to get guns across the border from Mexico to San Diego. Do you think you can come up with something?"

"Yes, Herr Major. I'll work on it. May I ask why you want the guns taken across?"

"Certainly. A precaution if the United States decides to join the Allies, an attack from within will demoralize the Americans."

"I will come up with something, Major."

Hans returned to his desk, but couldn't think clearly with all the noise around him. So he went outside and went for a walk around the base. He often did his best thinking while walking. He missed lunch and really didn't think too much about eating. He walked all afternoon and when everyone else was eating supper, he sat back at his desk and started making an outline.

He put his pen down at midnight and read over what he had. Then he'd sleep on it and review it again in the morning.

Hans fell asleep sitting at his desk, still holding his outline when someone opened the door to his office. It was Major Hammell. "Are you sick, Lieutenant? You look awful."

"No, no, I'm not sick. I fell asleep rereading the outline I was working on."

"You mean you were here all night?"

"Yes Sir. I finished my outline, but before I give it to you, I need to review it one more time."

"Certainly," and Hammell left and went back to his own office.

Hans went to his quarters first to clean up and put on some fresh clothes. Then he returned to his office and over a cup of coffee he read and studied his outline. When he was satisfied he went to see the Major.

"Yes, come in, Lieutenant."

"That request you made about getting guns into the United Sates—here is my outline."

Hammell took the outline and read and reread it twice more, "You did all this last night, Lieutenant?"

"Well, until I fell asleep around midnight."

"Unbelievable. I think we should go upstairs and see the Admiral and see what he thinks."

Canaris read through the outline with great interest. "When did you have time, Lieutenant, to figure all this out and write it up?"

"Last night, Herr Admiral."

"You mean you thought this up and put everything on paper last night?" Canaris asked and looked at Major Hammell who nodded his head slightly.

"Yes Herr Admiral. Major Hammell asked me to put together an idea how to get guns to the United States."

"Okay, now give us a rundown how you expect this idea to work," Canaris said.

"I volunteer, Herr Admiral, to go to Mexico to set this in motion. Whoever goes will have to be very fluent in Spanish. I am. I am trustworthy and I am very good at this kind of intelligence.

"I will have to travel to Spain right away to set up a contact and accounts with an antique Spanish furniture dealer. And I already have an individual in mind in Barcelona. And I think I can convince him to send guns hidden within the furniture and ship it to Mexico.

"I will have to set up a business in Tijuana, Mexico, which lies just south of the United States border and San Diego, California. I will also have to set up a business in San Diego where our intelligence officer who is already in San Diego can pick the guns up.

"The firearms should be manufactured in Spain, so they cannot be traced back to Germany. I will have to create another code to write to my furniture contact in Spain and the San Diego agent. Once I have taken delivery of the furniture and guns I will send a coded letter back to my contact so he can receive payment."

"This all seems so simple, are you sure you can do it and that it will work?" Canaris asked.

"Yes, Herr Admiral, I am sure. Mexico custom officials will not be looking for guns coming in from Spain, as I am sure the U.S. will not suspect Mexico.

"Of course I will need to know the agent's name in San Diego and how to contact him."

"You have convinced me, Lieutenant. Major you will be in charge of this operation and you'll have my written authorization to make it happen. Lieutenant Grubber, from this moment on you will answer to the Major. He will be your handler," Canaris said.

"Any questions?"

"Yes, Herr Admiral. There are many sections in the intelligence division that I will be needing access to. It will be easier if I was a Captain and not a Lieutenant researching this information."

"Any objections, Major?"

"None."

"Okay, Major make it happen."

* * *

Hans had the document people start work on his new identity, "I will need a birth certificate from Spain as well as passport for Enrico Flores. And a driver's license. I will be back in two weeks."

He drew money from payroll and flew to Madrid and then to Barcelona. As much as he would have liked to say hello to Luis and his wife, it would jeopardize his mission. He found the antique furniture store and Juan Perez was still in business. It took Hans two days to convince Señor Perez. But when Hans mentioned he would be amply compensated for his help, plus the sale of the antique furniture which would be used to hide the guns while being shipped, he agreed.

It took another two days to work out another code for communicating back and forth and another day to work out a deal with Star Z-45 (smg) machine guns. "Señor Perez will pay you for the guns when he picks them up."

"When will you need the first shipment, Captain?"

"Señor Perez will let you know."

Back at the antique store, "When will you want the first shipment?"

"I can't give you a date yet, but I will be back to see you before then and we'll set up a schedule."

* * *

Everything was set up in Spain for the purchase of the furniture and guns and on his flight back to Berlin, for the first time he understood that once he left Germany he knew he would never be able to come back.

He explained to Major Hammell how he had set things up. "Señor Perez will be the liaison between you and me, Major, and here is a copy of the code we will be using."

"How much more do you have to do here, Captain?"

"I should have everything done within a week. I am going to have to have the name of our agent in San Diego, Major, and how to get in touch with him."

"I'll have that information for you first thing tomorrow morning, Captain."

"There's one more point. I am going to need a considerable amount of money to set all this up and would it be possible to draw a year's advance on my wages?"

"Certainly. Just run it by payroll and figure up how much you'll need."

"Okay, Major, and thanks."

The agent in San Diego was Kerry Rupert, a good American name, so his father Elma and Susan Rupert figured. They had immigrated to the United States just months before the start of WWI. They had purchased false documents at a great expense to erase all effects of their German heritage. Their son Kerry was working on the Naval Air Station in San Diego as a civilian employee as a machinist. His father was custodian at the county hospital and Susan worked part time as a cook.

After Hans had read the file he returned it to Major Hammell. He put his address and contact in his briefcase.

Hans had no problem drawing an advance on his wages. But when he asked for $200,000.00 the clerk said, "I must have a voucher from Major Hammell."

"No problem." Hans went upstairs and was back in five minutes.

"That was quick, Captain."

"Major Hammell, this is a lot of money to be carrying with me. I would like to exchange some for raw diamonds. They will be easier to carry concealed."

"Do you know where you can purchase diamonds?"

"Yes, Major. The auction in Rotterdam, Netherlands."

"How long will it take you?"

"Flying round trip three days, top."

"How close are you to being ready?"

"This should be the last stop."

"Good, when you return, I want to go over everything with you."

He was already known at the auction so he used his Juan Esteban identity. The European economy had shown a little improvement in the last two years but the price for rough diamonds was still comparably low. He purchased one lot for $40,000.00 that he figured should have sold for $65,000.00 and he purchased another lot for $55,000.00 that he figured should have been worth almost $90,000.00. He would use the remaining $5,000.00 to purchase diamond cutting equipment in Spain and have it shipped with the furniture and guns.

All this planning and deception he found exciting. While working for the German cause he was also creating the foundations for a new life for himself.

* * *

Back at the Abwehr headquarters he asked the supply sergeant for a concealed money belt that would go around the waist, under his shirt. This would be a safe way to carry the money and diamonds and get them through Mexican customs.

"Come into my office, Captain—and close the door," Hammell said.

Hans closed the door and sat down. "Captain, do you have any reservations about going to Mexico and smuggling guns across the border to our agent there? Any reservations at all?"

"Not at all, Major. In fact I find all this rather exciting and exhilarating. And I think I have everything prepared."

"Normally I would not assign someone so new to operate so isolated. You will have to depend at all times on your own knowledge and survivability. If you get into trouble there will not be anyone who can help you."

"I understand that, Major, and I am still excited."

Major Hammell laughed then and said, "When this is all over I expect I'll be working for you, Captain. Now give me a rundown of your plans."

"Well, I have the money I need and some in diamonds. I have recruited two people in Barcelona who I can depend on to provide guns and ship them hidden in antique furniture to Mexico. When I get to Mexico I'll establish a Spanish antique furniture business—a cover to receiving the hidden guns. I will also establish a similar business in San Diego and hide the guns within the furniture to get them across the border. I'll contact our agent there. I have his name and address and recruit someone I can trust, perhaps his father, to manage that business and receive the guns and see that our agent gets them.

"I have created a code we all will use and I have already given you a copy.

"My passports and paperwork are already taken care of and all the information I'll need I have written in code in a notebook."

"It seems to me you have taken care of everything. What about your folks, Hans?"

"I have thought about that, but I think it best if they know nothing about what I do. I feel for my mother, but I stopped caring for my father years ago."

As a covert intelligence officer, Hammell understood Hans' decision. Hammell stood and instead of saluting Captain Grubber, he shook his hand and said, "Good luck, Hans, and never forget you will always be alone."

Chapter 5

Hans had made a hidden covey in the bottom of his traveling bag to hide his papers and forged passports. His money belt he kept with him.

When he boarded the airplane for Spain he had no regrets about leaving. There was nothing he was leaving behind. He never looked back.

In Barcelona he wanted to be careful not to meet Luis. But in a way he felt like he was coming home as he walked the streets. Before he went to make final arrangements with Lucas Perez at the furniture store, he ordered diamond cutting and polishing equipment to be delivered to Lucas Perez.

"What am I to do with this equipment, Señor?"

"Send it with the first shipment of furniture."

"When should I ship it, Señor?"

"Ship it one month from today. To the Flores Diamond and Furniture Cartel. I have already contacted the Delta De Lebre shipping company and they will be expecting the cargo a week before it is to be loaded.

"Delta De Lebre has two new victory class steamships and passage to Tampico will take about fifteen days. Weather permitting. Once I'm there I'll make pre-arrangements to have everything shipped to Tijuana. Once you have shipped the cargo, then follow my procedures to notify Major Hammell and then you will be paid."

"Everything is alright with me Señor. What are you, waging your own war? I don't want to know what you are doing.

But everything is okay."

"Thank you Lucas."

That evening instead of sleeping he went for a walk around Barcelona. He went by Antonio's shop, by his old rent, and he spent two hours walking in the park. Barcelona was more home to him than where he grew up.

The Delta De Lebre left port at night with the high tide. Hans Grubber was standing on the fantail watching the city lights disappear and experiencing a sense of loneliness. For Hans Grubber no longer existed. From this day on he would be Enrico Flores from Barcelona, Spain looking for citizenship in Mexico.

With nothing to do on board the freighter he became bored. The ship was equipped to handle four passengers, but he was the only one on this trip.

Because of the season, the Captain sailed a few knots faster and trimmed three days off the passage. So on the morning of the twelfth day Enrico walked into the main office of Delta De Lebre and asked to speak with the manager. "Yes, Señor, what can I do for you?"

"My name is Enrico Flores and I arrived this morning aboard your ship. In a month, an associate of mine in Barcelona will be sending some cargo for me aboard your ship. I am now on my way to Tijuana to establish an antique furniture business. The cargo that is being shipped will be stock for my store. I would like to make arrangements now to have it shipped to Tijuana, please. The address will be Flores Diamond Cutting and Antique Furniture Cartel."

"Surely, Señor Flores, we can take care of that here. Fill out these forms if you would. Will you be shipping much more in the future with us?"

"Yes. Once I have my business established I expect to use your shipping company often."

Enrico filled out the forms and handed them back to the manager. "When I get to Tijuana I will send you a letter informing you of my address."

Tampico appeared to be a prosperous city. It was clean and he would have liked to be able to stay a few days, but he had a schedule he needed to keep. So he boarded a train that would only take him as close as it was going to Tijuana, at Mexicali.

As he left the Atlantic coastal area, the air became very hot. Temperatures that he was not used to. But the air was drier, which helped.

In Chihuahua the train turned southwest to Los Mochis on the Pacific coast. The air was much cooler and fresher here.

Finally the train stopped at its northern terminal in Mexicali. Standing on the platform looking north he could see a little of the United States. From there he went by bus to Tijuana.

Tijuana was much more than he had expected. If not for his mission he could have a good time here.

He found a room to let by the day and then he laid down to sleep. Twelve days of rock and rolling on aboard the ship and for twelve days eating greasy food, and then the exasperating train ride to Mexicali. He was worn out.

He awoke the next afternoon after twelve hours of sleep. He ate a light lunch and then went about finding the perfect place for his cartel business. On the second day he found what he wanted. A vacant small warehouse just off main street. The building had a rock walled cellar with a dirt floor. The main floor was sturdy and sound with a living space above it.

He bought the property, hired carpenters to remodel and remake the first level with huge showroom windows. And he gutted and rebuilt the upstairs.

He purchased only enough furnishings for the upstairs so that he could move in. He had already forwarded his address to the manager of Delta De Lebre shipping. After a month his new store and apartment were finished and his first shipment of furniture and guns should be leaving Barcelona.

In the meantime he crossed the border into the United States and found it much quicker and easier than passing through any European custom check. He found a transit bus into

San Diego and then a taxi cab to the agent's address. He wasn't going to make contact yet. He simply wanted to be sure he could find the address. Not far away he found a park and decided this would be a good location for their first meeting.

He had brought paper and envelope with him to write a letter to Kerry Rupert and have it postmarked from this side of the border.

He said he was there by directions of a mutual friend and would be in the park close to his address on Friday evening at 7 pm. That would give him three days. Then he bought a stamp from a local drug store and dropped the letter in a mailbox.

Then he walked around the city some to get acquainted with it, and to find a building here he could establish an antique furniture business. Actually not too far from Rupert's address he found exactly what he was looking for.

A for sale sign was just being put up on a vacant building. Enrico introduced himself and said, "I would like to talk with you about purchasing this building." The owner showed him the interior and it was perfect. There wouldn't even have to be any remodeling and there was a delivery door in the rear.

"When would you like to close, Mr. Flores?"

"Would Friday morning at 10 o'clock be too soon?"

"No, that'll be fine. I'll have my attorney draw up the closing papers. How will you be financing this?"

"Would cash be acceptable?"

"Oh, most assuredly. If you don't mind me asking, what are your intentions with this old building?"

"I am in the Spanish antique furniture business."

Before leaving he wanted to obtain a mail address for his business and was surprised how easy it was. He was never asked for proof of identification.

On his way back across the border he thought of something that he had forgotten to do. He would need some American identification. He would have to have a banking account to operate a business in the U.S. He would also need invoices, receipts.

That night in his own home he forged an American passport, driver's license and the next time he was in San Diego he would exchange some pesos for dollars. It was 4 am before he laid down to sleep.

That morning he found a print shop in Tijuana and had all the necessary paper forms made up. Then he went to the Banco de Mexico and set up an account for the Flores Cartel. And obtained a certified bank draft in the amount of $30,000.00 in cash. His own personal money he kept at his home.

Thursday morning Enrico Flores crossed the border again and this time he was asked, "Didn't you come across two days ago? What is your business?"

"Yes Sir, I did cross two days ago and I am establishing a Spanish antique furniture business. And you'll probably see me many times in the future." He did not have to disclose how much money he was carrying with him.

Enrico was surprised how easy it was to set up a bank account. He made out a form requesting the name of the business, his name and address.

He kept $15,000.00 for the purchase price of the building plus that gave him $1000.00 to play with.

At 10 o'clock he met the owner of the building and in five minutes the building was his. His attorney said, "I'll have this recorded and send you the deed."

"Thank you."

Instead of going back to Tijuana and having to cross again tomorrow, he stayed in San Diego and walked about the Naval base. He was allowed inside the security gate. He had lunch at a nearby restaurant.

That night he stayed in a hotel and slept in late. It was almost noon before he awoke.

He was in the park early and when he noticed a lone man enter, he figured this was Mr. Rupert. He walked over and, "It is a nice evening."

"Yes it is. I was supposed to meet a friend here."

"If you are Kerry Rupert, I am your contact." They sat down on a park bench away from others.

"Mr. Rupert, I know of your mission here. I now have a new one for you. I am to get guns across the border to you to distribute to your contacts. I have set up a furniture business not far from here," and he gave Rupert the address.

"The first shipment of guns is on its way here, hidden inside the furniture. As soon as the shipment arrives I will bring them across to this new store. Now, it would be good if you could quit your job on the Naval base and manage this store and redirect the guns. I do not need to know who your contacts are or where the guns will be going. That is between you and your handler."

"I can quit my job on the base without any problem. I still have friends who work there and I should be able to get any worthwhile information from them that I can pass along.

"How do we run the business?"

"Just like any business. There is a bank account already set in place. Your income will come from the furniture sales. You will keep all records and I will occasionally review them."

"How soon will the first shipment come?"

"It is crossing the Atlantic now and I have already made arrangements to have it shipped to Tijuana. I'm thinking in six weeks we'll be in business. You probably shouldn't quit your job for another month. "

They talked long after the sun had set and then Enrico went back to his hotel. So far everything was going okay.

* * *

With both businesses set to go and arrangements had been made with Kerry Rupert, all there was to do now was wait until the first shipment arrived.

Four weeks later Enrico received a telegram from the shipping company that his cargo had arrived and had been sent on via truck service. Two trailer trucks actually, and should arrive soon.

Two days later the service trucks arrived and everything was unloaded into the warehouse portion of his store.

Enrico rode with the load across the border. He wanted the custom officials to believe he was on the up and up. They opened the trail box and saw it was full of furniture and said, "You're clear to leave."

Enrico stayed long enough to help Rupert unload everything and set the furniture up in the display room and then he returned to Tijuana. How Kerry Rupert moved the guns to his people was now out of Enrico's concern. He had fulfilled his part of the operation. Now to wait for another load.

While he waited he thought it would look better if he had a wife. Then people would be more convinced he was here permanently, without creating suspicions. So during the day he sold furniture and at night he cruised the bars. Which ever woman he chose she would have to meet certain criteria. First, she would have to be an asset to his business. She would have to come without a family. An orphan. She would have to be able to keep their business secret and she would have to be subservient and not a tigress.

In the meantime another shipment of two trailer loads arrived with more guns. They had sold many pieces from both stores and needed the new shipment. But Kerry Rupert only needed a few guns. He had not been able to dispense all of them. So Enrico dug a hole in his cellar and built a vault under the dirt floor to store the guns and ammo in. When he had finished, if you didn't know of the vault underground, you would never suspect there was one.

The furniture business was good and more so in San Diego. Enrico had to on occasion take some from his store across the border. By now the custom officials were used to his comings and goings and no longer inspected his cargo.

* * *

Major Hammell had received a letter from Kerry Rupert through his contacts and he was pleasantly surprised. He took it up to Admiral Canaris' office.

"Come in, Major. What is it?" he asked.

"I have a letter this morning from our agent Rupert in San Diego. The letter was forwarded through his contacts," Hammell gave the letter to the Admiral and then waited.

Canaris leaned back in his chair as he read. When he finished he said, "That young man, Major, surprises me. All on his own he has established a network for getting the guns across the U.S. border without question and a way for Rupert's contacts to pick them up. He is ingenious."

"I'll make payment to the Captain's furniture contact in Spain," Major Hammell said.

* * *

After a month of visiting practically every bar in Tijuana Enrico found the kind of woman he was looking for. Elena Carlos had a sinewy body, short black hair and a smile that had captivated him. And she was an orphan, no family. He was quite taken with her.

Three weeks later they were married. He told her about the furniture business, but not about smuggling guns. That would come later. But there was no way she was ever going to learn about his German heritage. There was nothing in his home or business that would tend to make anyone believe he was German.

Elena became pregnant early on. At first Enrico was furious, but as time passed he decided having a family would help to secure himself as a Mexican businessman.

One day after a new shipment had arrived Elena was helping Enrico to move the furniture around and she said, "Why

93

is this furniture so heavy, Enrico?"

That day he had to tell her about smuggling guns across the border to San Diego. "But why, Enrico?"

"There is a market for guns across the border and there is money to be made." That's all he was willing to tell her. And then to Elena's shock he added, "If you ever say a word about what I am doing, Elena, I will cut your throat."

She believed he would. "I will not say anything, Enrico, or ask any more questions about them."

Their furniture sales in both stores was increasing each month and Enrico had to write Lucas Perez in Barcelona to send more and a catalog. But that was creating an inventory of guns Enrico had to keep hidden.

* * *

Some months, Kerry Rupert in San Diego could disperse all of his guns and some months he couldn't, causing Enrico to keep a large number of guns buried in the cellar of his warehouse. The furniture was selling faster than the guns were being dispersed. At first Enrico was feeling guilty about making so much money and Germany paying the bill.

In mid-October of 1939, on the front page of the newspaper, was an article and photos about Germany's blitzkrieg into Poland. Enrico read the entire article with interest. Still he believed in the Führer's new ideas about how to improve life for the German people and any who chose to join Germany.

He had to do a lot of thinking on that.

Maybe Admiral Canaris knew something he wasn't telling others. He expected all along that Hitler would use military force against Europe. But deep down Enrico wanted to believe in the greater cause that would bring all of Europe together and strengthen the economy and better lives for everyone. So he continued to do his part in getting the guns across the border to San Diego.

There were times when Rupert would run out of guns and there were other times when he had to stockpile them. But the furniture kept selling. And customers were beginning to special order items.

The furniture business was doing so well, he set up his diamond cutting and polishing equipment and began cutting diamonds. He purchased some jewelry gold locally and began fashioning elegant jewelry.

The most expensive pieces he took across the border and sold at auction in Los Angeles. On these trips he would also purchase a few rough stones. And not once had it occurred to him to declare the jewelry or rough stones when crossing the border. Smuggling had become such a common practice, he never gave much thought to declaring the diamonds. He had made many friends at both crossings and they slowly began to let him pass back and forth without even looking at his cargo.

Elena gave birth to a boy in the spring of 1940 and Enrico named him Pietro Juan Flores. With the birth of his son changes started happening how Enrico felt about Germany and Der Führer's action to bring all of Europe under one rule. He knew then he would never return to Germany, no matter the outcome of Hitler's war.

And war is what Europe and the United States were calling it now. Hundreds of merchant vessels were being sunk in the Atlantic Ocean and the Nazis were rounding up all Jews and shipping them off to concentration camps. He wondered then about his mentor Karl Hermon and his wife in Kiel. He had always known the Hermons were Jewish but he had given it no thought at all.

One day while these thoughts were troubling him he wrote a coded letter to Lucas Perez in Barcelona and asked him to stop shipping any more guns. He said it had become very difficult to smuggle them across the border and for their agent in San Diego to disperse them. Which both were lies, but he wanted the gun shipments to stop. But he asked to continue shipping the furniture with an invoice and he would pay for them.

A reply from Perez never came. And the shipment of furniture and guns continued. Enrico had so many guns he had to purchase a vacant building away from Tijuana to store them. By now he had also purchased a van delivery truck that he could use to transport the guns to this new location and take furniture across the border to San Diego.

* * *

Another year had passed and Elena was pregnant again. The furniture business, even in spite of the war in Europe and over China, was doing exceedingly well. Enrico had to purchase a large building in San Diego and this new building also had a cellar to it, where more guns could be stored.

With war looming in both the East and West some of Kerry Rupert's contacts had been inscripted into the army. It was simply impossible to take care of the guns they had. They were stockpiling every month, with new deliveries. For the first time Enrico thought he might be exposed.

He was so afraid of being caught he started burying guns in the desert where no one would think to look.

England and France both had declared war against Germany and the flow of guns from Spain started to dwindle until the beginning of 1941 when they stopped altogether. But the furniture kept coming and Enrico was now paying for each shipment.

In the spring of 1941 Elena gave birth to a girl this time, and she was named Avilla Rose Flores. And the fighting in the East and West was accelerating. Every day now there was a new article on the front page of the newspaper.

Enrico's biggest concern now was, what would happen if Germany should win. Admiral Canaris didn't think Germany could. But so far all of Europe and Russia were taking an awful beating from German forces. He knew it would only be a matter of time until the United States joined the Allies in Europe and then there would not be any possibility of Germany winning the war.

With two kids to look after now, Elena stayed at home and Enrico had to hire someone and he installed a new lock on the cellar door. He was the only person allowed in there.

To slow the business some he increased prices on all furniture by 5%. Which slowed the market for three months. But in December of 1941 after Japan attacked Pearl Harbor in Hawaii, the San Diego business dried up and Enrico had to ship all the furniture back to Tijuana and he closed the doors, but kept ownership of the building. The guns had long since been moved. Kerry Rupert went back to work on the base fueling aircraft. Three months later and Kerry Rupert was inducted into the U.S. Army.

Business was still good in Tijuana, but Enrico needed another project to keep his mind busy. So he traveled to Ciudad Juarez across the border from El Paso, Texas and opened another furniture store.

It took the better part of a year to get the store set up in Ciudad Juarez. His wife Elena was beginning to complain about him being away from home so much. Before the store was set to go, people from across the border in El Paso were coming to see his furniture.

Even though the United States was now at war with Japan the Americans were still buying his antique looking furniture. He had found a good manager in Juarez, Carlos Camile. "Carlos, I expect your honesty and trustworthiness. If I discover you have been stealing from me I will take you out in the desert and cut your throat."

Chapter 6

The store in Juarez was selling almost as many pieces of furniture as the San Diego store had. Enrico now had a good trustworthy manager in the Tijuana store and when he wasn't working between the stores he would cut and fashion diamonds in specialty settings. They sold for a lot of money.

To make his San Diego crossing look legitimate he began foraging sale and purchase receipts. Something to show customs on both sides.

Germany was now fighting two fronts and Enrico couldn't imagine why Hitler had sent his forces into Russia. There was no possible way he could ever expect to defeat a country that was so expansive, with more resources than Germany. Germany was now occupying France and still waging war against the English and North Africa. Enrico said out loud, "The man is a lunatic." Then he began to wonder if this wasn't what Admiral Canaris was aware of when they talked with Francisco Franco in Spain.

He also surmised that Germany was too busy to come looking for him and their money. For the first time he was beginning to feel like a criminal. And in a sick way of thinking, he found this exciting.

On one trip to his warehouse store in San Diego he was told by a neighboring shopkeeper that Kerry Rupert had been killed in a battle on Midway Island. That was the only person in the western world who knew Enrico was German, but not his German name. Enrico found some comfort in this.

* * *

In 1944 the United States joined the Allies and declared war on Germany also. The end was near for Germany and Enrico could see this.

These Americans surprised Enrico. When Japan bombed Pearl Harbor they didn't know at the time, but they had kicked a hornet's nest. The Japanese did not believe the Americans would fight so aggressively and now they were bringing the war to Japan's front door. And all while the Americans were fighting the Japanese and the Germans, his furniture sales in Ciudad Juarez were better than the San Diego's store ever was. And the biggest buyers were from Texas. They had money to spend.

Reading the headlines in the newspaper every day, it was obvious to Enrico that Germany was losing the war. Just like Admiral Canaris had predicted. He often wondered what would become of the Admiral. Would he be held for war crimes? Would he have seen the fallacies and resigned? He liked the Admiral.

On June 8, 1944 the entire newspaper was about the Allied troops landing on the beach of Normandy and how the Allies were already pushing the German troops back towards Germany.

It was obvious now Germany was going to lose. It was only a matter of time. And this gave Enrico a sense of security. He would have been forgotten by now and probably the Abwehr, Hitler's intelligence division, did not even exist now. Everyone would be trying to protect themselves. And no one in the U.S. or Mexico knew about the gun smuggling operation he had been conducting. Not even his wife Elena.

When he left Germany he had $100,000.00 plus the value of the rough diamonds, and all of the furniture in both stores was paid for. Plus he still owned the building in San Diego, two buildings in Tijuana and now one in Juarez.

He threw the newspaper in the trash and started cutting a smoky rough diamond to be set in a special design.

Because so many young American men had been called up to serve, there was a great need for workers. Especially in the steel and munitions industries. So many Mexican men and women applied for work visas to fill that nitch. And many of these same Mexican workers could not afford furniture that Enrico had is his showroom.

German U boats had been attacking any merchant vessel sailing on the Atlantic. But somehow the Spanish shipping company was never targeted. Enrico thought this probably was due in part to the conversation Admiral Canaris had had with Franco, warning him to stay out of the war. The trade off had to be information about the Allies that Spain was providing to Germany.

By April of 1945 things were not looking good for Germany. Russia was closing in fast from the East and the Allies were closing in from the West. Many German troops had had enough. They were tired of fighting and they were hungry. They began to surrender by the tens-of-thousands.

Then on May 9, 1945, Enrico read on the front page of the newspaper that Germany had officially surrendered and the war in Europe was over. Enrico was now feeling safe. He knew his name would not appear on any reports or documents found at Abwehr headquarters. If there was anything left of it after the Allied bombing.

On September 4, 1945, the newspaper entry was all about the official surrender of Japan on September 2. Enrico supposed now that as the American troops came home more Mexican workers would be laid-off and return to Mexico. He also supposed that for a while his furniture business would slow down.

Soon after the end of Japan, Elena was not feeling good and Enrico took her to the hospital. Two days later doctors told him his wife had advanced cancer and there was nothing they could do except treat her for pain with morphine.

Four months later in January, Elena died leaving Enrico

with their two children, Pietro, 5, and Avilla, 4. There was no way he could care for two kids plus take care of business, so he hired a woman to live in, Maria Rosetta.

He tried staying around home more and working on cutting and faceting diamonds. He made another expensive setting with a large diamond. And with that and some smaller diamonds and settings he went to Los Angles to sell them.

Losing their mother was a great lose for Pietro and Avilla and they really didn't know their father Enrico. He had always been so busy and away from home. When he wasn't cutting and faceting diamonds he would spend time with his two kids, trying to get to know them. Maria had moved in and it took a while for the two kids to accept her. Not as a mother, but as a friend and someone who would look out after them.

* * *

A few years passed and Enrico was getting bored with his life. He heard about a coffee plantation that could be purchased near Chihuahua in a small village named Aldama. The owners of the plantation were elderly and their only son was not interested.

Enrico walked around the plantation and liked what he saw and he balked at the owner's selling price and left. He returned two days later with a counteroffer, which was only half of the asking price. But with one additional clause. Señor and Señora Rafael could continue living in the main house for as long as they wanted. The downstairs would be theirs and Enrico would have the upstairs and the office. He also agreed to keep the foreman and a few of the yearly workers. The Rafaels accepted without question and Enrico Flores was now a coffee plantation owner. He had enough money from the diamond business to purchase the plantation and set up a banking account for the farm.

"I want you to understand one thing, Señor Miguel, you have access to the plantation account. I will periodically inspect the books and if I discover that you have been stealing from me I'll cut your throat. Do we understand each other, Señor?"

"Yes Señor, I understand. You can trust me."

"Good."

* * *

Enrico would have liked to have moved his family to the plantation, if it were not for all the guns he had hidden beneath his warehouse and in the desert. And he was tired of travelling by rail and bus. There was a car that went with the plantation, but he decided to leave it there, for when he visited.

He needed his own airplane. There was a small private airfield in San Diego. After talking with people at the Piper aircraft company he decided to buy the Super-cub. "In the future if you want to attach pontoons you can with this airplane. It is also a verbal workhorse. But before I can let you fly it—you must have a pilot's license."

Enrico stayed in the apartment above his old store in San Diego while he studied and trained for his license. And like everything he did, with perfection. He studied manuals and aced the written test. And he was a natural in the cockpit. "Are you sure you have never flown before?" the instructor asked.

When he had his pilot's license he took his two kids for a ride out over the Pacific Ocean. And this airplane seemed to bring them closer together. They each started calling him Papa. Pietro was eleven and Avilla was ten.

* * *

With Miguel being a free hand to run the coffee plantation as he saw it, the plantation actually made a profit that first year. And he gave Miguel a nice bonus that year and a smaller one for each worker. His philosophy was to keep the workers happy and they would produce.

Twice a year he would take Pietro and Avilla with him in the airplane. The Rafaels were just like grandparents to them and more like a mother and father than his own.

Each year after that the plantation was showing more of a profit. Enrico Flores, aka Hans Grubber, was considered a wealthy man.

Two years later both of the Rafaels died and Enrico moved Pietro, Avilla and even Maria was willing to relocate to the plantation.

When Avilla turned fifteen he and Avilla flew aboard a new DC-3 passenger plane to Paris, France, where he enrolled her into a girls school. For two years and then to a university where she wanted to study accounting, foreign language and business management. She was gifted like her father with a brilliant mind. Pietro liked the plantation and he and Miguel got along very well.

Pietro was smart but not like his father or sister. He was more aggressive and Enrico had to keep reminding him that he cannot push the workers so hard or they'll quit.

* * *

While in Chihuahua one day he overheard a group of men talking, conversing, at a sidewalk café. Talking about some faction south of Mexico that was needing firearms. After all but one man had left, Enrico walked over to the other table and said, "Excuse me, Señor, but couldn't help but hear you talking about needing some guns. Is this true?"

"Who are you Señor?"

"Someone who might be able to help you. You don't need to know my name nor I yours."

"How do I know you are not federali?"

"Do I look like a federali, Señor?"

"No, you are too small."

"I don't need to know for what reason you are needing

guns, as long as they are not to be used against Mexico."

"I can assure you they will not be used in Mexico. What do you have?"

"I have three hundred star SMG machineguns, and ammo."

"How much are you asking, Señor?"

"$46,000.00, Señor. That comes with clips and ammo."

"$153 and change per gun; that is a good price.

"I will have to speak with my associates, Señor. You meet me here two days from now and you will have my answer."

"I will be here. There is one stipulation."

"What is it?"

"I don't want cash. You will pay me with rough diamonds. And let me assure you, Señor, do not try to pass off fakes. I know diamonds."

Enrico stood up and said as he was leaving, "In two days."

He went back to the plantation to look for a secluded field or old road where he could land with his plane loaded with guns. He didn't want to involve the plantation workers, or his family, so he looked for an area away from the plantation. After two hours of searching, he found an old abandoned gravel road that led to an abandoned quarry.

"This should be ideal," he said.

Two days later, an hour and a half before the meeting, he waited on a sidewalk bench across the street to wait to see who—and if anyone—would show up early.

Then right on time the same person arrives, gets a cup of coffee and sits at the same table. Enrico waited a few minutes to make sure he was alone. When he was satisfied he walked across the street and sat down.

"You're late."

"No, I was watching to see if anyone was watching from the sidelines."

"Are you satisfied?"

"I'm here. What have you and your associates decided?"

"We'll agree to your terms. It'll take a week though to come up with the rough diamonds."

"That'll be okay. It'll take me two weeks to gather the guns," Enrico said.

"I thought you said you already had the guns."

"I do. But they are not here."

"Okay, two weeks. Where will we meet?"

Enrico had already drawn a map. "Can you find this place?"

"That won't be a problem."

"This goes bad or if you fail to keep your word, I'll cut your throat," Enrico said in a mild tone and he looked him in the eyes when he said it.

The buyer believed every word of the threat. Particularly since it was given in such a mild tone to his words. "Okay, two weeks from today. What time?"

"7 pm."

* * *

Enrico flew back to Tijuana, crossed the border and spent the night in the apartment above the empty store. The next day he walked to the nearest gun and ammo store five blocks away and bought a .38 special revolver with a 2 ½ inch barrel. Something he could conceal in his pants pocket. He didn't fully trust the buyer.

Before driving back to Tijuana he checked to make sure he had taken all of the guns out. At the crossing the custom officials were use to seeing Enrico Flores. They simply waved him through.

That night before midnight he loaded into his car all the guns he had stored below the warehouse and drove out to his airplane and loaded them. He had already topped off his fuel tanks and he now put another five gallon can of gas inside also.

Just in case, he would be flying with another extra 1500 pounds.

He was tired, but if he left now he figured he could reach the plantation just as the sun was coming up.

It was a smooth flight down and when he landed both fuel tanks were reading empty. He came in on fumes. Miguel came out with an old panel truck to meet Enrico and he was shocked when he saw all of the guns. "Señor Flores, what is all this?"

"Miguel, not a word. You know what will happen to you if you breathe a word of what you see here."

"Sí, Señor."

The loaded panel truck was put in a shed and it was locked. "Miguel, please refuel the plane for me. I will be leaving again at noon."

"Sí, Señor." Miguel had no idea what business Enrico was in with so many guns, and he didn't want to know.

Enrico slept for four hours and then flew to Tijuana, refueled his plane, drove out to his desert cache and left the guns in his car under a blanket and some boxes and left that parked behind his store/warehouse while he slept another four hours.

The air was turbulent on his last trip and he decided to fly north of the Sierra Madre Mountains and then turn south to Aldama and his plantation. But this caused him to use more fuel and he had to set down at a small air strip near El Sueco.

This detour and refuel cost him two extra hours and the sun had been up for three hours when he landed at the plantation. Miguel didn't know how he knew, but he suspected he had better take the loaded panel truck out to meet Enrico. And he was surprised to see more guns and so many bullets. He didn't say a word. He only looked at his boss questioningly. Enrico was tired and didn't respond.

After putting the truck away, he lay down and slept for twelve hours.

A few days before the meeting with the buyer, Enrico drove out to the old field where they were to meet and walked around it, looking for likely spots where he could be ambushed. There were a few at the edges, so he decided to be there early and wait in the middle. This would give him good visibility all around. Satisfied he drove back to the plantation.

In the meantime, to launder money from the gun sale, he made out a forged receipt and sales invoice for diamonds that didn't yet exist.

He would stay on the plantation until after the sale, then he'd fly back to Tijuana and cut the diamonds and make some fashionable jewelry. The difference between his purchase receipt and his sales invoice of course was only $46,000.00. The money he would deposit in his bank account in Tijuana.

Two weeks had finally passed and Enrico drove the panel truck out into the middle of the deserted field and waited. It was 5 pm. For $46,000.00 he didn't mind the two hour wait. The .38 special he had purchased in San Diego was now loaded and in his pants pocket.

At 6:30 Enrico could see a dust cloud rising from the lower end and figured his buyer had arrived. He fingered his gun in his pocket again. A nervous response. He could see only one person in the pickup with a homemade cap over the back.

When the pickup stopped Enrico stepped out. "Do you have everything?" the buyer asked.

"Yes, and I guess this is where I ask to see what you have brought."

The buyer produced a small leather pouch and handed it to Enrico. He opened the pouch and emptied the diamonds in his hands and took out his loupe and fixed it to his eye and began examining the stones. The largest one had a slight imperfection which he could work around, but it did devalue the stone. The smaller ones were okay. "The large stone has an imperfection which lowers the value. According to my calculations I am missing one stone. It would be my guess you decided to make a little profit yourself."

"I assure you it is all there."

Enrico pulled out his .38 and stuck it in the man's face and said in a mild tone. "The other stone please. I should kill you for trying to cheat me. We will never do business again."

The mild even tone scared the buyer more than the gun, and he reluctantly produced the other stone. "I thought so. Now you can have the guns and ammo. But for my safety, I am going to stand back here where I can watch you load everything into your vehicle. And I would hurry if I were you."

Chapter 7

On the drive back to the plantation Enrico was relieved that he had finally gotten rid of all the guns and ammo. And made a tidy profit on them.

The next day he flew to Ciudad Juarez to check on business and the following day on to Tijuana. Where he remained for several days working the rough diamonds into fashionable jewelry. The large diamond with the slight blemish, this time he shaped it and cut facets without splitting the diamond. When he had finished he now had a beautiful piece of fine work that he was sure would sell for more than the total value of the guns.

When he had finished each stone to perfection, he crossed the border and voluntarily showed the officer his work. And of course to officially declare them. "Did you make this jewelry Señor Flores?" The custom officer asked.

"Yes, when I am not selling furniture."

He was early for the auction in Los Angeles and he waited excitedly anticipating how high the bids would go.

Once the doors were opened and after he had his display set up he walked around viewing the other displays. His was the smallest display, but his work was not unnoticed by others there. Many were impressed with the settings.

He finally sold his small collection for three times the $46,000.00. The amount of money was not important to him. What was was the fact he liked the rush, the excitement of getting away with it. Outsmarting his opponent. That's what was important to Enrico Flores.

He had outwitted the French, the English, the Scots, the Spaniards, his own countrymen, the Americans, the Mexicans and now whomever it had been that had bought his guns. Who would ever expect such a pleasant mild mannered businessman to be involved in such undertakings.

* * *

When Avilla graduated from the university she had a degree in accounting and business management, and she could speak fluent French, English and Russian. Like her father, while in college she had forged her own French documents and applied for a passport using her new name and identity: Belle Saucier.

She and her brother Pietro had been working on a plan for the last year and part of it was for Avilla to get a job with the French Consulate in Saigon, South Vietnam. South Vietnam was fighting a civil war with North Vietnam and had asked France for help. Two months before graduating Avilla was able to secure a position with the French Consulate in Saigon. Two weeks after graduating she was unpacking her bags at the Continental Hotel in Saigon. She was one of Ambassador Huber Ewing's assistants. Her job was to type and file all of his reports. No one at the Consulate was aware that she could speak and understand several languages besides French.

With her job now secured, Pietro could go ahead with their plans. But first he had to speak with his father about what he and his sister were doing.

* * *

"Papa, after we finish dinner I need to speak with you," Pietro said.

"Why can't you say what you have to say to me right here, now?"

"Because, Papa, there are too many ears listening. I must

110

speak with you in private." Enrico just nodded his head.

Neither one said another word until they were outside. "Where shall we go?" Enrico asked.

"Out in the coffee tree groves. It'll look as if we are only inspecting the trees."

They walked in silence out into the middle of the nearest grove. "Avilla and I have been working a year on how we can set up a network across the border to sell marijuana. The drug is becoming more and more popular. If we move now we can corner the market."

"And you couldn't talk with me about this?"

"Papa, you are never in one place long enough for anyone to have much of a conversation with you."

"All right, I'll give you that. Now explain your plans," Enrico said.

"First of all we need to grind our own coffee beans instead of selling them to a coffee manufacturer."

"And."

"And, we build our own coffee company across the border in El Paso. We sell our coffee throughout the United States. We buy marijuana in Mexico, in bales and ship them in the coffee beans across the border. The awful smell of the coffee beans will hide the smell of the marijuana."

"Okay so far. How does Avilla come into this plan, being in Vietnam?"

"She can easily buy opium and other narcotics in Vietnam and mail them here hidden in artifacts."

"You two have this all worked out I see. How soon does this go into operation?"

"I have already found an empty building on the north side of El Paso, at the city limits. We'll have to rebuild and get the equipment set up before we have to pick our crop."

* * *

Later as Enrico thought about the whole idea, the more he liked it and he liked his son's initiative and how well he had everything so well organized. And his daughter Avilla really surprised him. He understood now that when he was gone the two together would be able to take over the Flores Cartel and run it.

* * *

Avilla, like her father, possessed a very sharp mind and intellect. She could read or type any report and then be able to almost repeat word for word what it had said. At times she was typing some very confidential and secret reports for Ambassador Ewing.

One evening while she was sipping a drink in the Texas bar she could overhear two people in the corner speaking in low tones and in Russian. This piqued her interest immediately.

During the evening many soldiers on leave had asked her to dance. She had declined all. She was more interested with what the two Russians were saying.

Sometime later the music was of a slow waltz. She stood up and walked over to their table, "Would either of you gentlemen like to dance?"

They both looked at each other in surprise. "Well do you?" she asked again.

This time one of them stood up and Avilla led him to the dance floor.

As they were dancing the guy asked, "What's your name, honey?"

"Belle, and that's all you need to know."

"Okay, Belle—I'm Larry and that's all you need know."

Then in fluent Russian Belle whispered in his ear, "I have information to sell. Are you interested?"

"Yes, what's it going to cost me?"

"$5,000.00. And not in traceable bills. I want raw diamonds."

"What's the information, honey?"

"Not until you have the stones."

"It'll take time."

"Better not be more than two days or the information will be of no use."

"I'll see what I can do. How will I find you?"

"This is Wednesday. Friday—here at 10 o'clock in the evening. Oh, and a word of precaution. I know diamonds, so don't try to pass off fakes."

Avilla went back to her room, showered and went to bed. This whole thing this evening, she found exciting. She liked being Belle Saucier. But at the consulate she would have to remain Avilla Flores.

The next day one of the reports she had to type was with regards to the number of U.S. troops arriving. There were 10,000 troops now coming.

Friday evening before going to meet her contact she put the .41 caliber derringer her father had given her under her waistband and wore a loose fitting blouse to hide it. Like her father, she was at the bar early sitting at a corner table so she could see everyone. An escape route if she needed one was to her right through the women's restroom.

At exactly 10 o'clock Larry entered the bar and walked to her table.

"Sit down, Larry, and it would look better if you would kiss me."

"Sure enough, honey."

"Did you bring the stones?"

"I have them."

"I need to look at them in the light. Not here. In the ladies room. There's no one in there now."

She got up and walked towards the restroom door and Larry followed her. Once inside she checked the stalls to make sure they were alone and then she locked the door. She held out her hand and Larry gave her the diamonds. She fitted her loupe to her eye and looked at each of the three stones. They were not a fine grade, but they certainly were worth $5,000.00.

"They are real. United States has sent 10,000 additional troops. They are on their way now and will be landing in Saigon probably tomorrow or the next day."

"That's worth $5,000.00. How will I know when you have more information?"

"Do you come here often?"

"At least twice a week."

"What days?"

"Every Wednesday and then maybe again Friday or Saturday."

"Okay, when I have more info I'll look for you here on Wednesday."

"Okay, now we'd better dance at least once to make it look good," Larry said.

* * *

Avilla didn't think of herself as a spy or an enemy collaborator. It was business and it was exciting. She felt no allegiance towards any country. Not even Mexico.

She found someone who would help her to learn to speak Vietnamese. She was a good student and she learned very quickly. In two weeks she was understanding most conversations she would overhear on the streets. Though it took a while longer for her to speak it fluently.

About once a month she would meet Larry in the Texas bar and offer some new information. "I am taking a great risk obtaining this information. It has all proven good. So now I want $10,000.00 in raw diamonds." She got it without argument.

She had now found a source to obtain opium and other narcotics at very low prices. These she would hide in artifacts bought in Saigon and send them home to Pietro. Some of the artifacts were very valuable and Enrico put these in his furniture store for sale.

Pietro had by now established his drug pipeline from the coffee grinding factory in El Paso and Enrico found the markets for their coffee products. They were now calling their coffee, Texas Tea.

Enrico had to laugh how precisely the drug operation was working. And Pietro had been correct. There was a lot of money to be made. Once the custom officials at the El Paso border became used to the Flores' trucks hauling coffee beans, they began to only inspect their papers and not the load or truck.

* * *

In 1964 shortly after the Gulf of Tonkin incident, Avilla met with Larry on Wednesday night at the Texas bar. "I have some big information and this is going to cost you $50,000.00 in raw stones. And believe me the info will be worth it."

"Okay, I'll see what I can do. It might take longer to come up with that much so we meet Saturday."

Avilla was making enough selling information so she rented a suite on the top floor of the Continental Hotel. She didn't tell her co-workers about the suite. It was leased under Belle Saucier's name.

This was a dangerous game Avilla was engaged in, but she was getting off on the danger and excitement. She was feeling alive. There were times when she'd get lonely and wanting a partner for sex. But as of yet she hadn't seen anyone she wanted to bring back to her suite.

She had made some very close friends while living and studying in Paris. But now they were all but forgotten, and that life. Everything that she is or was is now there in Saigon as Belle Saucier.

* * *

Pietro had traveled to San Francisco, Mississippi and Washington D.C. establishing his drug pipeline. Where his father and sister were more intellectual and mild mannered, he was more aggressive and forceful. Threatening those he left to feed the pipeline with a terrible death if they should betray him.

After he had everything set, Pietro went for dinner in a side street restaurant that was well known for its delicious cuisine. He found an empty table in the center of the room and a beautiful dark haired waitress took his order. "Hello, I will be your waitress this evening. My name is April."

"Hello, April. I am Pietro."

"I have never seen you here before, Pietro."

"No, this is my first time here."

"While you wait for your meal, Pietro, you might enjoy the floor show. It is about to start. Loraine is the dancer—blonde, natural boobs and quite beautiful."

Pietro was enjoying watching Loraine. April was right, she was quite beautiful.

When he had finished eating he ordered another drink and watched the rest of Loraine's dance. When she was through, Pietro ordered another drink and watched the next dancer.

"Mr. Pietro," April said, "the restaurant is closing."

"Okay," and he handed her a $100.00 bill for her tip. This impressed her and she invited him back to her apartment, on the third floor.

As they were walking up the stairs Pietro asked, "What's your last name, April?"

"Bianca. My mother was from Juarez and my father was some trucker who already had a wife and family. My mother, Emily, was a great mother. She did the best by me that she could and she died from working too much when I was twelve. I never knew my father. When my mother died I moved to Florida and my mother's sister took care of me. When I was old enough to be on my own I came out to San Francisco. What about you?"

"My last name is Flores. My mother died when I and my

sister Avilla were both young. My father Enrico owns Flores Furniture stores in Mexico, Texas and California, a coffee bean plantation near Chihuahua and we recently built a coffee making manufacturing company in El Paso. Oh, and my father cuts and fashions diamonds when he has time. My sister Avilla works for the French Consulate in Saigon, South Vietnam.

"I think I have heard of the Flores Cartel," April said. "So you are setting up business here in San Francisco?"

"Yes."

"I'm horny. Let's skip drinks and I'll fix you breakfast tomorrow."

April gave Pietro quite a floor show herself as she removed her clothes and then removed his.

Pietro had a difficult time believing this was happening. And she was so beautiful. Her skin was a natural bronze color. Before morning he had fallen in love.

* * *

There was one incident in Mississippi when his contact shortchanged the funds he used to pay for the drugs. Pietro took him for a ride in the country until he found an abandoned quarry and then he shot him without saying a word. Then he found someone to take the place of the dead man.

Once a month Avilla would send a few raw diamonds along with the hidden narcotics for her father to cut and design jewelry with and he would wire her money in exchange.

There were times now when she would feel a little lonely. She couldn't hang out with co-workers, because beyond the walls of the Consulate she was Belle Saucier. So once in a while she would pick up some nice looking service guy, not at the Texas bar, but any of the many other lounges on Tudor Street.

Chapter 8

The Mekong Devil Squad was on their way back to Saigon with one prisoner, Colonel Cao Van Ky ,when Cpt. Sam Albright said, "Okay, men, we stay here until dark this evening." There was always two men on watch, one to watch the prisoner while the others slept two hours then their positions would change. They had been inside Cambodia's borders for two weeks.

Their orders were to level a military compound near Prey Veng and capture the commander alive and bring him back for interrogations.

While in Cambodia no one talked. All orders were given with hand signals. The squad of five had worked so long together each one knew what was expected of him. This was the third tour of duty for them all, and in all that time there had not been any casualties. Some had received a superficial wound or scratch, but that was all.

The squad had been helicoptered from Chau Doc across the border to a clearing fifty miles east of Prey Veng. And instead of the helicopter landing, the men jumped out when they were twenty feet above the ground.

It had only taken two days to cross the fifty miles, but they set up watch on the compound for four days, watching the schedule and routines and where the commander's quarters were.

All they had had to eat were cold rations and water. Water that they had to drop an antiseptic pill in their cups before drinking.

At 2 pm before leveling the compound, they entered the commander's quarters on their stomachs and secured him and removed him gagged from the compound before letting loose C-4 charges. As the charges exploded they made their escape. Moving as fast as they could. At the first sign of daylight, they hunkered down for the day.

The Col. was given cold rations to eat as well.

The Mekong Devils were actually a separate unit of the Green Berets. Only their orders usually came from the D.O.D. and not the Army chain of command. And because of their work and standing, they were allowed special privileges.

Lyle Kingsley had been working for his father on the Kingsley dairy farm in Maine when his draft notice arrived in the mail. He liked farming but he wanted to see the world and do things before settling down to farm life, so he did not object.

Besides his physical stature—five foot ten inches, one hundred and ninety pounds and not an ounce of fat, big square shoulders, good attitude and physical agility—he was asked to join the Green Berets and later the squad which became the Mekong Devils.

They carried a backpack, each had an M-16 and a .357 automatic side arm and the Yarborough knife; they each had a roll of duct tape and handcuffs.

When darkness came they each had had three hours of sleep. They were tired, but you wouldn't know it by watching them move out. Col Ky had had the most sleep and he was still exhausted. He had no idea how his captors were doing it.

Ky had no idea where they were taking him. But apparently they did, as they silently made their way through the thick vines and water. Moving as they were, Ky knew none of his troops would be alerted. He was beginning to wish his soldiers had such ability.

Two days later they crossed the border near Chau Doc, and Col Ky was turned over to the authorities for interrogations.

The Mekong Devils were flighted back to their base in

Saigon for some well deserved rest.

Cap'n Albright submitted his report and Lyle Kingsley showered, shaved, put on some clean clothes and stuck his .357 under his belt in back and pulled his shirt down over it to cover it. Then he walked to the Continental Hotel and unlocked Belle Saucier's suite door. There were still two hours left to her work day so he laid down for a nap.

He had met Belle a few months earlier at the Delta Bar and Lounge, two blocks down the street from the Texas Bar. Here the Delta offered floor shows and topless waitresses. He had seen this beautiful girl sitting by herself. He asked, "Are you with someone or can I join you?"

Belle looked up and immediately liked what she saw and said, "If you don't, I'll jump on your back."

As they were sipping drinks and talking Belle asked, "You like this sort of entertainment?"

"Well—it sure is better than looking at a rice paddy and getting shot at. What about you? It's a little unusual to find such an attractive girl sitting by herself watching nude performers."

"The girls—they are beautiful aren't they? I couldn't think of a better place to hook up with someone."

The two had first met just as he was finishing his second tour of duty. Because of Belle and finding someone to be with and love in this god forsaken place, he decided to volunteer for another tour. Of course along with that, he was promoted to Master Sergeant and a nice bonus for staying another tour. That had been a year ago and his third tour was about up.

Lyle was still asleep when Belle unlocked the door to her suite and was surprised and happy to see Lyle was back. Back safely from wherever he had been.

He had told her from the beginning of their relationship that he would never be able to tell her what he did or where he had been during his absence from Saigon. She only knew that whatever he did must be secret and covert. He would not even say anything about the others he worked with or their names.

And then when he asked her about her job all she would reveal is, "I work at the French Consulate, and like you I cannot say anymore."

Very quietly she undressed and washed up and then laid down on the bed beside him. He did not move. She unbuttoned his shirt. He still did not move. She unbuckled his belt and as she started to pull his pants down she looked at him and his eyes were still closed, but he was smiling.

"Okay, you," she said, "you can open your eyes now."

He did and then he pulled her over on top of him and kissed her and whispered in her ear. "It has been a long two weeks."

"Two weeks and three days," she replied.

They made love over and over and finally he rolled over on his back, spent. "You have worn me out, lady."

She laughed and laid on top of him again. For one more time.

While Belle was showering Lyle found a sheet of paper near her purse with strange writing on it. "Belle?"

"Yes."

"What's this paper with what appears to be written in Russian?"

"Oh that. On the way home some guy on a street corner was handing these out. I told him I was not interested, but he shoved it in my handbag anyhow. I didn't want to make a scene, so I just walked off. Probably some kind of propaganda if it is in Russian. Can you tell?" She had almost made a costly mistake. But she thought she had handled it well.

"I have no idea."

"Throw it away then. Are you going to shower?" Trying to change the subject.

"Yeah, I thought I'd let you go first."

Afterwards they walked down to the floating restaurant for supper. They had learned long ago not to eat fish. Particularly if it was local fish. The raw sewage from Saigon emptied into the river. At least the whole city smelled like it. They ate beef steaks which were shipped in from Argentina. World renown for its beef.

"How long are you back, Lyle?"

"Three days only. Cap'n said we already have another mission."

Walking back Belle suddenly stopped and said, "Lyle, we must stop and go back and call a taxi."

"Why?"

"Those three men ahead of us, I do not trust them." Actually she understood what they were saying—that they would kill the man and rob him and gag the woman and take her behind some buildings and rape her.

But she didn't want Lyle to know she had understood them. Once they were back at her suite, they had room service bring up a bottle of wine.

* * *

The next morning Lyle walked with Belle to the Consulate. "What are you going to do today, Lyle?"

"Oh, I'll probably go back to base and hang around. I'll be at your hotel before you."

They kissed and said goodbye.

Just as Lyle was passing through the main gate a transport plane was landing. *Probably more recruits arriving from the states,* he thought.

He found the Mekong Devils all in the rec center. "Thought you'd be holed up with your lovely lady, Lyle, instead of being on the base," Russ Jones said.

"She has to work."

"Hey man, you getting serious with her or not?" Phil Drew asked.

"If we were anywhere but Vietnam and in the middle of the war, I'd ask her to marry me," Lyle said.

122

"That serious uh, Lyle?" Cap'n Albright said.

"Sure is. She's the best thing that has ever happened to me."

"Tomorrow night, Lyle, you'll have to spend on base. Make sure you are here by 1800 hours.

"We have a briefing at 0630 hours."

For a good part of the day the Devils worked out in the exercise hall and then they went for a five mile run around the base and inside the security fence. Off in the distance they could hear rifle fire; probably at the rifle range. Cap'n Albright ran up beside Lyle and asked, "How many more tours are you going to do Sergeant?"

"I know this should be my last. I—we, all of us—have pushed our luck with three tours. If I can convince Belle to leave with me, she'll be the deciding question. If she won't or can't— well I'm not sure, Cap'n."

* * *

That night as Lyle and Belle were having supper at the Continental Hotel Lyle said, "My third tour is almost over, Belle. It is for everyone in the squad and we are thinking about not doing another tour, but going stateside. But I don't want to leave you. I would like it if you would go back with me. I'd even resign from the Army. I think too much of you, Belle, to leave and leave you here.

This is what Belle was dreading most of all. Lyle was too nice of a person to ever fit in her life and world as Avilla Flores. But at the same time, she hated the idea of being left alone in Saigon. All of a sudden she was beginning to feel lonely.

"While you are away on your next mission I'll do a lot of thinking, Lyle, and you'll have my answer when you come back. I promise."

* * *

The squad all gathered in a conference room that was routinely swept for electronic listening devices. When Col. Ames entered the room they all stood at attention. "At ease, men. At dark you will be helicoptered out to a clearing twenty miles due south of Phnum Penh and you are to make your way to the General Ky Duan estate here," and he pointed to the map. "The coordinates are in your papers, Captain Albright. Here is a high altitude photo of the estate. Today is Sunday; on Wednesday we have the information that a Congressional Lobbyist has arranged a private meeting with the General. The lobbyist, a Robert Howland, lobbies for a munitions company. We believe he is trying to sell ammunition to the Cambodia Army, possibly trying to prolong the war for the financial benefit of his company. He is a traitor and we want him brought back alive, gentlemen."

"Once you have Mr. Howland Wednesday night, you must proceed to this location here," and again he pointed to the map. "At exactly 0600 hours you will jettison a lift balloon and a C-124 plane will do an airlift extraction and reel him in and return here with Mr. Howland. Then you are to make your own extraction as swiftly as possible. Captain, you know the routine from there. Any questions? If not, make yourselves ready to depart at dark."

"Ah, Colonel, I do have one question," Lyle said.

"Yes, what is it Sergeant?"

"How is this Howland traveling to Cambodia?"

"He flew to Calcutta and from there in a private jet to Phnum Pehn," Col. Ames said.

"Thank you, gentlemen, I can't stress enough how important that Howland is returned alive." With that said, Col. Ames left.

"Okay, you guys know what you need and what you have to do. Be on the tarmac at 2000 hours," Cap'n said.

There was an important mission ahead now and Lyle put all thoughts of Belle on hold. At 2000 hours they boarded the transport helicopter and stopped in Chau Doc to refuel. At midnight under a moonless sky they were dropped off. There was no waste of time, wondering what to do now. Cap'n took the lead and they started out on a slow pace, until the moon came out at 0200. Then they could move right along. And because of the urgency of the mission they didn't stop for the day until an hour after sunrise.

While two stood watch three could sleep and then switch off every two hours. And again because of the urgency, they started out an hour before the sun had set. And like the night before the moon didn't come out until after midnight. But they had already traveled a good distance. And once there was now some light Cap'n picked up the pace.

By 0200 Monday morning they found the General's estate. It was a combination rubber and sugar plantation. They found a perfect spot to lay low on a knoll overlooking the main house. So far they had not seen any Cambodian soldiers only plantation workers. And those went out in the field to work.

A heavy storm blew in from the east, dumping three inches of rain. The Devils were soaking wet. But they never moved. The rain wasn't the worst of it. When the hot sun came after mid-afternoon the humidity was almost stifling. Because of the humidity their clothes would not dry and they spent the entire night soaking wet. After midnight when all the lights were out in the mansion and the worker's shelters, the team split up to reconnoiter the plantation to see what they were up against.

They found a nice bungalow on the opposite side of the mansion which wasn't visible from the knoll. There had only been two sets of foot tracks in the mud coming from the bungalow towards the workers living quarters. Probably staff. There weren't any caches of weapons or ammunitions. And no indication that troops were being billeted on the plantation. It looked like General Duan had a paradise farm in the middle of a war torn country.

Cap'n was beginning to think less of this man's rank. In his mind Duan didn't deserve the rank of general.

Kingsley and Jones had found a quick exit from the plantation once they had acquired Mr. Howland.

By day the team was well rested and positioned themselves back on the knoll. Shortly after daybreak a fancy car drove in and General Duan and two aides got out and went into the mansion.

Lyle Kingsley and Russ Jones were on watch at noon while the others were sleeping, when another vehicle pulled in front of the mansion and stopped. Lyle awoke the others and pointed. It was Mr. Howland sure enough, with an overnight bag and a briefcase. When Howland closed the door, the car drove off, leaving the General and Howland and the two aides.

Lyle wasn't sure if the workers had taken anything with them for lunch or not. But no one came in at noon to eat. He was wondering if Duan even fed them at noon.

"It is good for you to arrive, Mr. Howland. My country is happy to hear what you have to say," Duan said.

"General, I will come right to the point why I am here. The company I represent makes munitions of all kinds for the U.S. troops. This company is making a lot of money and it would be in the best interest of this company to the have the war prolonged as long as possible. And to show you the company's appreciation"— Howland opened his briefcase and removed a bunch of money,— "here is $10,000 now." And he gave it to General Duan.

"I have been authorized, General, to offer you $5,000.00 each month that the war is prolonged."

"And how would I receive this money?" Duan asked.

"It will be sent to a company representative in Hong Kong. He will forward it to another representative in Thailand and he will send it to you each month.

"And how am I to do this, Mr. Howland?"

"You are the highest ranking officer in the Cambodian Khmer Rouge Army and you are an adviser to Prince Norodom Sihanouk. This gives you a lot of opportunity to prolong the fighting."

126

"What is the name of this company?" General Duan asked.

"It will be best if you do not know."

"I understand. What you say is true. I will think on it tonight and you will have my answer in the morning. Now we enjoy a fine bottle of wine, Mr. Howland."

"I must say, General, your English is very good."

"Thank you. I traveled to Hong Kong to learn your language. It has been very useful."

The team could watch Duan and Howland talking, looking through binoculars. Apparently Gen. Duan felt safe on his own plantation as he had only two aides and they were seated in front of a large window.

The staff entered through the rear entrance to prepare food for their evening meal. The Devils ate another cold C-rations and water.

"This is a fine wine, General," Howland said.

"Thank you. Would you enjoy a short walk around my plantation, Mr. Howland? And maybe walk off some of that dinner?"

"I would enjoy a walk, General. But what about my papers and the money?"

"They will be safe here. Come," and he opened the front door.

Russ Jones nudged Cap'n when he saw the two emerge from the mansion. Cap'n shook his head no and made the sign for papers. They all understood. It was important to secure the briefcase along with Howland.

As Cap'n watched as the two walked out of sight, he was wishing he could hear what they were talking about. It would make the case against Robert Howland even stronger. He hoped there would be enough documentation in the briefcase when they secured it.

It was getting close to sunset and everyone was getting antsy, waiting. Duan and Howland had returned by a different route and were now inside. When it was dark out, the lights inside the mansion came on.

At 10 pm it was completely dark outside and the lights downstairs went out and then two windows upstairs were illuminated. Bedrooms. It was still four hours away so they all ate another cold ration with water and slept. The next few days would be long and tiring.

At 11 o'clock the lights upstairs went out, and all lights on the plantation were also out. Way, way off towards the east they could hear bombs going off. It sounded like hundreds—B-52s, carpet bombing.

Everyone except Cap'n was asleep. It was always like this just before the execution of the mission. So much adrenaline was surging through his veins nothing could make him relax and sleep. He kept watch on the mansion even in darkness, like a hawk watching a mouse.

By 2 am there was a slight sliver of a moon. Cap'n looked at his watch and all he did was snap his fingers. Lyle and Jones circled around to the back door while the other three went through the front. Once inside they methodically searched each room on the first level looking for the two aides. One was asleep in a living room chair and the other one was in the bathroom. Lyle motioned to the others that he had number two and to move back out of sight. Lyle stepped into another open doorway and waited. He didn't have long to wait. Number two came out and turned the light off and in that moment when your vision is obscured Lyle stepped out and grabbed the man by his head and snapped it. Number two was dead and dragged into another room along with number one.

One man remained on the first floor on guard while the other four went upstairs. They already knew which rooms they were in. Lyle and Jones took one and Cap'n and Phil Drew the other. The doors were already open. Lyle and Jones could see someone in bed with only a sheet pulled over him. Lyle reached down putting one hand behind his head and the other one over the man's mouth. The man awoke with a start, but there was nothing he could do caught in this vice like grip. Lyle whispered in his ear. "Do not speak, do not make a sound. If you do I will cut your throat. Do you understand me?"

The man managed to nod his head that he did. Lyle released his head and held one of the man's arms in a vice-tightening grip and his other hand he put on the man's chest to keep him from moving. Russ put a piece of cotton in the man's mouth and then he tied a gag around his head. Lyle pulled him to a sitting position and Russ gave him his clothes to pull on. In the moonlight Lyle and Russ could just make out the General's uniform.

General Duan was petrified, but he pulled on his clothes and then his shoes.

Lyle and Russ looked at each other and both shrugged their shoulders and Lyle indicated they were to take him. They were downstairs before Cap'n and Phil had Howland secured in like fashion.

While leash ropes were being tied around the prisoner's middle Lyle went back upstairs. He made both beds and made sure nothing was out of place. Fred Nickerson did the same thing downstairs.

Cap'n said in a low whisper, "If either of you try to escape, hold us up or cause any problems at all, your throat will be cut and you'll be left. Now we don't have much time, so let's go."

Lyle and Jones had found their escape route earlier, so they led the way at a fast pace. They had to be on time at the clearing.

* * *

Shortly after daylight the staff entered the mansion to prepare breakfast for the General and his guest. When the food was set on the table, the two men still had not come downstairs.

The two aides were nowhere to be seen and after checking upstairs and finding both beds made up and everything as it should be, the staff could only assume that the General's group had left during the night. The staff ate the breakfast then cleaned up and went back to their own quarters.

* * *

That very same morning Avilla left the hotel with her bags packed and hailed a taxi for the airport. After Lyle's last visit it became obvious to her that he was in love with her. And that just couldn't be. Being the sort of business she was in. And the truth beknown she was beginning to think too much of Lyle also. She had made contacts in the narcotics world here to supply Pietro. She had made thousands of dollars selling information to the Russians. She could have left a year ago, if not for Lyle Kingsley.

She seated herself in the taxi and her eyes filled with tears. She decided to spend a few days in Paris to shake off the effects of him, before flying home.

* * *

Pietro and April traveled to Florida to set up a pipeline for their drugs. April found more Spanish speaking people in Florida than they did in Mississippi and she was feeling at home. Pietro stayed with the Hispanic people thinking it would be easier to form a pipeline for the drugs with Spanish speaking people.

After two weeks he had the connections he wanted and then they moved on to D.C. Here he found it more difficult to connect with people he wanted and he was a week longer.

For now he skipped New York and stopped in Boston and found the right connections there very easy. From Boston he traveled north skipping Maine, figuring the economy there couldn't afford his drugs. They crossed the border into New Brunswick, Canada and after a month he had established links in Fredericton and Moncton.

"That is enough for now. Now all we have to do is see that our product gets to these connections," Pietro said.

"Will you supply them with only marijuana or stronger narcotics, Pietro?"

"I'll let them get started with marijuana and then start cocaine, acid and speed. These drugs will be more expensive so I'll let our connections build their pipeline. Before we start them on the hard stuff we'll have to make another trip along the route. Maybe we'll start up north next time and work our way home."

* * *

The marijuana business was going full scale. "I'm surprised, Pietro. I never thought there would be this kind of money in illegal drugs," Enrico said.

"Papa, there are millions of people out there looking for a way to escape their boring routines and escape for a few hours in an illusionary world. And if we do not capitalize on the drug trade someone else will."

"I have an idea how we can cut our purchasing cost and improve our profits," Pietro said.

"How?"

"We hire people to grow the marijuana and bale it. Instead of buying from a supplier. I'll contact someone we can trust to contact someone else to grow it, so the Flores name will not be involved.

"Okay, go ahead, Pietro."

The shipments of hard narcotics Avilla had arranged from Saigon were beginning to arrive and Pietro started supplying his closest dealers first to see how well the stronger drugs would be accepted.

* * *

The Devils and their two hostages were at the clearing before daylight and without saying a word Lyle and Jones and Fred and Phil circled the perimeter making sure it was secure. Cap'n secured the lift harness on Robert Howland and prepared the lift balloon launch at 6 am. General Duan watched with great interest. He had concluded by now that Mr. Howland had been the main target and he was as it is a consolation prize. He wasn't exactly sure what was going to happen to Howland, but he was relieved when he wasn't fitted with a like harness.

Mr. Howland had no idea what was going to happen. He was scared as hell and the color of his face—well, there wasn't any more color.

The two parties returned and only nodded to Cap'n, that everything was secure. General Duan noticed the Captain kept checking his watch. Whatever was to happen with Howland, he decided it had already been planned and scheduled for a particular time.

At 0559.30 hours Cap'n fired a flare gun straight overhead and then he jettisoned the lift balloon, trailing a cable behind it to Howland's harness. General Daun and now Howland knew what was about to happen. The balloon had reached its maximum altitude and the steady drone of an airplane could be heard. Then it was directly overhead and suddenly Mr. Howland was launched backwards into the air at 150 miles per hour and was being reeled into the belly of the C-124 cargo plane.

Even though General Daunt was still gagged, he began to laugh. He would never have believed it, if he had not seen it himself. He began to wonder what Mr. Howland was experiencing. He'd probably crapped in his own britches.

He was helped to his feet and they began to move away from the clearing as fast as they could travel.

From the clearing they changed course slightly to the east. They usually held up somewhere during the daylight, but because of the flare and the presence of the C-124 and the eventual discovery that General Duan was missing, Cap'n wanted to put as much distance as possible between them and the clearing. Everyone though, including Duan, was showing signs of exhaustion. Cap'n was surprised how much Duan was trying to keep the pace.

By noon Cap'n figured they had traveled about ten miles. Everyone needed a rest, so they located a slight knoll to hide and to watch their perimeter as they ate and rested. The gag was removed from Duan so he could eat and drink some water.

Everyone knew what was expected of them without a word being spoken. General Duan had never witnessed such articulate performance of duty with a group of men. He was impressed. He wasn't sure where they were taking him, but if he had to guess he would say Saigon. He began to wonder if he'd be imprisoned for the remainder of the war in South Vietnam or somewhere else.

At mid-afternoon Lyle was taking his turn at watch when he saw movement through the bushes a hundred and fifty yards away. He awoke Cap'n and gave him the signal, enemy were near. Then he awoke everyone else. Even General Duan, in case they had to retreat. When they had closed the distance by half, Cap'n could see it was a six man patrol. Doubtful they were looking for them so soon. Probably only a routine patrol. General Duan could see the patrol also and he made no effort to signal them.

When the patrol was only fifty yards out they turned east as if maybe returning to the Mekong River, Cap'n hoped. All of them breathed a sigh of relief.

Cap'n stayed on watch with Lyle while the others went back to sleep.

Just as the sun began to set the sky clouded and a gentle rain started. Not having any moonlight really slowed their progression. At least they had not seen anything more of the Khmer Rouge patrol.

In spite of the overcast and light rain, they made good speed that night. Just before daylight Russ Jones was out in front and then Lyle. They came to a stream flowing east towards the Mekong River. Russ waded into the water. He was waist deep when suddenly something had pulled him under water. Immediately Lyle dropped his rifle and pack and with his knife in hand he dove into the water. The rest of the team and General Duan stood on the stream bank watching. At first there was nothing. The water was almost calm when suddenly the water began to boil and for the first time they could see snake coils, then everything went calm again and Duan thought the snake had probably killed both men. He found himself actually hoping the two men would survive the coils and the big snake.

And then both men stood up and Russ had the dead snake's severed head still clamped on his wrist. And they were laughing as they climbed out of the stream. There was a noticeable sigh of relief. Even General Duan extended his hand to help the men out.

Duan then stood back and for the life of him he couldn't understand why the two men were laughing. One man emerged after being attacked by a huge snake and the head of the snake still clamped onto his wrist. *Who in hell are these men?* He and Mr. Howland had literally been lifted out of their beds and forced to race through the jungle cover to a clearing where Howland was swept away at 150 miles per hour into the belly of an airplane. All this and neither he nor Howland had been harmed. In all honesty he admired his captors.

Before crossing the stream the team removed the snake's head and an antiseptic was used to flush out the wounds and then with needle and thread the Cap'n closed the wounds and bandaged his wrist. Besides laughing there was no more noise made.

They crossed the stream and looked for cover for the daylight hours. They had lost valuable distance with the snake. They still had two days to go and they were low on K-rations.

They would have to make do.

Two days later they were at the extraction point and Cap'n radioed to base at Chau Doc. The gag was taken off the General and the men were talking, but quietly. The General still sensing he was in danger remained silent and calm. It was a thirty minute wait. And even though they were this close to friendly soil they maintained their vigilant security.

When Lt. Gary Dumond left Chau Doc to pick up the team he supposed there were only five. Now as he was hovering above them ready to land, he could see six men. Dumond set his helicopter down and the six men didn't waste any time with small talk. They were seated with Cap'n in front with Dumond, "Where did you pick up the sixth man?"

"Phnum Penn," Cap'n replied.

"You guys were in Phnum Penn? I'm surprised you made it back with no causalities. The big brass general—Ky Duan I think his name is, he's supposed to be untouchable," Dumond said.

Cap'n nodded his head to the rear. "You mean you have—?" Gary was speechless and couldn't finish the statement. He shook his head while laughing and said, "I'll be damned. You know, Cap'n, you guys have quite a reputation in all of Southeast Asia.

"Cap'n," General Duan said into his helmet mic., "What will happen to me now?"

"Because of Robert Howland you will be interrogated by our people. You will be treated as your rank defines, General."

"You're CIA?"

Cap'n didn't reply.

Everyone was so tired there was very little talking during the flight. And they all were smelly, filthy and needing a shave.

"Cap'n, does anyone know you have the General?" Dumond asked.

"No."

"Then boy, is the Colonel going to be surprised."

Lt. Dumond set his helicopter down at the Saigon base and walked with the team to headquarters.

"Colonel Ames Sir," his aide said.

"Yes what is it?"

"The Mekong Devils are back, Sir, and Sir, they have a surprise for you."

Col. Ames stood up from his desk and went out to welcome the Devils back. "What's this, Captain? You were only supposed to capture Robert Howland."

"Colonel, may I introduce you to General Ky Duan. The head, the very top brass Colonel, of the Khmer Rouge. General Duan this is Colonel Ames."

"Colonel," Duan was the first to speak.

"General Duan, my pleasure."

"But how, why? You were only supposed to capture Howland," Ames asked.

"Couldn't see leaving him behind, Sir. And he probably has additional information about Robert Howland's proposal. Besides we didn't want to just kill him, Sir. I might add he has been very cooperative ever since we secured him. He caused us absolutely no problem or delays."

"Very well, Cap'n. You and your men look like you need a rest and you certainly need to clean up."

"Yes Sir.

"Dismissed. I'll have my aide go after a security guard to take charge of the General."

Before the Cap'n and the team left, "Excuse me, Colonel Ames, I would like to say something to Cap'n before he leaves."

"Certainly."

"Cap'n—and all of you, I never have seen men work as you have. You should be—all of you—complemented on your successful mission. You at times treated me with dignity and respect. I wish to thank you at least, for that. Now, Colonel Ames, I am prepared to tell you anything you want to know. Your Mr. Howland, Colonel, is a traitor to his own people and country. He offered me a great amount of money if I was to do what he wanted. I had not yet given him my answer."

Cap'n waited until each of his men had left Col. Ames office and as he was leaving he said, "Good luck, General Duan."

Before the team went to their quarters to clean up they all escorted Russ Jones to the infirmary. He insisted his arm was alright. "No Jones, you're too good of a solider to be side-lined by a little snake bite," Cap'n said, and they all laughed.

At the infirmary the admitting nurse said, "You guys are filthy. Are you here to be washed down and your uniforms stripped off and burned?"

"No Lieutenant. Jones here has a snake bite on his arm." Russ held up his wrist.

"When did this happen?"

"Two days ago."

"What kind of snake?" she asked.

"I'm not sure, but its head was as big as a football."

"Okay, go to exam room #3, someone will be with you soon."

Capt. Brody followed behind them to the exam room. "Ah, gentlemen, this room is too small for all of you. Why don't you wait in the lounge."

Dr. Brody removed the dirty bandage wrap and asked, "How long has this wrap been on?"

"Two days." Then Jones had to explain why he couldn't have come in sooner.

Dr. Brody examined the stitched wounds for infection and found none. "Who stitched you up?"

"Cap'n."

"Explain what happened."

When Russ finished telling Dr. Brody the story he added, "It was one big fucking snake. I thought I was a goner until Lyle jumped in to help me."

"All I am going to do is wash your wrist and arm and wrap it with a clean bandage. You were lucky you had good friends looking out for you."

"Captain Brody, I am aware of this. We always look out for each other."

Chapter 9

The Mekong Devils went to their quarters and cleaned up and put on clean uniforms. And as much as Lyle wanted to leave and see Belle, that would have to wait for tomorrow. After cleaning up they went over to the mess hall to eat. It was not yet time to eat, but Col. Ames had given the cooks a direct order to fix anything they wanted. They all had lost weight after eating nothing but cold rations for eight days.

After they had all eaten as much as they could they had to return to Col. Ames office for debriefing and since Cap'n was senior leader, he had a written report to do.

General Duan had been allowed to clean up and was given clean clothes to wear. He would be interrogated in the morning by CIA specialists. For now he remained in a locked cell.

When the debriefing was over, Col. Ames said, "You men may leave. Captain Albright, I'd like you to stay for a moment."

When the others had left Col. Ames said, "Close the door please, Cap'n."

"The work your team has accomplished on this mission is outstanding and I'm sure the information we'll get from General Duan will be very useful. He seems willing to work with us. I am awarding each member of your team the Silver Star award. General Westmoreland will be here Tuesday and I think that would be a good time to make the presentations. I would ask that you keep this to yourself, Cap'n, and even though your men will be on leave, I want you to make sure they are here at 1200 hours. The presentations will take place after lunch."

"Yes Sir."

"Dismissed."

"Hey!" Cap'n hollered, "Hey Lyle! Wait up."

"What is it Cap'n?"

"I know after a mission you spend a lot of time with your lady friend, just make sure you are here at 0800 Monday."

"What's up, Cap'n?"

"Can't say. Just make sure you are here."

"Okay."

He cleaned up and shaved. There was a layer of green scum on his skin under his clothes. Everything, even his boots, was thrown away. Some guys while on these types of missions developed serious infections from the heat and swamps. Cap'n always stressed that they wash up as best they could every day while on a mission.

He was happy and left the base and headed for the Continental Hotel. He inhaled deeply. Yup, the Saigon stink was still there. He had had enough of South East Asia, the heat and humidity, insects, snakes and the Saigon stink. To say nothing of the enemy. He knew he had talked himself into calling it quits when this tour was over. He would talk with Belle about her leaving with him.

He inhaled again and the stink reminded him of the paper mill towns back home when he drove through them. Back home everybody would say after twenty minutes you wouldn't smell the paper mill stink, and those living in the mill towns never noticed the stench. He could never get used to the Saigon smell.

As he rode up the elevator he was so excited to be this close to seeing Belle he began sweating like a nervous kid on his first date. He unlocked her door. There was no one there. He checked his watch and her work day was over. He stood in the middle of the suite and looked all around. Something was wrong. All her personal things were gone. Her closet and bureau were empty. All of her clothes were gone. There was absolutely nothing there that would indicate Belle had ever lived there.

"What in hell is going on?" he said aloud.

He looked around her—or what had been her—bedroom. It was like she had never been here. Then he noticed something on the pillow, the one she always used. He walked around the bed and found a handful of uncut diamonds, no note, nothing but the diamonds. He picked them up and put them in his pocket and went out to the livingroom.

The diamonds were the only thing there that made any sense. But what was she trying to tell him by leaving a handful of diamonds on the pillow she used?

He sat down in the livingroom chair, staring up at the ceiling trying to make some sense of it all, "Maybe someone at the Consulate can tell me where she is or what happened. But their doors are closed on Sunday and Monday I have to report at 0800 to Cap'n," he said aloud to himself.

Not knowing what to do or where to look, he left the hotel and picked up a fifth of vodka and headed back to the base. The only drinking allowed on the base was at either of the clubs. He hid the fifth under his shirt and walked through the main gate and waved to the security guard.

Instead of going to his quarters he decided to go for a walk around the perimeter security fence. He took a drink of vodka and it burned his throat and all the way down to his stomach. He didn't care, he was looking for somehow to relieve his sadness. He was feeling so empty. He took another drink. This time it didn't burn as much. By his fourth drink the vodka was no longer burning. At lease he wasn't aware of it.

Out of sight of the buildings he sat down and leaned back against the fence, trying to put some sense into all that had happened. *Why had Belle just disappeared and then leave the diamonds as if they were supposed to be some kind of message. But what was she trying to tell me?*

He had another drink and another. The bottle was half empty now, and he wasn't feeling a bit better. A C-130 transport jet flew directly over his head and landed. "Another three hundred new recruits," he said. "You should go home!" he hollered.

He kept thinking about Belle and wondering where she was and why she left and why she didn't leave a letter explaining why. *And why the diamonds?*

There was only a little left in the vodka bottle now. And he was feeling worse than before he started drinking. He thought people drank and got drunk to feel better. He surely wasn't. He was beginning to feel sick and his heart was broken and mentally he was now in a deep black hole. He drank more vodka.

He leaned his head back against the fence and closed his eyes. He felt like he was spinning round and round. "Oh God I feel awful." But he finished the vodka and leaned over and began to puke his guts out. When that was over he leaned back against the fence and closed his eyes and again everything began spinning. And this time the spinning didn't stop when he opened his eyes. And he began puking again on his hands and knees. It was a long time this time before he stopped puking.

He sat back against the fence and he started puking again. Only nothing was coming out. He had the dry-heaves. When he was finished, his gut was hurting. He sat back down and this time instead of leaning back against the fence, he slumped to one side. And he passed out.

* * *

Early the next morning a fully loaded B-52 took off flying directly over Lyle passed-out. The noise of eight jet engines flying within two hundred feet of him was enough for Lyle to open his eyes. He recognized the noise of the huge bomber. He laid on the ground feeling worse than death. His insides were hurting and his stomach was sick, and his mouth was dirt dry. Eventually he pulled himself up to a sitting position. He laid back down trying to go back to sleep. But his insides were all jumbled up and he was sick.

He managed to stand and his head felt like it was about

to explode. "So this is what a hangover feels like."

Every time he tried to move he was wracked with more pain. He was feeling so bad he had not yet thought about Belle. Every time a jet would take off and fly directly overhead the noise and vibrations would jar his head. His head still felt like it could explode any moment. He needed to move though, to at least get out from under the flight path of incoming planes and those that were taking off.

On hands and knees and clinging to the fence he finally was able to stand. He was needing some water to drink, and he slowly began to make his way to his quarters. He was so dirty and shabby looking he was stopped twice by security MPs. "You'd better go sleep it off, fella," one MP said.

As he crossed the base compound to his quarters everyone would stop and stare. Before laying down he drank a lot of water and then he fell face down on his bed. Passed out again.

No one disturbed him until 0600 the next morning. "Out of bed, Sergeant," Cap'n said. "Get up and stand at attention!"

Lyle was feeling much better, physically, and jumped up and stood at attention, "Yes Sir, Cap'n."

"What has gotten into you, Sergeant? Look at yourself. Now shower, shave and put on your dress uniform. Then go to the mess hall and eat breakfast. General Westmoreland is going to inspect the troops this morning."

Lyle reported to the mess hall, in his dress uniform, for breakfast. As he was filling his tray he noticed the only ones wearing their dress uniforms were the members of the Mekong Devils. *What is going on?* he wondered.

"What's going on, Russ? We are the only ones in dress uniform," Lyle asked.

"Beats me. I'm following orders the same as you.

"What has happened to you anyhow, Lyle? I have never seen you like you were the last two days," Russ said.

"You know that girl I have been seeing?"

"Yeah, what about her? She's beautiful."

"She disappeared without a word."

"Do you think someone has kidnapped her?"

"No, she cleaned out her suite of all her personals. And she left me a gift."

"What did she leave you?"

"That's not important."

Cap'n joined them just then. "Well I must say, Sergeant, you are looking better. A little hollow eyed though."

Lyle drank some coffee and two eggs with bacon and got up and left. "What's his problem, Russ?" Cap'n asked.

"He said his girl packed up and disappeared without leaving a word."

"That'll do it every time," Cap'n said. "You make sure he is on the parade grounds at 0800."

"Yes, Cap'n," Russ said.

At 0800 Cap'n Albright escorted his team to the front of the parade ground. General Westmoreland stood at the podium and addressed everyone there, telling them what a great job they were doing for their country. And how he hoped the war would soon be over.

Still Lyle and his teammates, all except for Cap'n, were wondering why they were in dress uniform and none of the others. Then Col. Ames addressed the gathering. "We are here today to honor the five men of the Mekong Devil Team. Their missions are classified, but because of their latest effort we have gained much valuable information. It was a stupendous mission with results that went far beyond the original goal. And at this time I am very proud to announce that each member will be receiving the Silver Star Award for your diligence, your bravery and for going beyond what was asked of you.

"Now Mekong Devils if you would please come forward, General Westmoreland will give you your well-deserved awards."

Cap'n turned slightly to look at his team and he smiled and said, "For a job well done. Thank you."

Westmoreland shook the hand of each of them as did many others. There were also many news media people there trying to get their story.

Later as they were walking back to their quarters Lyle said, "Cap'n, I need to go off base and see if I can learn anything about Belle."

"Go ahead, Lyle, but tomorrow we have new people to train."

He changed out of his dress uniform and the first thing he did was to go back to the hotel and check her suite one more time. He walked instead of hailing a taxi. And for the first time since he had landed in Saigon, he was not now aware of the constant stench.

He decided to check first at the registration desk. "Excuse me, has Belle Saucier returned?"

"No Monsieur. When Miss Saucier left she said she would not be back."

"Thank you." There it was. She had left on her own accord. He had one more idea and he walked to the French Consulate.

"Yes Monsieur. What can I do for you?" the receptionist asked.

"I am looking for one of your employees. A Belle Saucier."

"I am sorry Monsieur. There is no one who works here with that name."

"How can that be? She said she has worked here at the Consulate for four years."

"I cannot help what she might have said to you Monsieur. But there never has been anyone with that name here at the Consulate."

Lyle said, "Thank you," and walked outside. He looked up at the sky and said, "What in hell is going on?"

There was nothing more he could do now. He eventually made his way back to base, in a foggy daze. It was like Belle Saucier never even existed. And leaving a small fortune in diamonds just blew his mind. Wanting to be alone he went for another long walk along the perimeter of the base. He tried sorting out all the pieces, everything he knew about Belle and he kept coming up empty. None of what he knew of Belle fit in the puzzle. Who was she?

He ate a meager supper and went for another walk. Cap'n kept watching Lyle and he wasn't happy with what he was seeing. Lyle wouldn't be the first soldier to lose his girlfriend or wife while serving in the swamps of South Vietnam and Lyle was handling it worse than he had ever seen.

The next morning the team met the new recruits who were beginning their training in special operations behind enemy lines. It became obvious to Cap'n, early on, that Lyle's heart nor his attention was in his work. "Sergeant Kingsley."

"Yes Sir."

"In my office now. The rest of you continue." Lyle stepped in behind the Cap'n and followed him to his office. He was feeling like a bawled-out school kid.

"Sit down, Lyle. In two days, Lyle, we have another mission into Cambodia. This one won't be as easy as the last one. And you can't go, Lyle. This woman of yours has fucked your brain right out of your head. You would be a danger to yourself, Lyle, plus the whole team. I hope you can understand this. You are the best man in the team. But I just can't let you go, Lyle.

"You—we have all done three tours here. Our third will be over before the team returns. I'm sending you home, Lyle. A thirty day emotional leave. Colonel Ames has okayed it. You need to put some distance between you, Lyle, and Southeast Asia. Hell, we all do. Come back after your leave and we'll talk about your future. With your ability, Lyle, you should be an officer. Colonel Ames has said after your leave he would fast track your request to O.C.S. So you have thirty days to think about it. Go home and enjoy being with your folks again. But clear your head, Lyle. You're no good to anyone, least of all to yourself like you are."

"Yes, Cap'n."

Chapter 10

That evening a C-130 left Saigon for Clark Air Base in the Philippines and at noon the following day he boarded another that was going to Ord Army Base in California. Here onboard the jet he was able to sleep. But in his dreams he was with Belle which did not help his physical emotions.

The jet stopped in Pearl Harbor for fuel, more soldiers boarded and two crates. Lyle stayed in his seat with his eyes closed trying to get back to the dream where Belle was there too.

He woke up and stopped thinking about Belle and started thinking how good it will be to see his folks. It had been four years now. And he was hungry. The first since discovering Belle gone.

It was almost noon when they landed at Ord Army Base. And the first thing he did was to go to the mess hall. When he had finished eating and several cups of black coffee he was surprisingly feeling much better. Then he began to wonder if half his emotional depression was not from all the vodka he had consumed. The only thing the stupor succeeded in doing was make him sick and throw him in a depression ditch. "If I hadn't had the vodka I'd probably be with the team now on the last mission," he said aloud. But as he had said all of his life, things happen for a reason. And yes, even Belle.

As he walked about the compound soldiers everywhere were looking at his Silver Star. That he proudly wore. He went next to see the base commander, Col. Alfred Dix.

"Your orders, Sergeant."

Lyle gave them to the Col. "Three tours in Vietnam? And your Captain Sam Albright and Colonel Ames both told you to take a thirty day emotional leave. I guess I can understand that after three tours." Col. Dix signed his papers and then said, "Take this to payroll and then you are free to leave."

"Thank you, Colonel Dix."

At the payroll office, "Do you have your papers, Sergeant?"

"Here," and Lyle handed them to him.

"Uhm, four years of back pay. Uhm, three years of those in a war zone. I'll be a few minutes, Sergeant. Why don't you have a seat."

Fifteen minutes later; "Sergeant, I'll need your signature here and here," and the clerk pointed.

"That's $21,443.16. Quite a chunk of change, Sergeant."

"Yes, would you have an envelope to put this in?"

"Certainly."

With the cash in his pocket Lyle was beginning to feel a bit better. It was late in the afternoon and he decided to find a motel.

He located an inexpensive motel on the outskirts of town. Once he was settled in his room he telephoned his parents. He forgot about the time difference and the phone rang several times before his mother Doreen answered, "Hello."

"Hello, Ma, This is Lyle." There was a long pause before she could speak again.

"Is that really you, Lyle? Are you still in Vietnam?"

"No Ma, I'm in California and I'll be home in four days."

Doreen was so happy she began to cry. Her crying awoke Henry and he asked, "Why are you crying, Doreen?"

"It's Lyle, Henry. He's coming home."

"Here, let me have the phone—Son, is this really you?"

"Sure is, Dad. I'm in California and I'll be home in four days."

"Are you flying into Portland or Bangor?"

"Neither one Dad. I'm going to buy a pickup truck tomorrow and drive across country. I'll see you in four days."

Lyle hung up the phone. He was glad he had called.

During the night he kept waking up from dreaming about Belle and needless to say he didn't sleep well. The next morning he was up early. Showered, shaved and packed his few belongings in his travel bag. He didn't have any clean civilian clothes, so he put his uniform back on with his Silver Star.

There was a small restaurant next door and he ordered breakfast with, "...a pot of black coffee, please."

"A pot?"

"Yes Ma'am. I'm a coffee drinker."

"Where are you stationed, soldier?"

"I'm heading back home to Maine now. I've spent the last three years in Vietnam."

"I lost my boyfriend over there. I have no idea why we are fighting there," the waitress said.

There were no car dealers in Ord so he boarded a bus for Santa Cruz. The bus went by a Ford dealership before stopping at the terminal. From there he took a taxi back to the Ford dealership.

There he bought a red and silver XLT 4x4 Ford pickup with a cab on back. He figured to buy a mattress for the back and sleep in his truck instead of paying for a motel room each night.

"Being in active duty young man, and with a Silver Star Medal I'll give you an additional 10% off. Now how would you like to finance this?"

"Cash."

"That'll do."

The pickup was his, the papers were all made out and he was able to purchase vehicle insurance through the Ford Motor Company and his travel bag in beside him. "Can you direct me where I can pick up a mattress for the back?"

Next door to the furniture store was a sporting goods store where he bought a pillow and sleeping bag. He was ready now to start for home. It was 2 pm when he headed east. And instead of taking the interstate he chose the scenic route. He'd pick up the interstate later when he needed to make up some time.

He drove until midnight and stopped at a truck stop for lunch and coffee and gas and just as the sun was coming up he crossed the Sierra Range into Nevada. He still wasn't tired so he kept driving until mid-morning. He pulled over in an opening and sacked out in the back for four hours.

There was enough to see during the daylight hours to keep his mind away from thinking about Belle. But during the night when there wasn't that much to see, thoughts of Belle started to come back. What bothered him the most was the fact that no one known as Belle Saucier ever worked at the French Consulate. *Who was she? Were her feelings for me genuine? If she didn't work at the Consulate, then what did she do?* And then there were times when he was simply missing her cheerfulness.

He was mesmerized by the desert and totally surprised how big the wheat and oat fields were. Sometimes they stretched along the roadside for miles.

He crossed the Mississippi River at St. Louis and picked up Interstate 70 and followed that to Pennsylvania and I-80 across to New York and I-95 north to Maine and to the end of I-95 in Houlton. His folks farm was only a few miles north of Houlton, between US Route 1 and the New Brunswick border.

About mid-afternoon on the fourth day he pulled into the driveway and shut the truck off. His Mom and Dad had heard him drive in and they came out to greet him. His mother was crying and there were tears in his eyes also.

He opened the pickup door and slid out and stood and stretched and inhaled a deep breathe. Suddenly it hit him; the manure smell of a dairy farm. Some people might think it was a repugnant odor, but for Lyle it was home. And he breathed in again.

Over supper he explained to them why Cap'n had sent

him home, but not everything about Belle. He knew there would be too many questions that he didn't have the answers to.

"I have to start milking. I gave Earl the day off."

"I'll change out of my uniform and help you, Dad."

"Are my clothes still in my room, Ma?"

"Yes."

He went upstairs to change. For now all thoughts of Belle were gone.

They had to clean out each cow first and scrape the manure into the gutter cleaner. While Lyle finished that Henry started milking. Lyle then grained each cow and fed the young calves and the bulls. Then he had to put hay down for each cow. By now Henry was three quarters through the milking herd of a hundred and ten.

"I had forgotten, Dad, how much work there is to milking."

When the milking was done, while Henry washed up the milking machines, Lyle spread out sawdust under the cows. Then he helped his Dad with the washing. "Six o'clock on the nose," his Dad said. "Time for supper now."

Doreen had been fixing a boiled dinner all day. And now as they opened the kitchen door the smell of the boiled dinner was waffing through the air. They washed up in the shed, and took off their boots and manure splattered coveralls.

Lyle ate until he couldn't eat any more. "This is sure good, Ma. I had forgotten just how good your cooking is."

"Have you room for dessert? I baked an apple pie this morning."

"Oh, not now, Ma. Maybe later before I go to bed."

They each had another cup of coffee and sat at the table talking. They wanted to know all about the Silver Star Medal. About the Mekong Team and what kind of work he had been doing for the last three years.

"It was in all the newspapers, Lyle, about you receiving the Silver Star. Everyone around here knows about it and about you."

"The work we did, Mom and Dad, is classified. We swore an oath never to discuss with anyone about what we did."

"Okay, Son, I won't ask again," his Dad said.

"What are your plans, Lyle?" his mother asked.

"I'm going to spend the rest of my leave here at home with you and Dad. Maybe we can put all the hay in before I have to leave."

"What about your future, Son?" his Dad asked.

"This is the end of our third tour—the Mekong Devils. Some are through with Army life. Cap'n talked with me before I left Saigon. He wants me to continue and go to Officer Candidate School. I didn't give him my answer. I said I'd think about it.

"Dad, if you would like to go to church tomorrow with Mom, I'll do the milking in the morning."

Before going to bed that night he went for a long walk around the edge of the hay fields. The grass would be ready to cut shortly. The moon wasn't full but there was enough light so he could see deer feeding on top of the slight knoll, silhouetted against the moon lighted skyline.

While in Vietnam he had missed home, but he never thought too much about farming or taking over the farm someday. But now he was beginning to understand just how much he had been missing it all and never realizing it. He was suddenly happy, out there alone in the field.

As he reached the top of the knoll the deer ran off and Lyle sat down with his back against one of the apple trees. Thoughts of Belle started drifting through his conscious mind. Not thoughts of love and sex, but he was wondering who she really was. He finally came to the conclusion that he would never know. So he stood up and continued his walk.

* * *

His father was up the next morning just like he had been doing for the last forty years. "Dad why don't you take the day

152

off? Let Earl and me do the chores and milking today. Take Ma out for dinner in a fancy restaurant and go for a drive."

"Are you sure you can handle it son?"

"Yes, Dad, I'm sure."

Earl Wingnaut drove in the yard then and Lyle went out to greet him. Earl was fifteen years older than Lyle and farming is all he had ever done in his life. But he could not ever manage his own financing. So he worked on other farms.

Lyle let Earl do the milking while he cleaned out and fed. Then after everything was washed up Earl asked, "Do you want me this afternoon, Lyle?"

"Yes, I gave Dad the day off." They both laughed.

After changing his clothes and cleaning up he drove to town to the Country Diner for breakfast. Working before breakfast had really made him hungry now. The diner was only about half full. He recognized only a few people. He chose a table in the corner.

"Why lookie here folks, we have us a real hero amongst us this morning."

Lyle would recognize that voice anywhere. "Good to see you too, Becky."

"When did you get back, Hon?" Becky asked.

"Yesterday afternoon."

"What are you having, Hon? Let me guess, your usual, right?"

"I'm surprised you'd remember," Lyle said.

"Hon, remember! You're the only one that ever ate here who ordered six eggs, fried potato, toast and a thick slice of ham; every morning you came in. Let me tell ya, Hon, all I have to do is holler to the cook 'Lyle's special.' You watch, I'll stay out here until he says your breakfast is ready."

Becky went around to all the tables filling their coffee cups. A few minutes later Becky came out with Lyle's breakfast. "What'd I tell you, Hon, and the toast isn't burnt."

"You're a sweetheart, Becky."

"Be careful, Lyle, you say things like that again I'll divorce my husband. Enjoy your breakfast."

His breakfast tasted just like he remembered. As he sat back in his chair sipping the last of his coffee he was thinking how good he was feeling being home and among familiar faces.

He left a good tip and paid for his breakfast. "Come back soon, Hon," Becky said.

He drove back to the farm and changed back into his work clothes and decided to check over the equipment before haying. And surprisingly enough his father and Earl had already done so and greased everything and there were bales of new baling twine in the toolshed.

So he made a pot of coffee and took that and a cup out on the porch. He said aloud, "You know, I didn't know until I was back how much I missed the farm. But I don't know if that's all I want to do in my life. Officer Candidate School sounds pretty tempting too. Whatever I decide I won't have to go back to Vietnam."

He sat out on the porch past noon. Enjoying the peace and his surroundings and the smell of the farm. He fell asleep in his chair with those happy thoughts going through his head.

When his folks drove in the driveway Lyle was still asleep on the porch. He woke up when he heard the kitchen screen door slam closed. He was still holding his coffee cup and the pot was cold.

Doreen reheated the coffee and then all three sat out on the porch talking. "I checked the haying equipment today and I guess you and Earl have already taken care of it."

"I didn't; Earl did. He's a good farm hand."

"He's a good man to have around," Lyle said.

"Lyle, your mother and I did some talking today. Tomorrow after milking and chores we are going in to talk with our attorney Don Haskel. Your mother and I have decided to turn the title of the farm over to you. Now wait a minute. That doesn't mean we expect you to give up your Army career. This is in case anything ever happens to us the farm and everything will already be in your name."

"You aren't getting tired of doing chores are you, Dad? Only kidding."

* * *

The next day after the morning milking and chores and then breakfast Henry showered and put on clean clothes. "We'll be back before pm milking. We're going to the restaurant again."

"Okay." Lyle was happy to see his folks take the time to get out and away from the farm.

That morning the Hood milk truck arrived to empty the three stainless milk tanks. The milk truck came every other day and the farm was averaging $2000.00 a week. Lyle first thought that seemed like a good income, but farming was getting more and more costly to operate. But his parents had managed to save a lot of money. But some of the farm equipment was old and needed replacing. That and other thoughts about the farm were running through his mind.

After chores were done he cleaned up and went for breakfast at the diner. While he waited for his order, he was thinking about his folks and maybe since he would be around for three more weeks, they should go on a vacation. He would talk to them about it over supper that night.

He fixed himself a cup of coffee and sat on the porch and put his feet up on the railing. A hummingbird flew within a few inches of his face and started a sideways dance. In a little bit another flew down and buzzed the first one. Then the chase was on.

He took another sip of his coffee. He could see a Sheriff's vehicle slowing down and turning into the driveway. He recognized the sheriff and walked down off the porch to greet him. "Hello, Jim. Would you like a cup of coffee?"

"I don't know how to say this Lyle except to come right

out with it. Your folks, Lyle, were involved in a head-on collision at 1 o'clock on Route 1. The other driver swerved across lanes right into your folks. Your Dad, Lyle, died instantly. Your mother died on the way to the hospital. I'm sorry, Lyle. I wish I didn't have to tell you this."

"Where are they now, Jim?"

"In the morgue at the hospital."

"What happened to the other driver?"

"He died instantly also. I've requested a blood alcohol test be done. I believe he was operating drunk. Are you going to be okay, Lyle? I mean you just came back from Vietnam and all."

"Thanks Jim. I'll have a lot to work through in my head, but I'll be okay."

"If there is anything I can do for you, all you have to do is ask."

"What about their belongings? The things Mom and Dad had with them?"

"I have everything with me, Lyle. I can release everything to you now I guess."

"All I have, Lyle, is the vehicle papers and this portfolio. I didn't go through it. The M.E. at the morgue will have their personal effects."

"Thanks, Jim."

First he had to telephone Earl Wingnaut. "Hello, Earl?"

"Yeah."

"Earl. This is Lyle. Can you help with milking tonight?"

"Sure."

"Can you come over as soon as possible?"

"Sure, I'll leave right now."

Lyle went back outside and started walking around the yard. It was nervous energy that he had to deal with.

When Earl drove in and saw Lyle walking around, he knew something wasn't right. "What's happened, Lyle?"

"It's my folks, Earl. They were both killed in a car accident this afternoon."

"Oh man, I'm so sorry, Lyle."

"Can you milk this evening and do the chores? I need to go to the morgue."

"Sure, no problem, Lyle. I'll be here in the morning too, to help you."

"Thank you Earl."

* * *

At the morgue the M.E. gave Lyle a few minutes to say goodbye to his folks. "When you are ready, Lyle, I have their effects in my office."

Lyle stood there looking at his Mom and Dad. Trying to find some reason to all this. There was so much he wanted to say, but the words just wouldn't come out. He was glad he had made it home before this happened.

After several minutes he knocked on the M.E.'s office door. "Come in, Lyle, I have everything in this box. Other than your mother's purse and your father's wallet there wasn't much besides their wedding rings. When you talk with a funeral director they will make arrangements to pick up the bodies."

"Thank you, Dr. Holt."

Lyle was back at the farm in time to help Earl feed the cows and wash up. "I'm going to need your help every day Earl, I probably won't be around much during the next two days."

"I understand, Lyle. I'll be here every day."

"Thank you, Earl."

Earl left and Lyle went into the kitchen to make a pot of coffee. He needed something in his stomach besides coffee, but he just couldn't bring himself to eat anything just yet. He took his coffee out on the porch and sat down. He finished that cup in five minutes, he poured another and went back to the porch. He knew this was going to be a long night.

He took a sip of coffee and then held the cup between his hands. In his world the word coincidence didn't exist. He believed that every event in life happens for a reason. Not that the event just happened. There was always an underlying reason for each event, be it happy or sad.

Then he began thinking about Belle. If she had not disappeared he would still have been in Vietnam. Never having the chance to see his parents again before they were killed in the accident. And that too he knew was not just a simple accident. It was a piece in the jigsaw puzzle of his life.

This was beginning to make him feel somewhat better and he took another sip of coffee. The last few days with his parents had been happy golden days. He took another sip of coffee and suddenly another thought hit him. Like a wake-up call. His parents had been at their attorney's office that day and had put the farm and everything with it in his name. "I'll be damned. As though they each knew this was going to happen, so they made these new arrangements so I would not have to. I'll be go-to-hell," he sipped his coffee.

For the first time since leaving the farm and the family, he was wishing that is older sister Sheerie was there with him now so he could talk with her "...about Mom and Dad," he finished his thought out loud.

His coffee cup was empty so he went back to the kitchen to refill it. The sun had just about set and still he didn't turn on a light inside the house. He had spent so much of the time during the three tours in Vietnam, in the dark, that darkness was so common he could easily find his way around.

He sat with his feet on the railing thinking about all the pieces of the puzzle that had been forming in his life to bring him to this moment. What if only one of the pieces had not happened? Where would he be then? These thoughts were intriguing. Was life—his life—that exacting? Where if one piece—event—had been different, changed, his life would be different? This was quite a load to think over. Especially since there was so much he would have to do in the next few days. The first thing he would have to do is go see a funeral director. Then Attorney Don

Haskel. Let alone decisions about the farm. As long as he could keep Earl Wingnaut he would be alright for a while.

He finished that cup and set it on the railing and decided to go for a walk around the fields. The moon was already out. Not full but there was enough light for him to see.

Not wanting to tread down the grass, he stayed on the field road which went up passed the knoll with the apple trees. He sat down leaning against one tree where he could look down across the hay field. As he was sitting there he happened to remember once, his father saying he would like his body buried under the apple trees on the knoll. "This would be a fitting place for them both. But I don't believe the state laws would allow it. Unless they were both cremated. I'll find out in the morning when I talk with Mr. Haskel."

During the night he had finally been able to come to terms about Belle. He accepted her now as only a piece of his puzzle. At times a very happy piece but at the end—*Well*, he thought, *all good things must come to an end.* And as much as he will always miss his Mom and Dad he had accepted their passing also as a piece to his life puzzle.

Now the sun was beginning to rise above the eastern hills and he walked off the knoll and began cleaning out the cow stalls and putting down clean sawdust. "I'm surprised to see you this morning, Lyle," Earl said as he began milking. "You don't look so good. You stay up all night?"

"Something like that."

He was hungry but he just couldn't bring himself to eat. Instead he showered and shaved and then drove to town to talk with Dunnett's Funeral Home. "Hello, Lyle. I'm so sorry about your Mom and Dad."

Fred Dunnett said, "I'll pick up the bodies this morning. Do you know what your folks wanted for final disposition of their bodies?"

"I'm not sure, Fred. I have to see Mr. Haskel from here and find out what is in their will. I'll let you know as soon as I can. I would prefer a memorial service, Fred, and not a religious funeral. Any idea when?"

"Let's see this is Tuesday, is Friday okay with you?"

"That will be fine. I know there will be many people who would like to come—what if we wait until Saturday?"

"That'll be okay, Lyle. If they wanted to be cremated I can have the bodies taken to the crematory in Bangor this afternoon and the ashes will be back before Saturday."

"Oh, and one other thing Lyle. If you could write up an obituary for your Mom and Dad I'll see that it gets in the papers."

"Okay, I'll work on it as soon as I can."

Lyle left the funeral home and went to see Don Haskel. "Come in, Lyle; I have been expecting you."

Mr. Haskel handed Lyle a copy of his parents will. It clearly said they both wanted their bodies cremated and their ashes placed on the knoll with the apple trees. The rest of the will was pretty much like his parents had said the evening before the accident, about putting everything in Lyle's name.

"You'll notice the farm business account is in your name, but not their savings. That will have to go through probate court and under the circumstances there won't be any problem."

Lyle thanked him and stopped at the funeral home on his way home. Earl had already left for the day. He was hungry but what he needed most was a couple of hours sleep.

After two hours of restful sleep, he rolled over and another thought hit him. He had three weeks left to his leave. What was he going to do with the farm? This was bothering him enough so he couldn't go back to sleep. He got up, made a pot of coffee and sliced a big piece of mincemeat pie and a piece of sharp cheese. The pie was delicious. No one could make mincemeat like his mother.

Earl arrived early and had a cup of coffee on the porch with Lyle. "I assume the farm is yours now, Lyle. Have you decided what you are going to do with it?"

"I've been thinking on that—I'm not sure yet what I'll do. If I close up the farm and sell off the herd—well, I only have three weeks left to my leave. And I can't close things up in only three weeks."

They each took a sip of their coffee and Earl said, "Seems to me, Lyle, you just answered your own question."

"Guess I did at that. I guess I needed someone to bounce ideas off. The funeral won't be until Saturday evening. That way I figured more people will be able to attend. Earl, I don't have any family, and I'd be proud if you and your wife Peggy would sit with me down front."

"I'd be honored."

"When would Dad pay you for your work?"

"Usually Saturday evening just before we started milking."

"Okay, I'll do the same. You keep your own hours, Earl."

In the barn Lyle did everything except the milking. He let Earl do that and then they both washed down everything. "You'd better get some sleep tonight. You look terrible."

Lyle cleaned himself up, then made a ham sandwich from the boiled dinner leftovers and then another piece of mincemeat pie and cheese. He let the coffee alone and drank water.

The next morning he was up early and feeling well rested.

* * *

After milking and chores that morning, he washed up and went to town for breakfast. "What'll you have, Hon?" Becky asked.

"You know what I want, Becky."

She hollered back to the cook, "The Lyle Special!" Everyone else looked up from their own plates. They had not seen a Lyle special on the menu.

"I'm sorry about your folks, Lyle. When is the funeral?"

"Thanks, Becky. It was quite a shock. The funeral is Saturday evening at six o'clock."

161

"We'll surely be there Lyle. They were both good people and this town will surely miss them."

When Becky brought Lyle's order out everyone was staring. They had never seen anyone eat a breakfast so big.

There wasn't much to do now until after the funeral and he knew now what he had to do. He still spent a lot of that time walking around the fields. The hay he noticed should be cut soon, before it goes to seed. And for that he would have to hire a few strong young boys.

During the days that followed, before the funeral, Lyle had finished the boiled dinner leftovers, the mincemeat and apple pies. He never had to do too much cooking for himself. The last four years the army had taken care of that. So he ate his meals at the diner; besides, he always enjoyed talking with Becky and seeing old friends.

On the day of the funeral Lyle and Earl started the afternoon milking early enough so they would have time to clean up and get to the church on time.

It was a huge church and it seemed as if the whole town had come to say their goodbyes and share some memorable stories. When it was all over and everyone had left Lyle breathed a sigh of relief. He was glad that it was all over with. That evening as the sun was beginning to set Lyle took his Mom and Dad's ashes to the apple tree knoll. He emptied both urns at the base of the center apple tree.

A light breeze started to blow. Lyle was talking to his Mom and Dad as if they were actually there telling them how much he loved them and saying goodbye. His eyes were full of tears and his throat hurt from holding back his grief. Just then the breeze started circling around the knoll, making a tighter and tighter circle until there was a small funnel. And when it passed over the ashes, they were picked up by the wind funnel. The ashes were swirling round and round in the funnel and the funnel lifted off the ground and rose into the night sky and disappeared.

"Goodbye, Mom and Dad."

Chapter 11

Earl took the next day off—Sunday. He figured Lyle could handle things by himself now. Lyle was also up to the challenge. He was slower than either his father or Earl, but when he had finished washing the milking machines, he was feeling good about himself.

Breakfast was at the diner and Sunday was Becky's day off. The diner just didn't seem the same without her soprano voice. This morning instead of a side of ham with his six eggs he had a steak. As he was eating he kept thinking about the farm and farming. And asking himself if he was ready to commit his life to the farm like his dad and granddad had done. Either way he knew he would have to take a trip to Bangor to the Army's recruiting office. Maybe he could file his discharge papers there. He was sure that he would have to give up the possibility of a career in the Army. And then maybe this was just another piece of the puzzle.

Earl would be back to work on Monday and he would talk with him. After he had finished the evening milking and chores he washed up and sat on the porch with his usual coffee and for the first time in a long time, he was feeling at peace with himself. He refilled his cup again, put his feet on the railing, took a deep breath. He no longer could smell the farm; to him the air was fresh. There were no more thoughts of Belle Saucier and most important, he was happy.

Eventually he fell asleep sitting there on the porch with his feet on the railing. When Earl drove in he saw Lyle on the porch and as he walked up the steps Lyle awoke with a start. He was still holding his cup. "Hey man, what did you sleep out here last night?" Earl asked. "Anything wrong?"

"No—just enjoying a cup of coffee last night and I must have fallen asleep." But he was hungry.

* * *

The next morning he put his uniform on and the Silver Star Medal and had breakfast at the diner. Earl would have to look after the farm today.

"What's this all about, Hon? You leaving us again to go back in the Army?" Becky asked.

"I'm still in the Army, Beck. I'm only on leave. But I'm going to Bangor to get out."

When he was on I-95, still a single lane on this northern end, he turned the radio off to listen to the ideas going through his mind. Everything on the farm was paid for. The farm was making a good profit and there was, as near as he could figure, somewhere over $80,000.00 in the farm account. He liked farming, but now the farm was his and he wasn't all that sure he wanted to be tied down to it seven days a week.

Before he knew it, he was driving over the Penobscot River in Medway. He had been so busy thinking about the farm he was oblivious to his surroundings.

After crossing the river, he began thinking about the Army and what Cap'n had said about him attending OCS and becoming an officer and making the Army his career. It was a wonderful opportunity. But he now had to refuse because of the farm.

There it was in his own thoughts. The farm was preventing him from making a life in the Army. Was this yet only another piece to his puzzle? The more he thought about it, the more convinced he was becoming. Everything that was happening was linked together; only a thread in the cloth of his life. Another piece to his puzzle. *What will I be when all the pieces come together?* "What will I be?" he then asked aloud. And this really began to make him wonder.

Then he realized he was getting off I-95 at the Union Street exit. Ten minutes later he walked through the door at the Army Recruiting office.

"Yes, how may I help you, Sergeant?"

"Is the Captain in?"

"Captain Greene isn't, but Major Masters is."

"I would like to speak with him if he is not busy."

"He just came in, go through that door, turn left and at the end of the hall."

"Thank you."

Lyle knocked on the door casing before entering and Masters looked up from his desk and saw Sgt. Kingsley standing there, "Yes, what is it, Sergeant?"

"A moment of your time Major."

"Certainly; come in. Sit down."

"Now, what is it that brings a decorated Master Sergeant to a recruiting office?" he had noticed the Silver Star.

"Major I am currently on a thirty-day leave from my unit in Saigon. My reenlistment is almost up and I have a situation that will prevent me from going back."

"Yes, what is it?"

"Both of my parents were killed two weeks ago in a motor vehicle accident. Now I am the sole survivor in the family with a huge dairy farm to operate."

"I'm sorry to hear about your folks, Sergeant. Do you have your orders with you?"

"Yes Sir," and he handed them to the Major.

"You are a member of the Mekong Devils?" Major asked in great surprise.

"Yes Sir."

"My word, Sergeant, do you realize your unit is the most talked about unit in the entire Army! You Mekong Devils have certainly earned a huge and enlightening reputation."

"Yes Sir, we all have done three tours in Vietnam."

"Well, I would say, Sergeant, you certainly have had your share of hell."

"There were times, Major, that that's exactly what it was."

"It says here your Captain, Captain Albright, and Colonel Ames have recommended you for O.C.S. Are you sure you want to be discharged?"

"There is no other choice, Sir."

"Very well, I can take care of everything from here. It'll take me an hour or an hour and a half, so if you would like to go out for coffee, feel free. Just be back here before noon."

Lyle left the building and found a deli two blocks away. He had a cup of coffee and an english muffin. He was back in the Major's office at twenty minutes to twelve.

"Sit down, Sergeant; I have everything here. All I need now is your signature."

After every form had been signed the Major stapled everything together and with Lyle's original orders and leave papers he handed them to Lyle. And then he shook his hand and said, "Thank you, Lyle, for your service and good luck to you."

"Thank you, Major."

During the drive home he decided what he was going to do about the farm. Before going home he stopped at the diner for supper.

* * *

The next morning after chores and milking Lyle said, "Earl, come to the diner with me for breakfast. We need to talk and keep track of this time. You'll be paid."

"Okay."

"Hi, Hon, so are you staying on the farm or not?" Becky asked.

"I'm officially discharged now. I'm a civilian again."

Becky took their orders and knowing Lyle and coffee, she put a pot and cups on their table.

"Earl, I asked you to breakfast because I want to talk with you about what I have decided to do about the farm. I think I'll sell off all the stock, the milking equipment, one tractor, one rake.

"After milking tomorrow morning I plan to go to Woodstock, New Brunswick. There is a man there who buys and sells dairy farms and equipment and stock. My Dad has used him in the past. Maybe I can sell him the hay also. Either way we'll harvest the hay and if we have to we'll store it in the barn and the hay shed. I'm thinking sometime of maybe raising beef cattle, so that's why I'm not going to sell off all of the equipment. I would like you to stay on until everything is sold."

"I didn't think you'd keep the dairy cows. It's a lot of work and you are stuck here seven days a week. You can count on me, Lyle. I'll stay until there is no more work. Okay?"

"Okay, and thanks, Earl."

Chapter 12

After leaving Saigon, Avilla flew directly back to Paris. Taking with her a suitcase of narcotics. After sleeping off some jetlag she went to see her drug agent who received the narcotics from Asia and shipped them to Mexico, hidden away in old Parisian furniture for the Flores Cartel.

When she was through in Paris, she flew home to Mexico City and then the coffee plantation near Chihuahua. She gave the rest of her uncut diamonds to her father and said, "There is a shipment of narcotics coming into Mexico City tomorrow on Air France's cargo jet. And we probably should be there to meet the cargo jet. We'll have to take one of the vans."

"Pietro is in San Francisco, so you and I will go, Avilla," Enrico said.

"What's he doing in San Francisco, Papa?"

"He and his wife April are setting up another pipeline for the narcotics you have been sending over.

"You never did say why you were leaving Saigon."

"Oh, I just thought it was time to come home." She had never said anything about the soldier she had been seeing in Saigon.

They sat in an air conditioned porch talking about the business and everything that had happened during her stay in Saigon. Avilla had never met April.

'"Is the narcotics business good, Papa?"

"We are making more money than I would have thought. But it costs much money to stay in business. There are lawyers

168

we have hired, police officers we have bought to look the other way and our own army for distribution. It is also more involved than I would have thought, but I say again we are making much money." Enrico started coughing and he excused himself and went into the bathroom. Avilla could hear him coughing and gasping.

The next morning the two of them left the plantation in one of the vans for Mexico City. "Maybe you should drive, Avilla." She didn't argue. Her father was looking pale.

As they rode out of sight of the plantation Avilla asked, "Papa, what is it with this cough you have?"

Just then he started coughing again and covered his mouth with his handkerchief. As he was folding it up again to put back in his pocket Avilla saw some blood on it. "Papa, are you going to tell me or do we stop here?"

"I started coughing about a year ago. At first I didn't think too much about it. But it wouldn't go away and once in a while I would cough up a bit of blood. I finally went to see a doctor and he said that I have an advanced cancer in my lungs."

"Oh, Papa, this isn't good. Why didn't you go see a doctor sooner?"

"I didn't think much about my coughing until I saw some blood."

"Did the doctor give you anything for it?

"Morphine for the discomfort."

"How long do you have, Papa?"

He was silent for a long time before answering. "The doctor said it could be weeks or even months. But he doubted if I'd live another year."

"Oh, Papa, I'm so sorry. You have always seemed like a rock to the family, always so strong and healthy."

They were silent for a long time. Avilla thought perhaps her father had gone to sleep. Then without any warning, "When I first came to Mexico I had no intentions of a criminal life. I have no Spanish blood in me, daughter. My real name is Hans

169

Grubber. Yes, I am German." He was quiet then.

Avilla was quiet also, trying to absorb this. "I think you better explain, Papa. You can't leave it like that."

"I am a small man, Avilla, and growing up in my home my father was ashamed of me, because I was so small. But I had a brilliant mind and I decided at a young age that if I was ever going to achieve anything I would have to use my mind. Like you, I have close to a photographic memory. When I finished school I went to Spain to study diamond cutting and the industry. I became very good at both. I changed my name to Juan Esteban; because of WWI I did not want to be discriminated against because I was German. So I forged the papers and became Juan.

"I stayed in Barcelona for several years, even after I became certified. But the Great Depression hit Spain, just like the whole world. Then this guy Hitler started preaching new ideas and a better economy and life for everybody. I was caught up in his ideas and returned to Germany, and I still had my papers for Hans Grubber. So once again I became Hans and went to work in Berlin for German intelligence, the Abwehr." He told her about his assignments to France and England and Scotland. About accompanying Admiral Canaris to Spain.

"I guess I was a little naive; we were talking with Francisco Franco, when Canaris told him Germany was going to attack Poland and asked to use Gibraltar as an attack base for the Atlantic and Mediterranean Sea. And then Canaris advises Franco to stay out of the war because Canaris was convinced Germany could not win." He started coughing again and spit up only a little blood.

"I was still encouraged with Hitler's ideas of a better world. Then one day I was asked to devise a plan to smuggle guns across the U.S. border from Mexico, with the intent to attack America from within if the United States didn't stay out of the war. Hence I left Hans Grubber behind and forged papers for Enrico Flores.

"After a while I lost my contact in San Diego, but the

gun shipments kept coming. When Germany surrendered I had a surplus of guns. I later found a market in Latin America.

"I liked the challenge and risk. I began smuggling diamonds. I always was smarter than anyone else. Your brother, Pietro, got us started in the narcotics business and I have to admit we are doing very good there. Only because I have always been here to control your brother. You and I, Avilla, have more intellect than Pietro and I think he needs to prove things to us and to himself. He is too ambitious, too aggressive and reckless, though.

He started coughing again and he spit up more blood. It took a little while to get his breathing under control.

"I have made all necessary arrangements, Avilla, so when I do pass everything will be in place. I have already signed documents giving you my power of attorney. When and if I can no longer manage affairs or I die. You and your brother will inherit the business equally. But remember this, Avilla: you will always have to watch Pietro.

"Do me a favor, Avilla."

"Sure, what?"

"Do not say anything to your brother about anything I have told you."

"Okay."

"When it is time for you to assume your power of attorney, my attorney will ask you and Pietro to his office where he'll make it official. That way Pietro will have nothing to say or complain about me choosing you and not him. In all honesty though, Avilla, Pietro does know how to make money. He's just too ambitious."

"I'll watch him, Papa—and Papa, thank you for telling me all about your past.

* * *

They left the airport at Mexico City two days later and

returned to the plantation. Pietro and April had returned from San Francisco. "I wondered where you had gone, Papa," Pietro said. "And it is good to see you looking so well, Avilla. Avilla, this is my wife April."

They hugged and April said, "Pietro has told me all about you, Avilla, and I am so happy to meet you."

"I am happy to meet you also, April.

"We have about $300,000.00 worth of narcotics hidden in furniture we brought back from Mexico City."

"That will come in handy. April and I were thinking about taking a little business vacation to Bar Harbor, Maine. Our contact in New Brunswick is requesting this stuff. After I have concluded business with him we all can spend some time on the beach and eat seafood."

"That sounds like fun, Pietro. Get out of this awful heat for a while," Avilla said.

"Yeah, and we can lay on the beach," April said.

"You better count me out. I—I have things that need my attention. You three go and have fun."

Avilla knew why her father would not go. But she kept it to herself.

* * *

Two days later the narcotics were hidden in amongst a load of coffee beans and taken across the border to El Paso. Pietro, April and Avilla took the bus across the border. Avilla went to secure motel rooms for the night and Pietro and April went to retrieve the suitcase of narcotics and then met Avilla at the motel. While she waited for the other two, she made flight reservations for the three of them with United Airlines to Boston. Stopping briefly in Chicago. From Boston she figured they would rent a car from Avis. She had no idea what to expect in Bangor if they were to fly into there.

Pietro and April arrived at the motel carrying the suitcase

of narcotics. "We'll have to divide this up between our three carry-on bags."

"I have reservations for 8 am tomorrow onboard United Airlines. First class."

"Do you know where we will be staying?" Avilla asked.

Pietro chuckled and said, "Yes, in our own condominium. Last week I had our man, Tomas Hernando in Boston, go up to Bar Harbor and purchase a nice condo and it is pretty much secluded in Cromwell Cove. There is a nice grassy lawn between the condo and the seashore. Oh by the way, before I forget it, we all need new names and identifications. I will be Juan Philipe and April—you call it, April."

"I like Zoe Philipe. It has a certain charm and ring."

"And I'll be Belle Saucier. I already have those papers."

That evening Avilla stayed up late into the night creating new identification papers for Pietro and April. When she had finished they looked genuine. She was a little surprised to find her brother so thorough and a little proud of him for being so cautious.

Chapter 13

On the drive home Lyle was feeling relieved that he no longer had to worry about the decision to stay in the army or not. He was discharged—with the excitement of starting a new life. He knew if his dad knew he was going to sell off the herd he would be disappointed. But not upset. He would understand.

He arrived at the farm in time to help Earl with the evening milking

"So you're a free man again," Earl said.

"Officially discharged. And it's a good feeling.

"Look Earl, I think I'll go to Woodstock in the morning instead of the next day, so I won't be here to help with the morning milking, but I should be back in time to help out with the evening milking."

Lyle was up earlier than usual the next morning and he pulled into the diner just as the front door was being unlocked.

"You're here early, Hon," Becky said.

"Yeah, I've got to see a man about a cow."

"Okay. Your usual."

"Sure, why not."

No one else had come in yet and while Becky waited for his order she sat down at the next table to talk. "So, have you decided what you're going to do about the Army?"

"I was discharged yesterday."

"What about the farm?"

"I'm keeping the farm but selling off the cows and some equipment."

"Are you staying around?"

"Unless I get a better offer."

Lyle's order was up and Becky got up to get it. He ate hungrily and said, "Thanks, got to go."

The time zone changed at the border so he figured he would be on time to find Mr. Getchell at his place of business. He also had a small farm just north of the Trans-Canada Highway Rt. 2 interchange.

It was a pleasant drive over. The air was still cool. Mr. Getchell was standing in his driveway when Lyle drove in. "Well, I'll be!" Getchell exclaimed as he walked over to Lyle's pickup. "Lyle Kingsley."

"Yes Sir, Mr. Getchell."

"What in the world brings you to Woodstock? Before you answer that let's go inside. I bet the Mrs. has some hot coffee."

"Mable!" he hollered from the shed as he kicked his barn boots off. "You don't have to take yours off, Lyle. Mable!"

"Stop that damn-blasted hollering. What do you want, Norman?"

"Have you any hot coffee?"

"You know better than that. You know there's always a hot pot on the stove."

"Well, me and Lyle would like a cup. Sit down, young man. Now what brings you to Woodstock?"

"Mr. Getchell—"

"None of that Mr. stuff. I ain't high society. It's Norman."

"Okay, Norman. Both of my folks were recently killed in an accident and I have decided to sell off the cows, and some equipment and the hay."

"Boy, the Lord sent you didn't he. Just yesterday—I have a market for a herd a little ways below here. Tell me, Lyle, what you have," and Norman got up for paper and pen.

"There are 110 milking cows, none of them are over five years old. 40 yearlings, 1 three year old bull, a two year old bull and six calves."

Norman wrote these figures down and asked, "What equipment?"

"Two International tractors, a 504 and one 460. One mowing machine, and one rake and two tag trailers."

"The equipment I'll have to see first. What about the hay?"

"It isn't mowed yet and it hasn't gone to seed either. Dad usually baled between 14,000 and 15,000 bales."

"Can you start mowing tomorrow? We're in for five days of hay making weather."

"I can. Can you pick up in the field?"

"I can do that. You mow and bale and I'll give you 75 cents a bale. Now, I need my adding machine to figure out the cows."

He was back in a few minutes with more paper and the adding machine. "I can give you $400 each per milking cow. $200 each yearling and $50 each calf.

"You say you have two bulls. I'll pay you beef prices for those two, $400.00 each."

After several minutes Norman said, "For the entire lot, $53,100.00."

"You make it an even $53,500.00 and we have a deal."

Norman hemmed and hawed about the price. Lyle knew he was tight with a dollar. But finally he gave in and said, "Okay $53,500 for all your livestock."

"When can you pick 'em up, Norman?"

"It'll take two trips with the big cattle rig, and I'll also have to bring the van truck for the two bulls. I can follow you back today for the two bulls and I can look at the equipment. My big rig is on the road today; this is Monday—about Wednesday morning, about 10 am. That'll give you time to finish milking. Mable, you wanta ride over to Maine?"

"No, you go, Norman. I have too many things to do right here."

"Okay. I'm ready if you are."

* * *

Earl was still there when Lyle returned to the farm. "Earl, this is Normal Getchell and he is going to buy the livestock, the equipment and the hay. And you can start mowing the first two sections. We will have to bale the hay, but he'll send a crew to pick the hay up."

"I'll get started right on it."

"Thanks, Earl."

They loaded the two bulls first and then Lyle showed Norman the two tractors and the rest of the equipment. "Everything is in good shape. $4500.00 for the two tractors. $150 for the mower, and $150 each for the two trailers, $4950.00."

"You're going to bankrupt me, boy. This money is hard to come by."

"I'll bet you already have a buyer in mind for the equipment, like you do for the livestock."

"If he mows today, you'll probably bale tomorrow afternoon? How many bales over these two sections?"

"There should be about 1600."

"Okay I'll have to have the big rig with a low bottom flat bed and a crew."

"I'll start baling at noon."

"The crew will be here at 3 o'clock. Do you have a buncher?"

"Yes."

"That'll help."

* * *

It actually took three trips to transport all of the livestock and two trips for the equipment and Norman was a week hauling all of the hay to Woodstock, a total of 16,043 bales. Lyle received a total of $70,752.00 for everything.

"What are you going to do with the milking machines and tanks?"

"Is there a market for it?"

"I might be able to find one. I'll give you a call when I find one."

They shook hands and Norman said, "Been good doing business with you, Lyle. And again I'm sorry about your folks. They were good people."

"Thank you, Norman."

Norman made their last pickup, and five days later Lyle received the last check. There was now $85,210.17 in the farm account and another $70,752. for sale of everything. Lyle put it all in a savings account.

"Well, Lyle," Earl said, "Everything is gone. What will you do now?"

"I'm going to cruise the woods and maybe cut some lumber this winter. I still have the 450 crawler and arch. Maybe when I figure out what I want to do, I might raise a few beef cattle."

"Well, if you ever need any help, call me."

"I will, Earl; without you I don't think I could have done everything." He reached in his pocket and handed Earl a check.

"You have already given me my wages, Lyle."

"I know. This isn't wages. Call it, for a better term, severance."

"But, Lyle, this check is for $6,000.00."

"And you earned every penny of it. I think Mom and Dad would have approved."

"I don't know how to thank you, Lyle."

"You just did. It is I who owes you a debt of thanks, Earl."

* * *

It was late when they drove into the yard of their new condo in Bar Harbor. Tomas Hernando was there to greet them. Avilla took an immediate disliking to the man. She hated his sleazy stares at her and April and she disliked his mannerisms.

She and April went inside while the two talked outside. Pietro signed the transfer of property forms and Tomas said, "I'll drop these off at the county registry of deeds tomorrow. I have taken care of everything. The electricity is on and so is the water. The house as advertised came complete with appliances and furniture for every room. Even towels and sheets. The property is yours, jefe. If there is anything else I can do for you, jefe, you only have to ask. After I drop the deed at the registry tomorrow, I will return to Boston."

"Thank you for your help, Tomas. I will remember this." Pietro knew Tomas was wanting to be invited in, but Pietro was going to show him who was the jefe. Instead he said, "Have a good trip back, Tomas."

The narcotics were locked up in a closet and the three unpacked what little they had. "This is beautiful, Pietro, and we own the entire condo?"

"The whole thing. The sun is setting, but let's go out and walk down to the shore."

The grass on the lawn looked as though it had been manicured. There was a hedge row that blocked the view from the neighboring condo and the other side was a dense patch of trees. Avilla kicked her shoes off and waded into the water. She screamed and exclaimed, "Wow! Is this water cold. This is the end of summer and it is still cold?"

"We are a long way north of Mexico, Sis."

They stayed down by the water until it was dark then they went back inside and stayed up for a long time talking.

Pietro telephoned Robert Newcomb and told him to meet him at the same gravel pit where they had met before.

"When are you going north to meet your Woodstock dealer?" Avilla asked.

"I was thinking the two of you drive me to the Bangor airport and I'll rent a Hertz car. Then you two can do some shopping. We'll need food and clothes. Remember to use cash always."

When Pietro and April went to bed Avilla went outside and walked down to the water's edge. She found a rock to sit on and bury her toes in the cool sand and listening to the surf break on the sandy shore. The moon was just climbing above the horizon and reflecting across the surface of the ocean. She was lonely and envied her brother's love for his wife April. She realized she could have had this kind of love with Lyle— She couldn't finish the thought, and mad at her life and herself, she walked out into the cold water. She was crying.

The water was so cold she didn't stay long. She dried her eyes and walked back to the condo.

They left the condo early the next morning and drove to the airport and had breakfast. Then Pietro said, "Plan to meet me at the main terminal entrance at 5 pm sharp. Don't be late."

Pietro took the small suitcase and left the airport headed north on I-95. Not wanting to stand out or to be noticed by the local residents he rented a two year old Ford. Figuring a car like the white Mercedes would look out of place in the country. In Bar Harbor a Mercedes would not stand out as much as it would up north.

He watched his speed closely all the way to the Houlton exit, not wanting to attract the attention of the police. He was wearing a dark colored Eisenhower jacket and in the right hand pocket he carried a snub nose .38 revolver. Just in case Mr. Newcomb might have different ideas.

He was hungry and was needing another cup of coffee. But he drove past a diner, not wanting to be seen by anyone. He wasn't long coming to the old dirt road that eventually stopped at an old gravel pit that was now beginning to grow up with weeds and bushes. Newcomb's car was already there.

* * *

"Have you got everything straightened out at the farm yet?" Becky asked.

"With the farm, yes."

"Then what is the problem?"

"Well—I hate to admit it, but all of my life someone has cooked my meals for me. My Mom—and she was a great cook—and then the Army. Now I'm having to do it myself."

"Ha, ha, ha!" Becky laughed, "What you need, Hon, is a wife." She brought Lyle his breakfast.

The day before Lyle had taken stock of the food stores at the house. Much of what was in the refrigerator had to be thrown out along with all the bread, cookies, muffins and one cake he did not know was there. He went through the pantry making a list of things he would have to get and the freezer in the shed. That was almost full of beef, pork, chicken and haddock.

From the diner he stopped at the IGA store. He had never had to go shopping before, either, and he felt like everyone was watching him. He finally had everything he would need and he drove home and started taking care of things.

When he had finished, he made a fried egg, ham and cheese sandwich and a pot of coffee and went out on the porch to eat. Afterwards he walked through the empty barn. He had already cleaned out every stall. There was still some grain left, which was okay, and there were probably five hundred bales of hay overhead in the loft. The two remaining tractors and other equipment was parked in the sheds.

He pulled out the lawn mower and mowed the two lawns. They were needing to be mowed and he worked up a sweat. Then he went inside and warmed the coffee left in the pot and took his cup out on the porch.

He sat down and was beginning to wonder if this was how his life was going to be, looking for anything to keep him busy. He said out loud, "As soon as the weather turns cold, I'll cut a few high grade logs."

And that reminded him he wanted to walk around and through the woods to see what there was for lumber. It had been several years since he was last in the woods, when he was a teenager, so he took his compass. He thought about taking his .357 in case he saw a coyote, but decided against it.

It was the last week in August and still warm. Not hot like Vietnam was year round. His father's woods road pretty much divided the three hundred acre wood lot in half. The old road he found in surprisingly good shape. He went off to the right or southerly to circle back to the road farther in. Here was a nice stand of hardwood; rock maple, yellow birch, ash and beechnut.

He broke away some of the outer bark on a few of the rock maple and on some he found pimples in the bark which meant the tree was birdseye. A very valuable wood. And those rock maple were tall, straight, and no limbs until the crown and some of them were three feet across the butt end.

Ash was a slow-growing tree and there were only a few that he would consider marketable. The yellow birch were like the rock maple, beautiful trees.

At the far south end of the lot the hardwood changed to softwood and the ground was spongy and wet and there were thickets of white cedar. He wondered if Ward Log Cabin was still in business behind the airport.

He started his circle back towards the woods road and here on dry knolls were stands of pine and spruce. Beautiful stands of lumber. "And they should be thinned, so the others can grow." He would check the hardwood market and if the price was too low, he'd start with the pine and spruce.

Back on the woods road again he made a loop on the other side towards the north. Again here he found a beautiful stand of hardwood mixed occasionally with pine. If these trees were harvested correctly there would be a yearly income for him for years to come. And then with a herd of beef cattle...

He was really beginning to feel better about his future now, and he could see a purpose. When he came to the north property line, a stone wall, he kept to the north planning to come out to an old gravel pit, infamous for teenage beer parties. That is until the county sheriff discovered this little hidey-hole, and that was the last of the beer parties. He came out to the pit and walked over to the top lip and looked over. There were two men and two cars parked there.

Lyle laid down behind a bush that he could see around and watch the two. Days of the Mekong Devils and survival had been reawakened. One man, small built, black hair, wearing casual clothes, brown slacks and a light colored shirt and a jacket, was holding a small suitcase.

The other guy was taller, hair down over the ears, blue jeans and a work shirt. He suspected he had stumbled onto a drug deal.

"Mr. Philipe, I want to see the merchandise. A quarter of a million dollars is a lot of money."

Lyle was right this is a drug deal.

Juan (Pietro) put the suitcase on the hood of the car and opened it. And then closed it. "Now I want to see the stones."

Robert Newcomb put his valises on the hood and opened it. Juan removed a loupe from his pocket and started examining the raw diamonds, not saying a word.

Lyle thought the taller fellow was beginning to act nervous. Robert hadn't expected Juan Philipe to be a diamond expert. He knew he was in big trouble. After fifteen minutes Juan put his loupe back in his pocket and put his hand in the right hand jacket pocket and removed a handgun.

Lyle saw this and couldn't believe what he was seeing. His first instinct was to get down there before someone got shot. Or him. He was wishing he had brought his handgun. There was no way he could get off the top of the bank without being seen.

Juan held the gun out and said, "Do you remember what I said if you ever tried to fuck me over?"

Robert just stared at Juan.

"These stones, Robert, aren't even industrial quality. Did you not suppose I would examine them?" Still Robert remained silent.

Juan pointed the gun at Robert's chest and pulled the trigger. Robert was dead before he hit the ground. Juan closed the valise and put that and the suitcase in his trunk, stepped over Robert and closed the door of his car and drove off. Lyle was now able to see the license plate, and he repeated the plate numbers several times so he would not forget.

As soon as the car was out of sight, Lyle jumped off the lip and landed on soft sand and slid to the bottom. He checked the victim and he was dead. There was nothing else in the victim's car, and he took the keys—just in case.

It was a five mile hike back to the farm if he walked the road. Shorter but slower through the woods. He chose the woods just in case the shooter was to come back for some reason or might be waiting at the mouth of the road for some reason.

He had already hiked a few miles through the wood lot, but he was nowhere near as tired as he had been on missions. He sucked it up and started for home through the woods.

He checked his watch as he left the gravel pit. 12:50 pm. "The shooting was about 12:35 pm." All while he was hiking he kept talking out loud about everything he had seen and heard. He could run through the hardwoods but he was slower going through the softwoods. And when he had decided on this route, he had forgotten about the cedar swamp.

He was going over his boot tops in black mud and stumbling over fallen trees and roots. By the time he reached the farm it had taken him over an hour to take what he thought would have been the quickest route. There wasn't time to remove his muddy boots and clothes. He immediately telephoned the Sheriff's office. The phone rang.

"Sheriff's Office."

"Is this you, Jim? This is Lyle Kingsley!"

"This is Jim. You sound all out of breath, Lyle. What's up?"

"Jim, I just witnessed a murder. You'd better get out here as soon as you can. I'm at the farm."

"Okay Lyle, I'm on my way. It'll only be a few minutes."

While he waited for Sheriff Fye, Lyle did change his boots. But his clothes were still covered with mud.

Fifteen minutes later Sheriff Fye came screaming up the highway and when he pulled into the dooryard, all four tires were screeching on the pavement.

Lyle jumped in the passenger's seat and said, "Up to the old Pivey gravel pit, Jim."

On the way up Lyle told Jim everything he had seen and heard. "There's been a lot of drugs on the streets this last year. We'll have the name of the dealer in New Brunswick at least."

They walked away from the cruiser towards the fallen victim, "Where were you, Lyle?"

Lyle pointed and said, "I was on top of the bank laying down. When I first saw them they were asking to see the drugs and the diamonds. I don't know how long they were here before that or who arrived first."

Jim rolled the victim over and saw the entrance wound in the chest. "Yeah, he's dead alright. Shot right in the heart. What caliber did you thing the gun was?"

"It was a snub-nose revolver, so there's no empty ejected shell. My guess would be a .38."

"Well, I'd better call for an M.E. then we can look the car over,"

Jim radioed back to the dispatcher and asked that M.E. Douglas be notified of a dead body at the ole Pivey gravel pit. "Okay, it'll be a while before the M. E. arrives. Let's go through this car."

While they waited for the M.E. to arrive, Jim photographed everything, including the dead body and the tire tracks left by the other vehicle. Lyle walked out the road to the highway and back, looking for anything that might have been thrown out. "I didn't find anything, Jim."

Jim popped the trunk and it was clean. There was nothing inside and only the registration papers in the glove box. "According to this registration the car belongs to Robert J. Newcomb of Woodstock, New Brunswick. I'll have to notify the R.M.C.P.s tomorrow. Maybe they'll know this Newcomb guy deals in drugs."

The M. E. showed up an hour later. "Hello, Jim."

"Dr. Douglas."

"Before I turn the body over where was he hit?"

"In the chest."

Douglas lifted the back of the shirt, "There's no exit wound. The bullet is still in the body. That's good. Okay, let's roll it over." Douglas went through the pockets and pulled out three uncut diamonds. "Is this what this is all about?" Jim put those in an evidence bag, dated it and signed it.

"Okay, will you two help me put the body in a body bag?"

The body was then put inside the M.E.'s vehicle. Lyle, I'll want some of that sand put into this container. The sand that was under the chest. About two inches deep.

"Anything else, Jim?" Douglas asked.

"Only your lab results as soon as possible."

Douglas left with the body and Jim radioed the dispatcher again to have a wrecker sent out.

Tomorrow I'll have a deputy come out and comb both sides of the road with a K-9. If anything was thrown the dog will find it. But my guess is this guy, whoever he is, is smart and didn't throw anything away.

While they waited for the wrecker Jim called the dispatcher again and gave her the license number of the shooter's vehicle, "And get that on the air as soon as possible and the description of the car. A 1966 or 67' Ford, sedan, light brown in color, one person, small built. And then call Augusta for a registration owner and address. Have you got all of that, Jacky?"

"Yes, Sheriff."

"Good."

"This has turned out to be one hell of a day, Lyle. It'll

be a long night for me. But I guess that comes with the job. You getting hungry, Lyle?"

"Sure am."

"Yeah, me too. Once the wrecker gets here we can leave."

* * *

Pietro drove out the gravel pit road to the highway without stopping once, then on I-95 south. He wanted to race ahead and put much distance between him and the gravel pit. But neither did he want to attract attention to himself. So he drove the speed limit and passing any in his way. His biggest concern was he had lost a profitable dealer. Now, after the air had cleared, he would have to find someone to replace Robert Newcomb.

He figured he had several hours before the body was discovered. "At least it wasn't a total failure, I have both the drugs and the diamonds. Even though they are of a poor grade. But I'm betting Papa will be able to fashion them into some beautiful jewelry."

In spite of having just taken a life, he was feeling smug.

He returned the rental an hour earlier than he had thought, now he had to wait at the main terminal entrance for April and Avilla. He was nervous, carrying the suitcase with the drugs and the valise of diamonds. He found a men's room and emptied the diamonds into the suitcase and left the valise in the bathroom stall, after wiping his finger prints off.

Avilla and April were on time. "Did everything go okay?" April asked.

"No, he tried to pawn off a low-grade of stones that might be worth fifty or sixty thousand. So we still have the drugs. Maybe before we go back to Mexico we'll all go to New Brunswick and find another dealer. These drugs are so addictive the users will be looking hard for a new fix."

Both Avilla and April knew there was something Pietro

was not telling them. He was more nervous than usual and he couldn't sit still.

The next morning while April was preparing breakfast Avilla went outside and walked down to the shore. The sun was already up and promising a nice day. The air was a little cool compared to what she was used to so she went back in and turned the TV on and switched to a local channel.

The newscast that morning was all about one topic. A drug related homicide in Houlton the day before. Avilla was shocked and stunned. She hollered, "Pietro, what in fuck did you do yesterday? Pietro! You come out here! Pietro, you get your ass out here!" By now April was also wondering what was going on.

When Pietro walked into the living room, Avilla started all over again. "Pietro what in fuck did you do yesterday?!" she demanded to know.

"What are you talking about?"

"You killed that man, didn't you?!" she was still yelling.

"So what if I did. Big deal."

"You jackass! It's all over the news. Papa was correct when he said you were reckless."

"Shut up and let me listen to what's being said." They all were silent then listening to the news commentator.

"Yesterday there was a drug deal going down in Houlton that turned bad. In an old gravel pit just north of town, Lyle Kingsley witnessed one individual shoot another man supposedly over some inferior grade raw diamonds that were supposed to pay for a shipment of narcotics. The victim has been identified as Robert Newcomb of Woodstock, New Brunswick. The shooter is identified as a small built man about 5'7", 130 pounds. Black hair, maybe of Spanish origin. Wearing an Eisenhower jacket and driving a Hertz rental car, brown Ford sedan, registration number 739-002, a state of Maine plate. The car was rented in Bangor by a Juan Philipe. But doubtful if that is his real name."

April switched channels again and again. All channels were broadcasting the same thing.

"You put us all in jeopardy, Pietro," April said. She looked at Avilla. For as angry and as loud as she was only minutes ago she was now very quiet. "Anything wrong, Avilla? I mean other than Pietro killing that man and jeopardizing all of us?"

* * *

Sheriff Jim Fye worked all night on the homicide. The license plate number came back to the Hertz rental car in Bangor and when he called Hertz, he was told the car had been rented by a Juan Philipe. And a driver's license and address in Massachusetts. He then drove to Bangor and had the vehicle impounded at the Penobscot County Sheriff impound. A tech crew went over the inside of the car for fingerprints and it had been wiped clean.

"Sheriff Fye."

"Yes."

"For security reasons, we have a security camera which will have a photo of Mr. Philipe."

"Oh you are a sweetheart, Madeline."

She rewound the tape and fast forwarded it to the time on the rental slip. "Here Sheriff, he is just coming through the door."

"Hold it right there. Good. That's a good picture of him. Can you print that?"

"Sure can. It'll take a couple of minutes." Madeline disappeared in the back room.

When she returned she was carrying an 8x10 glossy print of Juan Philipe. "Thank goodness for modern technology. And thank you, Madeline."

"Hope you catch him."

Jim beat-footed back to his office in Houlton and asked the dispatcher to put the photo out. "An A.P.B., Jacky, to all law enforcement agencies. The CIA, DEA, and FBI. The turnpike authority, all airports big and small and the Coast Guard and Border Patrol and Customs. If this guy is still in Maine I don't want him leaving."

"Oh and Jacky, I'm going to lay down for a while in one of the cells. I need a couple of hours sleep."

All of this information and photo went out on wire by 6 am. At 8 am the day dispatcher, Fred, rapped on the cell door where Jim was sleeping. Begrudgingly Jim opened his eyes and said, "What in hell do you want? I said I wanted to get a couple of hours sleep, Jacky."

"Sheriff, Jacky went home, this is Fred."

"Oh, what is it Fred?"

"Ah, Sir, there is a phone call I think you should take in your office."

Jim stood up, stretched and stumbled his way to his office, "Hello, this is Sheriff Fye."

"Sheriff, this is FBI Special Agent Henry Jones. I don't have a lot of time to explain. But myself, CIA and DEA are boarding a military jet at Hanscom Field, Lexington, Massachusetts and we'll be at the Houlton International Airport by 11 am. Pick us up." That was the end of the conversation.

"No niceties or anything. Hum.

"Fred, get me Lyle Kingsley on line 1!" he hollered.

"Hello, Lyle, this is Jim Fye. Hope you haven't any plans, but you need to be in my office at 11 am."

"What's going on, Jim?"

"All I'm going to say now is *yesterday*. Just be here, okay?"

"Okay."

* * *

The breakfast April had been making went untouched. All that any of them wanted was coffee. At 9 o'clock Avilla turned the TV back on. The commentator was still telling about the homicide in Houlton, "Jesus Christ!" Avilla screamed, "Pietro, they have your picture on the TV now!"

Everyone was silent for a few minutes. Not knowing what to do or say. Finally April asked, "How could they have your photo, Pietro? Where did you go yesterday?"

"Only to Houlton. I made no other stop. They must have gotten it from the car rental."

"How are we ever going to leave here now, Pietro?" April asked.

"We don't for a while. We stay right here and let this blow over. As long as I don't go outside nobody sees me, I don't think there should be any problems. No one knows anything about you two. So you'll be able to go out and get food."

* * *

At 10 o'clock that morning Sheriff Fye received another phone call from the R.C.M.P. office in Woodstock. "I would like to speak with Sheriff Fye, please."

"Speaking."

"This is Lieutenant Jacobs, R.C.M.P. in Woodstock. Thank you for your notification of Robert Newcomb. He has been on our watch list for some time now. We never could figure out where the drugs were coming from. If you need any more information just call me."

"Thank you, Lieutenant."

This morning Lyle made breakfast at home. And then sat out on the porch until it was time to leave. Before leaving he put on his shoulder holster, checked the action of his .357 and slipped it in the shoulder holster and pulled on a windbreaker to conceal it.

Lyle was in Jim's office a few minutes early. At 11:15, Jim and three other men, all dressed in suits, accompanied him. Jim closed the door, "Sit down everyone. Lyle Kingsley this is

Agent Don Beverly, CIA, this is FBI Special Agent Henry Jones and this Hurley McRandall, DEA. Gentlemen, Lyle Kinsley.

CIA agent Don Beverly spoke first. "You stirred up quite a hornets nest when you posted that photo of Juan Philipe."

Then DEA agent Hurley McRandall said, "We have been after Philipe for a long time, but we never knew what he looked like, until this morning. He is suspected of creating a drug pipeline over most of the United States. And now it seems he is trying to move into Canada. He is like a ghost. Changing his name and identification wherever he goes. No one is sure what his real name is."

"There have been other drug related homicides where a person with Philipe's description has become a person of interest. If indeed it is the same person, it sounds like he is getting reckless," agent Jones said.

"And when you're in the drug business as deep as Philipe is, you cannot be reckless," DEA agent McRandall said.

"Because this is an interstate crime the FBI is now involved," agent Jones said.

"When Berlin fell in 1945 our people were in charge of recovering German documents. They had managed to burn many documents, but there were boxes of complete files found that dated back to 1936. I have reviewed one set of files with great interest.

"There seems to be a very intelligent young soldier who had no record of any kind of training. In fact before this, his files say he spent a few years in Barcelona, Spain, where he became a certified diamond cutter."

At the mention of diamonds started Lyle searching his mind.

"A search was made in Spain for a certified diamond cutter with the same name, Hans Grubber. There never was found a Hans Grubber.

"Back to Hans Grubber in Berlin. Without any training whatsoever he was made a Lieutenant and within a year,

Captain. So we have to assume this Grubber is a very careful and intelligent individual. And he was assigned to the Abwehr. Germany's Intelligence Division. He was sent to France, England and Scotland to retrieve information on their economy and ship building. At that time he was using the name Juan Esteban.

"Sometime later Grubber apparently devised a plan how to smuggle guns into the United States. Germany was planning to attack us from within. The last record we have of Captain Hans Grubber he was given a year's income in advance. And that was the last we have on Hans Grubber."

"Then years later, after the war, Juan Esteban surfaced in southern Mexico and sold three hundred guns for $46,000.00 to an individual who wanted to resell them in Latin America."

Lyle had been listening with great interest and now he spoke up. "It would appear to me, Agent Beverly, that whoever bought the three hundred guns must have been a CIA agent. Otherwise how would you know how many guns and for $46,000.00?"

Everyone was looking at agent Beverly. "You are quite correct, Mr. Kingsley. But you don't need to know any more than that." Jim looked at Lyle and smiled and winked.

DEA agent McRandall said, "We were able to capture one of the cartel's dealers in Florida and we learned the major players will have a yellow spider web—"

Lyle interrupted and said, "A yellow two inch spider web tattoo and a black spider in the center of the web."

Now everyone went silent and were looking at Lyle.

"You have our attention, Lyle; continue," Jim said.

"I met this young woman in Saigon that I fell for. She had this same tattoo with the spider on the inside of her right leg just above the ankle. Her name was Belle Saucier. She said she was from Paris and worked for the French Consulate there in Saigon. I know she was fluent in Russian and I also think she could understand Vietnamese. Although I never heard her speak it. She said her father was a diamond cutter. When I returned to Saigon after my last mission she had left without explaining why or where she was going. Not a word. When I checked at the French Consulate I was told that a Belle Saucier had never worked there."

"France, you say. Did you ever see any confirmation of this?" DEA agent McRandall asked.

"No."

CIA agent Beverly asked, "What was your unit Mr. Kingsley?"

"The Mekong Devils." That lit up Beverly's eyes.

"And what were your missions?"

"You do not have high enough clearance to know, Sir."

"Have you seen the photo that was put out on the wire, Mr. Kingsley?" Jones asked.

"I'd prefer if you just called me Lyle. No I have not seen it."

Jim handed his photo to Lyle. "That's him. There's no doubt about it." And then Lyle asked, "Do you think this Belle Saucier could be part of this drug cartel?"

Beverly spoke up first. "It is all looking as if Belle might in fact be this Hans Grubber's daughter and maybe a brother also, to this Philipe."

"We have information that narcotics were coming out of southeast Asia via France. But the trail stopped there."

FBI Agent Jones spoke up now, "If you are certain, Lyle, that this man in the photo is the same man you saw shoot Robert Newcomb, then I think we can get an indictment in federal court. You will be expected to testify, Lyle, at the Grand Jury Hearing."

"Yes Sir, no problem."

"Good, we'll have to put you in protective custody until then." Jim knew this wasn't going to go over well with Lyle.

"No, I don't think so."

"Lyle, if you don't come in for protective custody you may not live to see the hearing. There is no doubt in my mind that Philipe will try to kill you to prevent you from testifying. And the whole case depends upon your testimony, it is imperative that you come in for your protection."

"Let's say you get your indictment and somehow he escapes and goes back wherever he calls home. You won't have anything."

"What are you suggesting, Lyle?" Jim asked.

"You make him come to me."

"Come to you?! Out of the question," Jones said.

"Wait a minute, Henry. Let's hear him out," Beverly said, "Continue, Lyle."

"I know a place I can go, where they can't come at me without me seeing them first. What I want from you or the FBI, is that you put it on the TV that I am the only witness and will be testifying at the Grand Jury hearing. This information, if they are still close—and I think they are—will make them come after me. You see they won't have a choice."

"I'm still not convinced," Jones said. "If this went wrong it would end my FBI career."

"I don't agree with you, Henry. In fact I think it is an excellent idea. And I'm not worried about Lyle. You see, Henry, the Mekong Devils were the most feared unit in Southeast Asia. They all had done three tours and the only casualty was when Mr. Russ Jones was attacked by a huge snake that coiled around him and pulled him underwater, in the dark of the night. Lyle didn't hesitate, he dove in and after several minutes Jones was cut free of the snake, when he emerged from the water the snakes head had been cut off and was still clamped to Jones' arm. You see, Henry, Lyle has seen more combat and danger than anyone in this room will ever see. I say let Lyle do this." Then Beverly started laughing and said, "And God help this cartel if they do come after you, Lyle."

"Okay. I'll agree to it. But I need to know where you'll be and I must be in constant contact with you," Jones said.

"That won't happen, sir. The only person I know and trust in this room is Jim Fye. He'll know where I'll be and any communication to me or from me will be via Jim."

"I don't know about this," Jones said, "What do you think, Sheriff? You know Lyle better than the rest of us."

"I think Lyle can take care of himself," Jim said.

"You're the expert, Mr. Jones," Lyle said, "What do you think will be his next move?"

"I would expect him to lay low until they think we aren't looking anymore. So we'll run this about you and the grand jury for two more days and stop. Just long enough for him or his team to get the word. And I believe they—or he is still in Maine. If he is then I would suspect he has a team here helping, or he couldn't stay hidden for long. And the way we have every exit under security, he won't be able to get by us. So when you are ready, Lyle, you and Sheriff Fye set your plan into action."

"Now if no one else has any more questions, I think we should be leaving," agent Beverly said.

"You be careful, Lyle, I mean it," Beverly added.

"Have a good flight back," Jim said.

"I probably shouldn't have to ask this, Lyle, but are you sure you can do this? I mean without getting yourself killed?"

"I'm sure, Jim."

"You know sometime I'd like to hear more about the Mekong Devils, Lyle.

"I have an idea what you have in mind, and when you are ready you let me know. And here, you better take this portable radio with you, in case you need help or need to talk."

It was 3 pm and too late to do much. Tomorrow he would motor up to the family camp on Driftwood Lake. For now he'd pulled the sixteen foot boat out of the barn and serviced the 40hp Evinrude motor. He needed to know what was at the camp and what or how much he'd be needing. He was surprised how this day's events were awakening his survival skills and alertness. In his mind he was now operating like he had for three years in Vietnam. His senses were fully alert again. Always watching in his peripheral vision for any sudden movement or something that didn't belong. And one thing was for sure he would have his .357 with him always.

He drained the oil from the foot of the outboard motor and then filled it. He changed the plugs and then secured it to a metal barrel and filled the barrel with water. The motor started with the second crank. He let it run for a few minutes to get all of the old gas through it. Then he re-secured it to the back of the boat. He found a life preserver and a Porter's Paddle made from ash.

He would have liked to make the trip up the lake now, but it was too late in the afternoon. "I'll get an early start in the morning."

* * *

Pietro was becoming a nervous wreck. He hated being shut up inside. Once in a while he would try to sneak out the back door so he could at least walk down to the beach and sit on the shore. But Avilla remembered what her father had said and she watched him like a hawk. He would try to argue with her and she would verbally put him down. "This is your fault, Pietro, and you brought this down not only on yourself, but me, April and father and everything we have been working for. You get noticed, Pietro, and you'll bring us all down. Now shut up and deal with it." She was angry and Pietro was just a little bit afraid of her. He had never seen his sister like this.

Avilla was angry at her brother also because it was Lyle Kingsley that would eventually destroy them. When she left Saigon she knew then she was falling in love with the guy and she also knew they could never have a life together. And right now Lyle was a big obstacle in their path—her path—and in the end if it came down to her life or his, she decided he would have to go. "Business is business."

"Did you say something, Avilla?" April asked.

"Oh, just thinking out loud."

197

Still morning, noon and the evening news channels were broadcasting the headline story of a drug related shooting in Houlton.

* * *

Lyle made his own breakfast the next morning and stacked the dishes in the sink, closed the kitchen door and drove to the public boat landing on Driftwood Lake.

The lake this morning was like a mirror. Tree swallows were skimming just above the surface for a breakfast of flies. Big brook trout were also after the flies, some jumping clear out of the water after a fly. There was no one else on the lake yet and Lyle opened the throttle. The boat rode up and settled, riding the crest of the wake beneath him.

It was a four mile trip to Deep Cove, and the camp was at the end. The cove was forded by a high ledge wall on the left and on the right the ledge wall rose only maybe ten or twelve above the water. But on this side there was a fine, sandy shore. Boaters and canoers would often stop here for a picnic and to lay in the sun. On top of the ledge were red pine and white spruce trees embedded in a thick layer of moss.

There was a sandy shore in front of the camp also and the water remained shallow for two hundred feet away from shore. Fifty feet from shore he had to cut the throttle and tilt the motor up so it wouldn't drag on bottom. The last ten feet he had to jump out and pull the boat in.

He tied the boat up and walked around the camp first. No broken windows or doors. That was good. The pine needles and leaves out front needed to be raked. He opened the shed double doors, and everything was okay there also. The woodshed was full and two extra 100# propane tanks in the shed. He opened the root cellar dug into the bank next. He wasn't sure what he would find there. It took a minute for his eyes to adjust to the dim lighting. It was empty except for the shelves. The sandy floor was clean, albeit a little damp. But then again, it was always damp.

So far everything was okay. He unlocked the back door and walked into a coat and boots room, then the kitchen door. There was a slight musty smell but everything was dry and clean. No mouse droppings even. The beds in the three bedrooms and been stripped of sheets and blankets and he found those in cedar chests in each room.

There was a radio tower on top of the ledge behind the camp that he and his sister Sheerie had erected. His father had installed a radio phone using the tower. And it was still there, inside the window seat. All he would have to do is plug it in and attach a battery. His mother would never leave canned food, sugar or flour at the camp so he knew there wouldn't be any food. Everything was alright.

Before leaving he pushed the wharf, on two iron wagon wheels, into the water and tied it off to two trees. All he needed to do now was to stock the camp with food. And he had no idea for how long.

Satisfied he motored back to the landing and loaded the boat back on the trailer and drove home. It was still early, only 9 am.

He parked the boat and trailer out of the way at the end of the driveway and then drove to town to talk with the insurance company covering his house and farm. "Come in, Lyle, I have been expecting you after I heard you had sold off the stock. So what can I do for you?"

Lyle listed his equipment he still had and, "I want more coverage on the house, barn, other buildings and equipment."

"The house is covered for $100,000.00 which isn't enough."

"I agree. Knock it up to $200,000.00."

"The barn is underinsured also at $10,000.00"

"Double that. And probably another $100,000.00 on the three tractors and other equipment."

"I'll have a statement ready for you in a day or so, Lyle."

"No, that won't work, I'll wait if you figure out how much more I owe you. I may be going on a trip. That's why I want to be sure there is adequate coverage."

"Certainly. Would you like some coffee while you wait?"

"Yes."

An hour later, "Here you are, Lyle."

Lyle looked it over and wrote out a check. "Thanks, Ed."

His next stop was at Fogg's gunshop. He and his father had always had shotguns and deer rifles, but he wanted something more in line of the Ruger mini-14 or the AR-15, .223 caliber. The same rifles being used in Vietnam.

"Hello, Lyle, how can I help you today?"

"Do you have an AR-15 or mini-14?"

"No AR-15s but I have one Ruger mini-14 with wooden stock."

"That'll do. And can you attach a 3x9 power scope and laser bore sight it?"

"Sure, it'll only take a few minutes."

"I'll want a twenty round clip too—make that two—and two boxes of shells. And one box .357 magnums, hollow point loads. Oh and I'll need a sling for the rifle."

While James was busy attaching the scope and bore sighting it, Lyle walked around the shop to work off some nervous energy.

"Here, Lyle, see how that fits you."

Lyle put the rifle to his shoulder and looked through the scope. "That's good, James."

"Okay, it'll only take me a couple of minutes to bore sight it."

Five minutes later James said, "There, Lyle, before you go hunting you probably should try a few shots. You might have to make a small adjustment."

"Thanks, James; how much?"

"For everything, how's $290.00?"

"Fair enough."

He left the store and he was hungry, so he stopped at the diner.

"Hello, Hon."

"Hi Becky." He sat in the corner with his back to the wall. The noon rush hour was gone and when Becky brought his order he said. "Sit down, Becky."

"You're serious aren't you?" She sat and looked at Lyle, "What's up, Hon?"

"I need you to do something for me."

"Sure what?"

"No one can know anything about this, Becky."

"You have me scared now, Hon."

"Soon someone will most likely stop here. They'll seem friendly enough and they'll ask you if you know me. You are to tell them you do. Next, they'll ask if you know where I am. I want you to tell them I'm at my camp on Driftwood Lake. Can you do this, Becky?"

"Sure, I can do it. But what is all this about, Hon?"

"Better if you don't know, Becky."

"Okay, I'll trust you, Hon. I always have."

"And not a word to anyone about this. Not even your husband, Becky."

"Something tells me, Hon, this isn't some game is it?"

As he was leaving Becky said in a low voice, "You be careful, Hon, whatever it is you are doing."

"Thanks, Becky."

"One question, though. What makes you think someone will stop here and inquire?"

"This diner is close to I-95. They'll probably stop for lunch or just a cup of coffee. This is the most logical place to inquire. Just play along, Becky."

"I will, Hon."

On the drive home he couldn't help but wonder if he had done the right thing involving Becky. He hoped so.

He put everything in the house and then went grocery shopping at the IGA. Before he was done he had filled three shopping carts and he knew later he would need more.

The next morning on the south side of town were self-storage sheds. He went down first to make sure there was one available. Then he returned home and carried his father's safe out to his pickup: all of the firearms, photo albums and everything that could not be replaced if the house was to burn.

When he had everything locked up in the self-storage shed he returned home and packed his clothes and anything else he thought he would need. And the battery for the radio phone.

He had planned to wait until morning to go up to camp, but he had this gut feeling. And he telephoned Jim Fye.

"Hello."

"Jim, Lyle here. I have everything taken care of and I'm heading to my camp on Driftwood now."

"I thought that's where you'd go."

"I'll have a radio telephone there. I'll check in with you once in a while. The number at camp is 555-1798."

"Okay, be careful, Lyle."

"Thanks, Jim."

The boat was loaded heavy and it was beginning to get dark as he was tying up to the wharf. And it was dark before he had everything in the camp for the night. He pulled the boat up on shore some and tied it off again. The eggs, fresh vegetables, meats and bread he took to the root cellar. The rest could remain on the floor until he felt more like taking care of it in the morning. The chainsaw, oil and gas and tools he put in the shed.

He opened some windows to let the camp air out and then he sat down, exhausted. He was hungry but he didn't feel much like cooking so he opened a can of chicken noodle soup and ate it cold. Then he went to bed.

Early the next morning he used the radio phone and called Jim. He answered on the second ring. "Just checking in, Jim. Can you hear me okay?"

"You're coming in clear."

"Early morning is best, before the atmosphere is plugged with too many frequencies. I'll call when I have something."

Avilla had been sitting on a rock near the shore listening to the surf. What a peaceful sound it was making. She wished her life could be that peaceful. She knew what had to be done and she stood up, stretched and went back inside. Pietro and April both were in the kitchen. She poured herself a cup of coffee and sat at the table with them. Pietro spoke before Avilla could say what was on her mind. "We are going to have to kill this Lyle before he can testify in the grand jury. Without his testimony they have no case. It is obvious I cannot go up and take care of him, so you two or one of you will have to go."

"I have a better idea," Avilla said.

"What?"

"One of us goes up, finds where he lives and anything else she can learn about Lyle. Then you, Pietro, contact your man in Boston, Tomas Hernando, and he sends a couple of his boys to shoot him. It'll cost, but what other choice do we have? You can pay him with those diamonds."

"Okay, which one of you goes up?"

Avilla waited to see if April would volunteer. When she didn't Avilla finally said, "I can't." They both looked at her. She continued. "I personally know Lyle Kingsley. From Saigon. That's why I left. He was falling in love with me—and, I really liked him. But if it comes down to him dying or me spending the rest of my life in prison, then he has to go. If I go, he would naturally suspect something and maybe connect me with you, Pietro."

"I see your point, Sis. Tell us all you can about him," Pietro said.

"He isn't going down easy. In Vietnam he was with Special Forces and quite capable. He would go out on missions, sometimes for two weeks at a time. He is alert and strong. He will have to be ambushed. He did three tours without even a scratch."

"Do you still have feelings for him, Avilla?" April asked.

"Like I said it is either him or me."

"Okay, April, I guess you have to go and the sooner the better," Pietro said.

"Avilla, how fast can you forge me another driver's license? Use the name Juli Compos from Boston."

* * *

The next morning she put on a pair of really tight fitting shorts, a loose fitting top and no bra and she put her bikini in her bag, with towel and toiletries.

This was her life that was at stake and it only took Avilla an hour to have a plausible looking Massachusetts driving license. "I should be up there by noon. Don't expect me back until tomorrow."

As she was getting on I-95 in Bangor her stomach began growling and she now wished she had eaten breakfast. As she drove north she couldn't help but think how desolate and lifeless this state seemed to be. A road sign said '120 miles to Houlton.' She guessed she would be there by noon or a little after.

It was a perfect day for a drive. There was no humidity, blue sky and warm temperatures. If this drive had not been so important for her well-being she would have enjoyed it more.

After leaving Bangor she had seen no evidence of a town. Only an occasional building near an exit or on ramp. She sailed across the overpass at Oakfield and saw a few more homes and a train passing underneath her.

Finally a sign saying Houlton exit '1 mile.' She had decided to stop somewhere and inquire where she might find Lyle Kingsley. She already had rehearsed a story to front her inquiry.

Once she was off I-95 she saw a diner sign. "This will be

a good place to inquire and get a bite to eat." She pulled in and got out and walked into the diner. It was a little past noon and there were only a few patrons. But all heads turned to look at her. She had become used to turning men's heads wherever she went.

She found an empty table in the corner. The same one Lyle would choose. "Hi, Hon, what can I get for you?" Becky asked.

"I'll start with a coffee, regular, and your tuna fish salad special." As Becky was getting her coffee she was thinking she was now glad she had left her rings in the drawer at the condo. It will help strengthen her story, she hoped.

Becky was busy taking money from the last of the other guests. Then she brought over a cup of coffee.

"You aren't from around here are you, Honey?"

"No, but why do you ask?"

"Well, someone as pretty as you wouldn't go unnoticed around here."

"I'm actually looking for a friend I met a few years ago," Becky didn't expect this is what Lyle was talking about. But a beautiful woman could be a hell of a lot more dangerous than a man with a gun.

"Actually I decided to leave my husband to look Lyle up. We had a pretty good time for a short while."

"Where's your husband now?" Becky asked playing along.

April looked at the clock and said, "Right about now he'd be halfway across the Atlantic on his way to Italy."

"On business?" Becky asked.

"No, he's a pilot for Pan Am. I used to be a stewardess for Pan Am. Then he seduced me into the mile high club. We were married shortly afterwards. Then he convinced me to give up flying and now I hear he is sticking it to every new stewardess that happens to land his flight. I've had enough. I took my rings off and left them on a letter I left for him. He'll be back in another two days. I've had it with him. That's why I decided to do some traveling of my own and Lyle did ask me to come by if I was ever in this part of the country."

Becky got up to get her tuna fish salad. Then she sat back at April's table. "What's your name, Honey?"

"Juli Compos." April took a bite of the salad and said, "My this is good. Just a touch of vinegar right?"

"That's right. Not many people can taste it."

"Lyle said his folks have a dairy farm but he never said where."

"Well, that's easy enough. When you leave here go north on the highway for about three miles and you can't miss it. Except there ain't no one there."

"What happened?"

"Lyle was home only for a few days when both of his parents were killed by a drunk driver. It was hard on him. He had to give up the military and now he has sold off all the livestock and hay and equipment. He said he needed to be alone so he went to the family camp on Driftwood Lake. I tried to tell him he shouldn't cut himself off from people. That he should have his friends around. But Honey—looking at you I think you are just what the doctor ordered. I think you could strengthen him out. If you know what I mean."

"How do I find Driftwood, Becky?"

"Four miles beyond the farm. You'll see signs and a boat rental shop. You motor towards the other shore, but not all the way over, then turn to the north or left and watch for a long cove on the right. There'll be high ledge rocks on both sides. There is a sandy shore on the right people use for picnics and sun tanning and such. The camp is at the end of the cove. You'll see it from the sandy beach. Girl to girl if I were you and wanted to screw the hell out of him, I'd take along a big jug of wine."

April choked when Becky said that and spit up.

"Oh, excuse me," April said. "I just wasn't expecting that. But I'll keep it in mind," and then she laughed and so did Becky.

April paid for her meal and as she was going out the door Becky said, "Good luck to you, Honey."

"Thank you Becky—for everything."

Sure enough the farm was easy enough to find and it looked empty. Four miles more and just like Becky said a big sign saying Driftwood Lake and there was a boat rental shop. She liked Becky, her no-pretense way of saying what she meant. Then she laughed, "Yeah, screw the hell out of him," and she kept laughing until she turned.

She had been out on the ocean many times with Pietro and she knew how to operate a motor. The biggest motor she could get was a 25hp. "Sorry, Ma'am, we don't have anything bigger."

"That'll be fine."

There was a little chop on the water but not enough to slow her down. The cove was just like Becky had described. It looked like a fjord you'll see in pictures of Norway. Really quite pretty. And there was a sandy beach and the camp at the end.

She got out and pulled the boat up some so it wouldn't float away. She grabbed her towel, her bikini, the wine and a plastic cup. She spread the towel out on the sand and then turned her back to the camp and took all of her clothes off. And taking her sweet time about it. Then she bent over to pull on her bikini bottom, what there was of it, and she stayed bent over until her back started to ache. "There, that should get his attention."

And it did. Lyle had heard a motor coming closer so he got out his binoculars. He had seen other girls disrobe there on the beach, but not staying bent over for so long giving him a bird's eye view of her butt. "So this is what they have sent. The most dangerous weapon against a man. Almost ain't fair."

He watched her with great interest. He supposed she, in her own way, was inviting him to join her. That certainly was a thought, then he decided to wait and see if she would come to him. If this cartel was smart, before they planned to execute an operation like this, they would send someone to reconnoiter. A reconnaissance move. Smart actually. He decided to have some fun, since he was aware and play hard to get and see if she would come to him.

When she stretched out on the blanket, he made sure the radio phone was unplugged from the battery and stored in the window seat along with his rifle and automatic .357 handgun, and the portable radio Jim had given him.

He checked and double checked making sure nothing was out and visible that he didn't want seen. Then he made a cup of coffee and with binoculars sat on the porch steps. He was finding this whole thing interesting, and he wondered how far she would go. When he wasn't sipping coffee he'd watch her with the binoculars. "She surely is a raven beauty, and what a body." She poured another cup of wine rolling on her left side facing away from the camp. Even with the binoculars he couldn't be sure if she had any bottoms on or not. From that distance it looked like a string around her waist.

As April lay there in the warm sunshine she began thinking about Pietro, their life together and the mess they were now in because of him. Maybe she should really leave him. "But would he come after me and shoot me. I know too much about his drug business for him to let me go." These thoughts were depressing her.

She was getting a little bit upset that this Lyle had not come over to see her. She had certainly opened the door. The barn door wide open. She downed that cup of wine and poured another. This time facing the camp. Then she laid on her back and began daydreaming about letting this guy have his way with her.

Two hours went by and still he didn't come. Any other man would have come running with their tongue hanging out like a dog.

It wouldn't be long and she would lose the sun, so thinking she would probably come to the camp, he went out to the root cellar and got some hamburg and enough vegetables to make a green salad and bread. He put everything on the counter and went back to the porch.

The sun was behind the ledges and April pulled on her shirt, only, and put everything back in the boat and looked towards the camp. "There finally." Lyle was standing on his wharf waving his arm beckoning her to come in.

April smiled, she liked what she could see from the beach. She had a little difficulty pushing the boat back in the water. But she did manage.

He stood on the wharf watching her motor in. He had no idea what he was going to say. Probably something stupid. She was thinking the same.

He indicated the open side of the wharf. She brought it in perfectly and shut it off. He held the boat while she stood up and climbed out. "Ouch. I didn't think I slept long enough to get burned."

All Lyle could think to say was "Hi."

"Well, are we just going to stand here staring at each other or are you going to invite me in?"

"I'm sorry. It's—well it's just that beautiful girls don't drop in every day. Yes come up to the camp."

"Can I bring the wine?"

"Sure, that would taste good. I was about to make something to eat. Are you hungry?"

"Yes. What's your wife going to say when you walk in with another woman?"

"I'm not married and no girlfriend. By the way my name is Lyle Kingsley."

"Juli Compos."

"Hope you are hungry. I was about to fix a green salad and fry a hamburger on bread."

"That sounds good. I tell you what, you fry the hamburgers and I'll make the salad. Looks like you were expecting company."

"Oh, when I saw you sunbathing—well I was just hoping."

"This burn is still hurting. Would you have anything to put on it?"

"I don't know, but I'll look. Maybe my mother had some hind of hand cream or something."

"Oh, do your folks come out here often?"

"Well, I've been gone for four and a half years and I'm not sure how often they used the camp. Before I went into the Army we used to come out often.

"This was their bedroom here. You can look in the drawers and closet. I'll look out here."

"You said this was their room."

"Yes, they died a few days after I was back from Vietnam."

"Oh I'm sorry. What happened?"

"A drunk crossed the centerline and hit my Mom and Dad head-on. That bureau was my Mom's you might find something there."

Lyle kept looking in the kitchen cabinet.

"Found it, hand lotion, this will work. You'll have to put it on my back please."

She walked out and turned her back to him and took her shirt off. Lyle noticed that her back was burned. He had seen worse. But boy! Did she have a beautiful body. As he was rubbing the lotion in he began to enjoy this.

"There how's that, Juli?" as he put his arm around her and held his hand against her flat belly. That too was feeling good. She responded with a slight move, and leaned back against him. "You are one beautiful woman, Juli. But what are you doing out here?"

She turned around to face him and hugged him and said, "I'll tell you everything after we eat."

"How do you like your hamburg?"

"Medium. I don't suppose you'd have any salad dressing?"

"I think I forgot that."

"How about some vegetable oil and vinegar?"

210

"There is that. In the cabinet there," and he pointed.

She found salt, pepper and garlic powder. "Oh this is going to be great."

"Hamburgers are ready."

"The salad is too," and she poured the wine.

Juli ate one hamburger while Lyle ate two.

"There I feel better. I'll do dishes if you clean the table. Does this pump work?"

"Yes. There's hot water in that kettle on the stove top."

"I have never used a hand pump before."

"Welcome to the woods."

When the dishes were washed and the kitchen cleaned, Lyle poured them another glass of wine and they sat on the couch.

"This is a nice log cabin."

"My grandfather built it when he was in his early twenties. He wasn't so sure he wanted to be a farmer all of his life. He had a chance to buy this land for the pine and spruce lumber. He and another helper built this cabin from the spruce that were on the wood lot and then spent the next winter here cutting huge pine and spruce trees. He only took the biggest and left the rest. Well the big trees out there now is what he left. Want to go for a walk? I'll show you."

"Okay, I could use some exercise.

"Coming in the cove I saw a tower on top of the ledge. What is that?"

"That—my sister Sheerie was older than me and she didn't want to be out here without a radio. Dad said if we got a tower on top he'd help us put it up. We would pick up railroad spikes and we would hammer them into cracks in the ledge. When we had finished we had a nice ladder. My dad said he didn't believe we would ever do it. With rope and pulley it was easy to haul the tower to the top. And Sheerie had her radio."

"Where is Sheerie now?"

"No one knows. When she graduated from high school,

she said she wasn't going to spend her life on a farm and she left. The next Christmas my folks received a Christmas card. That was the last we heard from her. I don't know now whether she is still alive or not."

"These are beautiful trees. Where does this path go?"

"It was the twitch trail the work horses used to drag the logs off this point across the ice to the mill that used to be at the outlet. My sister and I would keep the bushes cut out and we used to play out here. It'll go out to the point of land. To the left is a huge swamp. I've tried many times to find a way across it and never did. Here we are."

"What a beautiful spot for a house."

"This is a nice place to watch the sun rise. Sheerie and I used to set up a tent here and before it was light a loon would always swim out front and wake us up. In time to watch the sun. We'd better start back."

"You really miss your sister, don't you?"

"Yeah, she was my big sister. She was three years older.

"Now tell me about you. You have recently had a wedding ring on your finger."

"Good observation. Yes, right now he should be landing in Italy. He's a pilot for Pan Am. That's where I met him. I was a stewardess for Pan Am." She told him the same story she had told Becky.

"So what are you going to do now?"

"Tour the country and maybe go back to work when I run out of money. But on the west coast —and not for Pan Am."

They walked in silence for a ways. Lyle thinking that she sure was some cool cookie. She told a good story.

"You keep mentioning a farm? What about the farm?"

"Oh, my great grandfather started the farm and then my grandfather, my Dad. He was a little disappointed when I decided to go into the Army and not stay on and continue the tradition. When my Mom and Dad died I was still in the Army, on leave. There were 110 milking cows plus young stock. I had no choice but to ask for an early out. I was so busy making arrangements for my parents and trying to keep the farm going. I finally sold off the livestock and most of the equipment. So everything sits empty now."

"Aren't you afraid of vandalism or somebody burning it down only to watch it burn?"

"Well, if someone burns it, they would actually be doing me a great favor."

"How? I don't understand."

"That house is over 150 years old. There is no insulation and sometimes in the winter with a north wind, snow will be blown through around the window jambs. If it burns I'd build a new big log house with a nice porch on the front. And maybe someday raise beef cattle and in the winter cut some lumber off the wood lot. I've sold off much of anything that would be worth stealing, so no I don't worry about it."

"You know Lyle, I find life up here so different than what I have been so used to all of my life, living in cities. I could really get used to this country life."

"It ain't bad."

April began laughing then, "What's so funny," Lyle asked.

"That word ain't. I have never heard it used until today. At the diner Becky used it and you have used it twice now."

"Hum, I never thought too much about it."

"You know Lyle, I'd like to spend the night with you, it's too dark for me to motor back. And I ain't been on the water at night." They both laughed. Lyle put his arm around her. April was a little unnerved by this at first. This wasn't why she was here. But his arm around her waist did feel good and she snuggled a little closer and she could feel him holding her tighter.

And Lyle was surprised too. This isn't how he had thought it would go. In spite of who she was he kinda liked her. *What piece of the puzzle is she?*

"How big is the farm, Lyle?"

"There is 400 acres in field, which I just baled over

16,000 bales, and 300 acres in wood."

"If I had more time I'd like to see it."

Back at camp now just as the sun was setting below the horizon Juli poured them another milk-size glass of wine and they sat on the porch. Juli in Lyle's lap. She unbuttoned his shirt and pulled it off and then pulled her top off also and leaned back against him. All she had on now was the string for a bikini.

"How is your back and shoulders now?" Lyle asked.

She noticed the concern in his voice. "It is feeling much better. In a day or two it'll probably peel like a snake skin. You are so warm, Lyle, I could stay like this all night."

"You aren't cold? I mean you really don't have any clothes on, you know."

"I ain't a bit cold," and they both laughed.

Lyle began caressing her back gently and then ran his fingers through her hair and patted her head like a kitten. And she began rubbing her hand over his stomach and chest.

Just touching her soft skin and silky hair was making him excited. And Juli was almost beyond excited from his caresses. She began wiggling only slightly at first in his lap and then with more intensity.

In one fluid motion he stood up with Juli in his arms. She had her arm around his neck and shoulders and kissed him with tenderness and then with real desire. On the way to his bedroom he turned off the gas lights and pulled the covers back on the bed. He set Juli down on her feet and he began to slowly inch her bikini off. He was taking too long and she grabbed his hand and said, "You take your clothes off! I can't wait any longer," and pulled her bikini down and kicked it off.

She stood there waiting for him to pull his shorts down. When he had his clothes off she wrapped her arms around him and kissed him with hot passion. Still holding each other and kissing they seemed to just melt into the bed.

Caution and suspicion forgotten, Lyle eased himself slowly on top of her and resting on his elbows he cupped her face in his hands and kissed her tenderly at first and then with real passion and hunger. Juli (April) responded with as much passion and hunger. She had never experienced love making like this. Someone who cared about her needs and hunger, while satisfying her, he was also satisfying his own needs.

Over and over they made love. He rolled onto his back and she sat on him and straddled him, all the time not losing their motion. When she tired she laid on her stomach and he laid on her backside. And all the time he was trying to please and satisfy her.

Hours later in complete exhaustion Lyle reached up and shut the gas light off. He lay on his back and Juli cuddled up as close as she could get and lay her head on his chest and he put his arm around her and held her close.

They both lay still, but much awake. And each thinking similar thoughts. *If this was only a reconnaissance tactic, then she was damned good at it,* Lyle was thinking, *and quite obviously the most dangerous weapon they could have sent.* He was so completely impaled with her. He couldn't get enough of her. And this was dangerous. Even with his senses on total alert, this petite, beautiful woman had so easily overpowered him. How had that happened? He could hear her gentle breathing and assumed she had fallen asleep.

Tears were running down her face, as she had to remind herself why she was there. This wasn't how it was supposed to be. But somehow she had let this man inside her protective shroud she had always put up around her to protect herself. Without trying he had gotten to her with his honesty, compassion and he obviously had a great deal of love as it was so clearly demonstrated for his family. Without knowing what he was doing, he had shown her compassion and love that she had never known was possible before. Pietro had never shown her so much concern, compassion or love. How could this happen?

Sometime later they both fell asleep.

* * *

Neither one moved all night fearing they would awaken the other. But just before daylight two loons out front started calling. April had never heard loons before and didn't know what they were and she lay motionless. Every few seconds one of them would call and the second one would answer. She shook Lyle's shoulder to wake him. "Lyle," she whispered.

"What?"

"What is that sound? It's awful creepy, whatever it is."

The loon called again and the other one answered. "That, Lyle. What is it?"

He didn't laugh, he said, "Those are two loons saying good morning. They do that every morning since I have been coming here."

He got out of bed and pulled her to her feet. "Come, I'll show you." They went outside down to the wharf. The loons called again. Lyle pointed, "Those big black and white birds." He cupped his hands together and blew through them making the same sound as the loons. One loon answered.

"That's amazing. Hey the sun isn't even all the way up yet."

"Yeah, this is the best part of the day."

"Well maybe, but I'm not through with you yet." She took his hand and ran back inside to the bed. She pushed him down on his back and she laid on top of him.

"I can't get enough of you, Lyle."

When they were spent, sweating and breathing heavy, they went back to sleep with April still laying on top of him. He had his arms around her.

They woke up some time later and April said, "Let's go wash up in the lake." She threw the covers back and pulled him out of bed. "Come on, where's your soap?"

"Kitchen sink."

"Two towels, will you?"

They waded out to their waists and soaped up and dove under to rinse the soap off. Then they swam around playing, and then standing in deeper water, toe to toe Lyle leaned down and kissed her softly. No man had ever kissed her like that before.

This wasn't going as planned. "Come, I'm hungry. What do you want for breakfast?"

"You."

"Honestly."

"Honestly."

"We just cleaned up. But I'm game if you are."

"Okay, how about bacon and scrambled eggs, with toast and coffee."

"Okay, you make the bed and I'll cook." This wasn't how it was supposed to go, but she was enjoying herself.

While April tended the bacon and eggs, Lyle poured the coffee. "Now go sit down, Lyle; I'm cooking this morning."

He sat in the rocking chair occasionally looking at her. She seemed so happy to be doing just what she was doing.

"Everything is ready."

They sat beside each other, instead of at opposite ends of the table. Lyle was liking this. She was getting to him.

"These eggs are good. What did you do different?"

"Oh I found some spices in the cupboard."

"Well they sure are good."

"How long are you going to stay out here, Lyle?"

"I'm not sure now. I thought by getting away by myself I'd be able to work through everything. But I feel like a new person since yesterday."

"Is there any hurry about you leaving?"

"No, not really. There's nothing that I need to do."

"Then I'd stay right here. This is such a beautiful spot."

"When I first came out here I was thinking about spending the winter. Do some ice fishing and trap beaver in the swamp I told you about yesterday."

"Well, maybe you should. I've only ever seen snow at a distance."

When they had finished eating Lyle helped her to pick

things up and wash the dishes.

They both knew what must come next. "If I wanted to get in touch with you how would I do it?"

Before he knew what he was doing he gave her his telephone number to his radio phone. Then he showed her the telephone and said, "It's best to call or for me to use it in the early morning or after 6 pm. That way there is less air traffic."

"Don't be too surprised if I call sometime."

They walked down to her boat arm in arm. "I have really enjoyed my stay, Lyle, and your company."

"I shall miss you," Lyle said. He kissed her goodbye then and steadied the boat while she climbed in and started the motor.

"The water will be calm now, so you won't have any trouble crossing the lake. But you be careful."

"I will."

Lyle stood on the end of the wharf watching as she motored to the mouth of the cove. She turned the boat a little so she could look back. He was still standing on the wharf and waving. She waved back.

Chapter 14

April turned onto I-95 south and she burst into tears again. She had cried all the way across the lake. She wished she didn't have to go back. And she couldn't understand why Lyle had caused such a reaction with her. If Lyle had asked her to stay, she thought now she would have.

The more she thought about him and his location, as she drove along, she began to see the whole setup objectively. Like she was above Deep Cove looking down at the camp and not driving. Then it occurred to her that he was there not to get over the passing of his folks or selling the livestock. "What a brilliant strategic move. You are there at your camp, Lyle, because you know Pietro will be coming for you and there, even inside your camp, you can observe the only possible approaches for an attack."

Now she began thinking how she could help him without giving herself away. She was afraid of what Pietro would do to her. Avilla, she wasn't sure. But her mind was made up. She was going to leave Pietro and the cartel at her first opportunity.

She was beginning to feel better. She was even smiling.

* * *

When Lyle saw the boat swing around and Juli (April) turn to look at him and wave back, filled him with an ecstatic joy. Was he wrong in thinking she had come only for reconnaissance? That's exactly what he had thought at first. But later he was not so sure. He sat on the porch all day sipping coffee and wondering. "Will I ever see her again? God I hope so."

The strangest thing about the last twenty-four hours, he had never had these feeling about another woman in all of his life. Not even Belle, 'if that was her name.'

Then he started to think about the attack that he knew would come and it was time to prepare for it. He emptied his coffee cup and put that in the sink. Then he took his rifle and .357 out of the window seat and made sure they were loaded. He put his shoulder holster and gun back on, and left the mini-14 loaded leaning next to the porch door.

Then he went outside looking for his best stance. If they come by boat, and he was certain they would, and probably with their own boat and probably a big one, they would not be able to come any closer than a hundred feet from shore. So that meant they would probably use two automatic weapons to riddle the camp in hopes he would be inside. *But I won't be. My boat is on the left side of the wharf facing the lake, so I should be on the right out of their line of fire.* Off to the right about fifty feet was a huge white pine tree. It would be big enough to shield him completely. *Anyway, they won't be looking this way. They'll be concentrating on the camp. All this will work out fine as long as I hear them coming.*

He walked the path to the point. He doubted if the attack would come from this direction. As he was walking back he had an idea. But there was nothing he could do today.

For supper he warmed up a can of soup with bread. At 5:30 he turned his radio phone on.

* * *

April was in a hurry now to get back. But she also knew better than to attract attention by speeding. The sooner she was back the sooner she might be able to sneak out and leave.

At twelve she drove into the communal parking area with

the next door condo. Avilla was there like she was waiting for her return. There were also two old ladies walking towards the parking area from the neighboring condo. April opened the door and Avilla was standing there. When she closed the door Avilla reached up and grabbed the back of her head with a handful of hair and pushed her up against the door. Pressing her body against April's. April was shocked and didn't know what to think.

Then Avilla whispered in her ear. "Play along April, I'll explain later." Then she kissed April with full lip contact and pulling her head into her own and grinding her body against April. Still April had no idea what was going on. Avilla was kissing her like she would her lover as they were about to climax. Avilla looked at the two ladies and they were watching with mouths open in surprise, but they were not leaving.

Avilla said, "Play along April. Act like you are enjoying this."

So April wrapped her arms around Avilla and began kissing her back. The two old ladies were still watching. After several minutes of this and the two ladies were still watching Avilla waved to them. They threw their noses up in the air and stormed back inside their own condo. Then Avilla backed away from April.

"What was that all about, Avilla?"

"I wanted to give those two biddies the idea that we are lovers. That way they won't be looking for a man here."

"Hmm, have you done this sort of thing often?"

"A couple of times in Paris to discourage unwanted or nuisance boys."

"Hmm."

"How'd it go?"

"Okay, I'll tell you inside with Pietro."

Pietro was sitting in the kitchen. April swallowed hard. She had to make this convincing.

"Both of his parents were killed in an automobile accident only days after he arrived back from Vietnam. It was pretty hard on him. He said he needed to get his head back on his shoulders. So he is now at the family camp on Driftwood Lake just north of Houlton. I asked him how long he would be staying and he said until he could work things out in his head."

"Did he say anything about me shooting Newcomb?"

"Not a word. I had lunch at a diner and no one was talking about it. I guess it was old news."

"How do we get to the camp?"

"I'll draw you a map." Avilla gave her a sheet of paper and pen. She roughly drew the shape of the lake. "The public boat landing is here. You can see it from the highway. About six miles north of I-95. You go straight across the lake and turn north and watch for a cove with ledges on both sides. The camp is here at the end of the cove." And she drew a square.

"There is a path that goes out to a point and stops at the lake, about a quarter of a mile long. Over here is all swamp. There are only two approaches."

"Did you see any guns?"

"No."

"Anyone else there?"

"No."

"Any close by camps?"

"No."

"This seems like a duck walk. Should be easy enough. Did you sleep with him?"

"How else do you think I could get all this information."

"You bitch! You think that is funny?"

She didn't like being called a bitch and she said, "Yeah, I slept with him and I fucked him all night."

Pietro back handed her and she fell to the floor. She picked herself up and went in the bathroom and closed the door.

"When this is all over I'm going to get rid of her."

"Not so soon, brother. We still need her. When are the two coming from Boston?"

"I'll call Hernando now and tell him whoever comes to

bring a boat suitable for a big lake."

April could hear all of this. She waited until they had moved into the living room before coming out. "Pietro, I'm sorry I said those things to you. I really am."

Avilla said, "We're just all under a lot of stress until we can finish this. April lets go shopping, we are out of food and drink here."

"Okay. I need to change my clothes first though." She closed the door behind her and took her clothes off and put on clean tan slacks and a button down blouse. She also put several $100.00 bills in her front pocket.

"I'm ready if you are, Avilla," April bent over and kissed Pietro.

As they were walking out to the car April was hoping the two old women wouldn't be there. "I'll drive, April."

"Okay."

"I think we'll drive out to Ellsworth to that big supermarket on the main road. I don't like shopping around here."

"Okay." That was more than okay with April. There was an Avis car rental close to the supermarket and this was her chance to escape.

"I really feel bad about Lyle losing both parents at the same time."

"It really knocked him for a loop. Did he ever tell you about his sister Sheerie?"

"No, he never mentioned he had a sister."

"Well, in a way he doesn't. She was quite a bit older and when she finished high school she left for the big city and bright lights. He said they received one Christmas card post marked from New York. That was the last they ever heard from her. Being at the family camp brings back a lot of family memories.

"I have an idea, Avilla, drop me off at the florist shop just before the supermarket. I want to get something special for Pietro and something for the house. When I'm through I'll walk over to the supermarket."

"Okay, I'm apt to be a while."

April got out and actually walked into the florist shop, in case Avilla was watching. When she thought it safe she left and went next door to Avis and rented a car. "I'm going to be in Houlton for a while, could I have this car picked up tonight or tomorrow morning?"

"Certainly. Just include the address on this rental form."

April did and paid the man and asked, "Now could I use your telephone?"

"Surely."

"Thank you," and she dialed Lyle's number. She hoped he would answer. If not she was driving up regardless.

"Hello."

"You did answer."

"Juli?"

"Yes. Listen, Lyle. I haven't much time. I would like to come back now. I need to talk with you, Lyle. Just me."

Lyle found himself saying, "Of course," against better judgment. "When will you be here?"

"Can you meet me at the landing at 7 pm?"

"I'll be there."

"Okay. I must leave here—and Lyle. I love you."

* * *

A month before Avilla, Pietro and April left for Maine Enrico had been having sporadic minor chest pains, along with his lung cancer. And he was told he was having angina attacks. A precursor to a heart attack. "You have partially blocked arteries Señor and hypertension. No coffee, no dairy products and no red or fatty meat. And stop worrying."

He didn't say anything to Avilla and Pietro because he didn't want to worry them. So he kept his discomfort to himself.

But now his son's picture was on the evening news wanted for a drug related homicide. This news caused a massive heart attack and he died sitting up in his chair. Avilla and Pietro would never know anything about their father.

* * *

When April had said, "I love you," he didn't respond. He was glad she was coming back, but they had a lot of talking to do.

He was at the landing a little early and April was standing on the wharf waiting. He pulled the boat in and she jumped in. "Okay."

"No luggage?"

"No. Just me. Not even a toothbrush." On the ride up to camp she rode facing him and smiling. And that smile melted away any doubts he may have had.

"I'm glad you came back."

"Me too. I thought about you all the way down I-95. I couldn't think of anything else, Lyle. That, and the truth. I owe you that. But not until we get to camp."

"Okay."

* * *

Avilla drove back to the condo without April. She carried in the groceries. "Where's April, Avilla?"

"I don't know, Pietro."

"What do you mean you don't know!" he yelled.

"Just that, Pietro. She went into the florist shop close to the supermarket. I saw her go in. She said she was sorry for what she had said to you and wanted to buy something special for you and some flowers for the house. She said she would meet me at the supermarket. She never showed up. I went into the florist shop and the woman said she could remember her coming in but left soon after without buying anything. She had no idea where she went."

"Damn, damn! Did she run off?"

"I don't know, Pietro, what happened to her."

"Was there a car rental place near the supermarket?"

"Yes, that has to be it. Beside the florist shop was an Avis rental."

"That bitch ran off with him. Now we have to kill them both, Avilla. Them or it'll be us."

"When is the crew coming from Boston?"

"Hernando said about midnight."

* * *

April caught the edge of the wharf and pulled them in and held it while Lyle climbed out. He pulled the boat up on shore some more, then tied it. April stepped out standing toe to toe with Lyle.

"Before either of us say anything, Lyle, I want you to know I really do love you."

He put his arms around her and hugged her for a long time without saying a word. Then he asked, "When are they coming, Juli?"

"You knew all along that someone was coming didn't you? Of course you did. That's why you are here in such a strategic place. And Lyle, my name is not Juli. It's April, April Bianca and I'm from Florida and I'm not married to Pietro. We only pretended to be to make his father happy.

"Let's go up to the porch and talk, Lyle. There is more I must tell you."

She sat in his lap like she had done the night before. "Pietro contacted his man in Boston. Hernando. He is sending two of his men with a boat. They are supposed to arrive at the condo in Bar Harbor at midnight. I told Pietro that you were here because you were having a hard time accepting the death of your parents and that you were depressed and not right in the head. I also told him there were only two approaches, that's why they'll come by boat. I doubt if Pietro comes himself. But he may, because I really pissed him off. When he asked me if I slept with you I said yes and that I fucked you all night. He back handed me and I fell to the floor. I didn't care though. On the drive back I came up with a plan to escape."

"I want you to know, Lyle, I had nothing to do with him shooting that man. Avilla and I both were in Bar Harbor."

Lyle sat quiet. Taking all this in while holding April close to him. She laid her head on his shoulder.

"Were you ever involved with his drug business?"

"No, he took me along for convenience. A show piece, nothing more.

"You knew yesterday that I was here for information about you didn't you?"

"I was expecting someone and I guess I was suspicious of you for quite a while. But there was something about you that I didn't want to let go. You were honestly so happy and this made me happy. Even when you left this morning I was still suspicious, but I could also see how you felt about me. You couldn't lie about that. And then when you turned your boat to look back to see if I was still watching—well I knew then I had seen the real you and I was already hoping you'd come back or call. I knew you were real."

"I've come clean, Lyle. There is something about you I would like to know."

"Okay. What?"

"What did you do in Vietnam for three tours?"

"That's a fair question and I suppose this is a time for honesty. I was a member of the Mekong Devils, a covert special operations team. We were assigned special missions in North Vietnam, Laos, Cambodia and sometimes in South Vietnam. That's all I can tell you April, under threat of arrest."

"I guess I can accept that much. Thank you.

"Avilla and Pietro have been under a lot of pressure since the homicide has been broadcast on all the news media. Pietro is losing it. And Avilla—well you wouldn't recognize her now." She then told him about Avilla forcefully kissing her and grinding her body against her.

"That's beginning to explain a lot."

"How do you mean, Lyle?"

"Well, I came back ahead of schedule from one mission and I was at Avilla's—only her name then was Belle Saucier— well I was there early and I laid on her bed for a nap and found a pair of blue women's panties under her pillow. They were too small for her and I know for a fact she did not have any blue ones. Yellow, white and orange. No blue. I wonder now if that was why she left without a word."

"I don't know about that, but I heard her say she would shoot both you and I if she had a chance. She has become as scary as Pietro.

"I'm assuming you have guns here."

"Yeah, two."

"Pietro asked and I told him I didn't see any, so he'll probably think you'll be an easy target."

"When did you first think you started to change in what you were here for?"

April laughed some and then said, "While I was sun bathing. I gave you quite a show, especially when I turned my back to you and stayed bent over."

"I was watching with binoculars."

"I figured you would be. When you didn't come right over with your tongue hanging out like a dog, I knew then you were not like most men. You were different. When I came to you and saw you—well, something shot through me like a bolt of lightning from my head to my feet and back to my head again. I knew then the reason I was there was all wrong.

"Knowing why I was here, I was surprised when you said you would meet me at the landing."

"Last night when you were sitting in my lap, like you are now, you were not nervous. I could feel your warmth and a goodness all about you. And I knew then you were real. And in the morning I hated to see you leave, although I knew you had to for my plans to work."

It was totally dark out, with no moon for another two nights. The air was a little cooler but Lyle was comfortable. "Are you warm enough?"

"I am as long as I can snuggle up to you.

"I never was a flight stewardess. That was only my cover story."

They sat there in the dark holding onto each other, enjoying each other's warmth and embrace and not worrying about what tomorrow would bring.

"Are you worried about tomorrow, Lyle?"

"No, but I don't want you to get hurt either."

"You know I feel safe with you."

"I think we should go to bed. We'll need the sleep. I expect to be up early tomorrow."

"What if they come during the night?"

"No problem. The loons will wake us long before they could get close."

He stood up with April in his arms and she put her arms around his neck. "I love you, April. You came into my world and you touched my soul making me see things differently now. Thank you, April."

* * *

Carlos and Emilio rented an almost new Criscraft boat with a 60hp Evinrude motor and had it attached to their '66 Pontiac station wagon car. Tomas Hernando paid them $5,000.00 in advance and there would be another $15,000.00 when the job was done. All they were taking with them were two throw away automatic machine pistols. That would be disposed of at the completion of the job.

Once they were on I-95 north it was a straight shot to Houlton. They had to stop in Augusta for gas and sandwiches.

They exited 95 and headed east towards Bar Harbor and pulled into the parking area of the condo a little past midnight.

Avilla stayed up, because she was so angry about April running off. When she saw lights turn into the parking area she awoke Pietro. "Go out and bring them in."

Carlos and Emilio were still sitting in their car when Avilla walked up. Carlos rolled the window down. "Who sent you? And the answer better be correct," she said.

"Tomas Hernando."

"Good, come in. Follow me."

Pietro had a map open on the table and Avilla had redrawn April's map of Driftwood Lake, Deep Cove and the camp. "You launch your boat here about sunrise or as near as you can. You'll have to motor to the opposite shore and turn left and watch for the mouth of this cove. There are ledge walls on both sides of the cove and the camp is here at the end. Now the information I have he is there alone. His folks were killed recently in an accident and he is depressed and out of sorts. My information has him there and no guns. It's a simple job. Oh, one more little bit. There are no other camps anywhere near this one, and the ledge walls should muffle the sound of your guns."

"Do you want us to burn the camp with the body in it?" Carlos asked.

"No, the smoke would be too much of an alarm. Now do not speed on the highway. This would only attract attention. You back track to Bangor and take I-95 and get off at the Houlton exit. It is the last exit. Turn left on Rt. 1. The lake is about six miles north. Look for a sign that says boat rental. The public boat launch is there also. Now do not waste any more time."

"Emilio, there ain't no way we can be there at sunrise. It took us three hours to go to Bar Harbor and back. There! That sign says Houlton another one hundred and twenty miles. It's 4 o'clock now, we might be there an hour and a half after sunrise."

"That should be alright Carlos. You heard him say there ain't no more camps anywhere near his. And he ain't got no guns. This'll be the easiest twenty grand we ever earn. I'm going to catch me a nap, wake me in an hour and I'll spell you, so you can get some sleep."

Carlos stopped at the Medway exit, "Hey Emilio, you gotta drive I can't stay awake no more."

"Okay Carlos."

* * *

April had never known love like this. Until yesterday they were total strangers and she had lied her way here for information about Lyle for Pietro, to send two goons in to kill him. Something had happened to them both. She loved Lyle now with more love than she ever thought possible. He was good for her and she wanted to think she was good for him too. This wasn't supposed to have happened, but since it did, she would give Lyle her heart and soul. The way he had just told her how he loved her brought tears to her eyes. She kissed him lightly on his lips. "Lyle, I have never known love coming from me for you like it is now. I love you."

And they fell asleep with thoughts of love for each other spinning an aura around them.

Just at daylight the two loons started calling out front and April awoke with a start and bolted upright. "Lyle," and she shook his shoulders. "Lyle, the loons are calling."

Lyle opened his eyes and saw the thinning darkness and said, "That's probably just the loons saying good morning. But I do think we should get up."

They dressed in silence and then Lyle laid the .357 on the table and put the rifle back by the door.

"We should eat something, Lyle."

"Yes it'll look good if they see smoke." He started a small wood fire while April started making an egg omelet and toast. Lyle put coffee on to make and then he stood by the big window to watch.

"When they come April, I want you to take this handgun and go to the root cellar, go through both doors. They'll have 9mm machine pistols and that won't penetrate the logs or the double doors. I'll be behind that large pine tree. I'll have good cover. They'll probably spray the camp with bullets hoping that one kills me."

"How do you know they'll have 9mm machine pistols?"

"Well, they're from the city, with that city consciousness they probably have no knowledge of the wilderness."

"How do you know all this?"

"In Vietnam it was my job to know the enemy and what to expect."

"You seem so nonchalant about all this," April said.

"Well, this is how I lived for three tours in Vietnam."

"Well, I'm glad you're not over there now. And I feel better knowing you are so good about knowing what you are doing. Breakfast is ready."

"This is good, April, I think you're a better cook than me."

After breakfast, "Why don't you keep watch, Lyle, while I pick up and wash dishes and make the bed."

Lyle poured another cup of coffee and sat down where he could watch the cove. The water was like glass. Not a ripple. There were a few early morning clouds lifting, but everything was promising a nice day. April had finished everything and she poured a cup of coffee and sat beside Lyle on the couch.

In spite of Lyle's self confidence that he could deal and handle this, April still was apprehensive. They had been up for two hours now.

"Maybe they aren't coming today," Lyle said.

"I don't know, I heard Pietro and Avilla talking about today," April said.

Lyle got up to pour another cup and as he looked up the cove from standing he said, "They are here, April. They're just coming around the ledge. It's time for you to go to the root cellar."

"I'd like to help you, Lyle."

"You will, April, if you go to the cellar. Please, now, before they get any closer."

"Okay, you be careful, Lyle."

"I will." They both went out the back door and Lyle circled around and out of sight to the pine tree.

"Emilio," Carlos said, "There's the camp. And smoke in the chimney. Get ready. I'll slow down so not to raise any attention. When you empty one clip reload fast."

"Okay, Carlos."

They motored in toward the camp going slow. They were so intent looking straight at the camp they did not see Lyle watching from behind the pine tree. "Let me swing the bow around to the left some. So we can both spray the camp." Carlos stopped and put the motor in neutral and picked up his pistol machine gun.

"Ok, Emilio, now."

The bullets were flying everywhere. Mostly into the ground in front of the camp. After the first volly was fired, Lyle took aim on Emilio's stomach and pulled the trigger. He screamed and fell to the bottom of the boat. He next aimed at Carlos' right knee and pulled the trigger. Carlos screamed worse than Emilio and he dropped his gun in the water. "Damn it! Emilio can you drive this boat?!" Carlos screamed. "He shot me in the knee and I can't move!"

"He got me in the stomach, Carlos! It hurts like hell but I'll try!"

"If you don't, Emilio, we're sitting ducks our here for him. Now move it! Damn you!"

Emilio managed to get to the controls and he pushed the throttle forward. They were both still screaming. April came running from the root cellar. "Who were they, Lyle?" she asked all out of breath.

"Probably just a couple of goons. It wasn't Pietro. Come, we better go inside and call Jim Fye."

"Hello, Sheriff's Office."

"Give me Sheriff Fye and in a hurry."

"Jim Fye here."

"Jim, Lyle. You better get to the boat landing as soon as you can. We were attacked. Two goons in a Criscraft boat, 60hp Evinrude motor and blood and shells all over the bottom. One is shot in the stomach, the other in the right knee. One gun was dropped in the lake here and we'll go after it. The other one they'll probably drop in the lake. You'd better call for an ambulance. They're going to need it. No sirens, Jim, or you'll scare them off. I'll dig out some bullets and bring those and the gun in when we find them. Better hurry, Jim."

"Okay."

Jim started towards the boat landing and as he drove he asked his dispatcher to start an ambulance, "and no sirens."

"Who's we? Who in hell is up there with him?" He used his blue light all the way and no siren and he pulled into the parking lot of the boat landing just as the boat was coming in. He backed off and waited until the boat was all the way in.

They were in now and Jim withdrew his gun and started walking towards them. There was a lot of moaning and cursing. "Hello boys. Bad day?"

"You have a crazy guy up there that took potshots at us and hit us both."

"What, was he right in the boat with you?"

"Of course not! You stupid or something!" Carlos said still holding his knee.

"Then if he wasn't in the boat with you two. Then these empty 9mm shells must be from your guns."

"We ain't got no guns."

"Okay boys you rest easy now. There is an ambulance on the way. And—if either of you try to throw any of these empty shells out I'll gladly shoot you in the other knee. Do you get my drift?

"Oh , yeah, you two are also under arrest for attempted

homicide. Do you boys know your Miranda rights? Where you don't have to answer any of my questions, because anything you do say will be used against you in court."

"We ain't saying a word, Sheriff. Not until we have talked with an attorney."

"Do you boys have a favorite attorney you want me to call for you?" Jim asked.

"Can't remember his number."

"Well if you'd like there are several fine attorneys here in Houlton and I'm sure the court will appoint one for you. Well, here's the ambulance now."

"Two with gunshot wounds. One in the right knee and the other in the stomach. And they are both under arrest for attempted homicide. I can't let you transport them until one of my deputies shows up to ride down with the two. Here he is now."

"Charlie, you'll have to go with these two to the hospital. They both are under arrest for attempted homicide. We'll have to work out a security detail later. I'm thinking they both will have to remain in the hospital for a few days.

"Sheriff Fye to dispatch."

"Go ahead, Sheriff."

"Would you call Deputy Beal out and have him pick up this boat and impound it, photograph it and collect the empty shells for ballistic testing."

Jim took a breath, stretched and said out loud, "Who is we?" As far as he knew Lyle was at camp by himself.

* * *

April ran over and hugged Lyle. "Are you okay?" she asked.

"Yes, do you want to go swimming?"

"Not really. Why?"

"One of them dropped his gun over the side and we need

to recover it. If I stand where I was I should be able to guide you close to it. The water isn't deep. Probably not even up to your neck."

"Okay." She walked over to the wharf and took her clothes off and started wading out.

"Go out about another hundred feet."

"I'm glad this water isn't any colder."

"A little more and I think to your left some. Okay go left now. Okay walk straight away from me towards the ledge. You're close. It should be right around you there."

"If I'm close, why not come in and help me look."

"Okay." Lyle took his clothes off and waded out where April was. "You stand right here and I'll make a widening circle around you."

"Hey! I think I just stepped on an empty shell."

"Can you go down and get it?"

"I'll try." She went down head first walking around on her hands. Her feet were sticking above the water. Once she was down there she could see the sun reflecting off two of the brass casings. She came up with them both.

"I have two Lyle."

"Hang on to'em."

She dove down again with her legs sticking up walking around on the bottom on her hands. She spun around and there only about three feet away was the gun. She swam over and picked it up and surfaced. She was excited and she yelled, "I got it!, I got it Lyle!"

Lyle turned to look at her. Sure enough, she had it. "It might still be loaded, so be careful."

Lyle swam over to her and said, "Good job. You cold?"

"I'd tell you how cold, but it wouldn't be very ladylike." They both laughed.

"Let's go in."

Lyle put his arm around her and they started for shore. "I'm glad there aren't any other camps in here," April said.

"Why?"

"Why? Look at us, Lyle. We're both naked and I'm carrying a pistol machine gun."

"Oh." They both laughed and started running for shore. They picked up their clothes and walked to camp.

"We'll probably have at least two days before they try again. We need to go into town for food and a few things. We'll have to stop and talk with Sheriff Fye too."

"Okay."

After getting dressed Lyle went out to dig spent bullets out of the logs in the front of the camp. Very few had hit the camp. He did manage to dig out three, there were many more he knew in the ground, but these three should be enough.

Then he sat down and wrote out a thorough report for Fye of what happened there that day. Then he called him. And he was surprised when Jim answered.

"Did you get those two, Jim?"

"They're both in the hospital under my deputy's charge. I'll need a written report from you."

"Already written and we have empty casings and the gun that went overboard. We'll be in about 2 pm. We'll come to your office, Jim."

"I'll have a lot of questions, Lyle."

"See you at 2 o'clock."

"We'd better leave now, you'll need clothes also. We need more food and I have a couple of ideas." He strapped on his shoulder holster and .357. Then he pulled on a wind breaker to conceal it.

* * *

"We'll stop first and get you some clothes."

Lyle stayed right by her side all through the ladies section and while she picked out some underwear and bras. Other women were staring at him. He didn't care. He was there to protect April. She picked out several outfits and a pair of hiking shoes. "This should be okay for a while."

People who knew Lyle were all wondering who the beautiful woman was that was with him. "Okay, now where?" she asked.

"Foggs gun shop to get you a .12 gauge automatic shotgun."

"And a box of 00B shells please. And a carrying case."

"I take it that's for me."

"Yes. It'll be a better gun for you. If you have never used one I'll go over it with you and then you can fire a couple of practice shots. What time is it?"

"Almost two."

They pulled into the Sheriff's office and Lyle said, "Better let me introduce you okay?"

"Okay."

"Hello, Lyle; Jim said to go right in."

"Thanks, Dave."

"Close the door, Lyle."

"Jim, I'd like you to meet my girlfriend April Bianca from Florida, April, Sheriff Jim Fye."

"When have you had time to meet her, Lyle?"

"We actually met at an airport in San Francisco a few years ago. She was a stewardess. I told her if she was ever in this part of the country to look me up."

"Not exactly good timing. How long is she going to be visiting?"

"For a while. Here, here's my report."

April handed him the gun and empty shells she had found. "There is still one in the chamber, Sheriff. There may be fingerprints on the shell," April said.

Lyle gave Jim the three slugs he dug out of the camp.

"Any idea who these two were, Lyle?"

"No, probably a couple of goons from Boston hired by one of Pietro's lieutenants."

"Do you think he'll try again?"

"He'll have to. I'm the only witness for the prosecution. I think he is probably still in Maine. Do me a favor would you, Jim?"

"Sure, if I can. What is it?"

"When you release this to the media, don't say they were shot. Just say you apprehended two suspects in an attempted homicide. This will make Pietro more nervous and scared and he's more apt to make mistakes. He'll try again, I can almost guarantee it."

"How long are you prepared to stay at camp?"

"Until this is over."

"How about you, Miss Bianca?"

"I'm with Lyle."

"You take care of her, Lyle. This isn't any game you're playing."

They left and Sheriff Fye called the news media and gave them the story that two would be assassins had been captured at the public boat landing at Driftwood Lake in Houlton. No names who they were after, or the fact that the two themselves had been wounded.

Jim's next call was to the FBI Special Agent Henry Jones. Jim gave Jones the entire story and added "Lyle's plan is working."

"The Federal Grand Jury doesn't convene for another six weeks. If Philipe isn't captured by then or Lyle's plan doesn't work, we have no other choice but to go ahead with the Grand Jury."

"I understand, Henry. I'll keep you informed."

"I'm hungry, April; are you?"

"Yes."

Lyle pulled into the diner parking lot. The rush hour

had passed and there was only one other vehicle there. As they walked in April knew she would have some explaining to do with Becky.

"Hi, Hon." Lyle smiled. Something he hadn't done much of since losing his folks, that is until April came into his life. "Well, Juli, I see you took my advice."

"April, Becky."

They sat down and Becky went to get their coffee. "What was that all about?" Lyle asked.

"Oh, just girl talk."

"Any of that special left, Becky?"

"The beef stew, yeah. Two bowls?" She looked at April.

"That sounds good."

While the stew was warming on the stove Becky watched Lyle and April. Holding hands across the table and talking to each other like they both were really happy.

When the stew was ready she brought out three bowls and a plate of fresh biscuits. When Becky saw the surprise on April's face she said, "Get used to it, Hon, Lyle has a hollow leg. He puts away more food than anyone else I serve in here."

She went back to the counter, watching the two of them. They were really happy. She poured herself a cup of coffee and sat down at the table next to theirs.

"I can't remember, Lyle, when I have seen you this happy. April, you must have screwed his brains out." They both spit up and choked on their stew, April was a little embarrassed. Lyle, he was just surprised.

"I told you, Lyle, that's all you needed to strengthen you out." April stopped her coughing and looked sheepishly at Lyle and then at Becky. Lyle only shrugged his shoulders.

"Well, I'll let you two finish eating."

"Is she always like this?"

"You'll get used to it. She says what's on her mind. I think that's one reason they do such a good business here."

"I like her," April said.

"Her husband does the cooking. He learned how growing up in a lumber camp."

"Well he learned well; this food is good."

As they were paying for their meal Becky asked, "When you two gonna get married?"

April said, "I haven't asked him yet, Becky."

"Then what are you waiting for? You two were meant for each other. Hell anyone could tell that just by watching the two of you."

"Thanks, Becky," Lyle said.

"Besides food, what other ideas do you have?"

"I want to pick up four 20# propane bottles and after we have been to the IGA we'll stop at the farm on the way back for barbed wire. I have an idea how we can use that."

At the IGA, April was picking up things Lyle would never have thought of. "We'll eat pretty good for a while."

At the farm Lyle said, "I'll have to get the wire from the shed, if you want to go in and look around help yourself. The door isn't locked."

She knew Lyle was in a hurry so she didn't stay inside for long. When she came back out he was just loading the last roll of wire. "It's a nice old house. We'll have quite a load going up the lake."

"Yeah, that's for sure. It'll be a slower trip, I think. When this is all over we'll come back and move in here. That is if you like the old house."

"I don't care if we live in the barn, Lyle, as long as I am with you."

"Okay, we'd better get going or it'll be dark before we cross the lake. In the dark it is very difficult to see the mouth of the cove."

"Sounds like you have tried."

"I have."

With everything loaded in the boat there was just room

enough for them to sit down. And Lyle had been correct, there was too much weight for the boat to plane out. But what the heck, it was a nice night and they followed the shoreline to find the cove.

The food, clothes and new shotgun were brought in, the rest could wait for morning.

As they were eating a light supper April asked, "Do you really think he'll try again so soon?"

"Well, he won't know until he hears the evening news that his two goons were captured, and he won't know that they were shot and he'll have no idea if they got us or not. I expect maybe in two or three days he'll send someone else."

"You're waiting for Pietro, aren't you?"

"Well it won't be over until he is either dead or in jail."

"Don't forget Avilla; I think she is just as dangerous as he is."

* * *

Pietro and Avilla had just sat down at the kitchen table when the evening news came on:

"Two men were arrested today in Houlton for an attempted homicide. At this time we do not know if this has anything to do with the drug related homicide a week ago. The names of the men who were arrested have not been released."

Pietro threw his glass against the wall and milk and broken glass went everywhere. "Jesus, can't these guys do anything right! What am I going to have to do? Go up there and shoot this bastard myself?"

"It may come to that, Pietro. But I think another team should be sent in first," Avilla said.

"I am so tired of being shut up in here! It's driving me crazy!"

Avilla was so sick of listening to her brother rant, she actually thought about abandoning Pietro. But with April out there she could bring her down. She had no alternative but stay and see this through. But then she was gone. She had had enough of her brother Pietro.

Pietro called Hernando in Boston. "Tomas, you sent two fools. They got themselves arrested before the job was finished. What in hell do you think I pay you for? For incompetency? Look you, find two more men who aren't complete idiots. If I go down Tomas, we all go down."

"Look Pietro give me a couple of days to come up with something and put together a team."

"I don't care how much it costs Tomas. I have $250,000.00 in raw diamonds right here. You put together a team and the diamonds are yours."

"Okay Pietro. I'll call you two days from now."

* * *

"I wish I knew for sure where that bitch ran off to. If she was taken by the police she could do us a lot of damage," Pietro whined.

"Look Pietro, she can't be made to testify against her husband."

"That's just it, Avilla, we only pretended to be married for Papa's sake. I wouldn't have even considered marrying that bitch. She's pretty and damned good in bed. I hauled her around with me only for a show piece and someone I could always have sex with. And she never had anything to do, really, with the drug business and she was not around when I shot those other two men."

"Then stop your whining." She was really beginning to get worried about Pietro.

She left the room, thinking she would like to get her hands on April one more time. Particularly if she ran off with Lyle. She denied herself Lyle's affection and now she was jealous thinking maybe April had taken her place. The more she thought of April the angrier she became.

* * *

In bed that night April said, "Lyle, you could have told Sheriff Fye that I know where Pietro is staying. Why didn't you?"

"Part of it I guess I'm trying to keep you out of it. And part of it is if they know they would go storming in and innocent people could get hurt."

"When this is all over, there'll be some tough questions to answer."

"I know. I'll be there with you April."

"Lyle?"

"What?"

"How old are you?"

"Twenty-eight. Why?"

"I'm older than you. I'm thirty. Will that make a difference? I mean most men would prefer younger women."

"That's strange."

"What's so strange?"

"All this time I was thinking I was a couple of years older. All of your features are perfect. No, you being older doesn't bother me in the least."

"I'm glad. You know I find life is strange. I mean, I'm originally from Mexico. My father was a trucker from the states. I left Mexico and lived with an aunt in Florida. And here I am now, northern Maine and in bed with the love of my life."

"Everything in life, April, is another piece of the puzzle of life. Not long ago I was asking myself these same questions. Especially when both of my parents died, together, right after I returned from Vietnam. I look at you April, and I suppose you are an important piece of my puzzle of life. As I think I am in your puzzle of life. There Is no doubt in my mind that all of this has happened for you and me April. To bring us together. All of the gears in the universe were in sync and clicked into place all together at the same time and brought us together."

"I have never believed in coincidences. Everything I believe happens for a reason. I laid awake all night that first night we spent together thinking about this same thing. And this is the only answer I could find."

April started crying hard and she buried her face in his chest. Lyle put both arms around her and held her to him. After a while she cleared her throat and said, "I'm sorry, Lyle, for that crying spell. It's just that I could feel so much love coming from you and all of a sudden my love for you burst forth and I couldn't control my emotions. I never want to leave your side, Lyle. I love you so much."

They lay awake for hours talking. Just talking. And they slept in late the next morning. Why not? They were not going anywhere and the only thing needing to be done was to set the booby-traps.

They were up at 8 o'clock and after breakfast April helped Lyle first unload the boat. She carried one propane tank following Lyle carrying two rolls of barbed wire. "I figure the next attack will probably be from this path. We set traps like this in Laos."

There was a natural oval opening about hundred feet long and Lyle secured the roll to a tree and let the wire unwind. So when the deadfalls are pulled, hundreds of coils of wire would be pulled across the narrow opening. He didn't have hollow bamboo to work with here, but with April's help he was able to make do.

"So how does this work?"

"You see that wire close to the ground?"

"Yeah."

"That's the trip wire which will release the deadfall over there and that will allow these barbwire coils to be pulled across the opening. This will entangle whoever gets caught in it."

"Did it work for you in Laos?"

"Not the first time, but it did the next time we used it. It actually is quite effective. Now just in case they are able to free themselves, that's where this propane bottle comes to play. This is a good bomb. We set this about halfway to the camp clearing and cover this side with brush so they can't see it. But we can. Now we have to clear a swath to the root cellar and cut a shooting hole through the wood on this end of the cellar."

When everything was done on this end, it was time for lunch. "You learn all of this in Vietnam?"

"Well, some of it. Some was learned in training for covert missions. When you train for it, it becomes easy. A good defense is a good offense. When they come at us next time, they will have the illusion that they are attacking us. Well in a way I suppose they are. But we will turn the table on them and attack. They won't be expecting it. Just like the last two."

When they had finished eating April helped him set the other three gas bottles. "Gas is lighter than water, so these bottles will float. But we'll have to secure them to an anchor so they don't float away. We'll put two in the water and the third one we'll keep back here for back up if the first two don't stop them. We'll need two anchors and some rope. We should have both in the shed."

April found a boat anchor and Lyle found a cinder block. "This will do fine."

"There's rope on that nail behind you."

"This will do. Now a knife." They carried everything down to the wharf.

"Now what?" April asked.

"We take our clothes off again and wade out to set these."

"If I didn't know better I'd say you're doing this just to see me naked."

"Nothing wrong in that. I like seeing you naked."

"Well, tonight you put on some soft music, a little wine and candle light and I'll dance naked for you."

"Promise?"

"Promise."

"Okay, let's set these. I'll tie one end of the rope to this block and you bring that gas bottle. It'll float so all you have to do is drag it behind you."

Lyle waded out about fifty feet from the end of the wharf and set over ten feet, as if guiding a boat to the wharf. "Okay you hold the bottle upside down and I'll go under and cut the rope to length and tie it to the bottle."

He was down there a lot longer than April thought he could stay under without breathing.

"I was wondering when you'd come up for air."

"You can let go now. I don't think it'll float off." The water was only to their waist.

The next one was another twenty feet from the first bottle. Also set as if to guide a boat to the wharf and away from maybe submerged obstacles in the water. Upside down they looked more like buoys than gas bottles.

"What about the third one?"

"If they get by the first two, since our boat is on that side they'll have to come in here. I thought about putting it under the wharf, but that would take out our boat also. So we'll bury it in the bank here. I'll have to go get a spade."

He dug out a hole so that the camp side of the bottle would be uncovered while covering the water side so it couldn't be seen.

"Where will you be?"

"We'd better build a blind over there," and he pointed away from the camp to the ledge. "If they get this far they will not be looking to the side. They'll concentrate on the camp."

They made a blind of ledge rocks and camouflaged it with bushes in front. "From here we can see all three bottles."

"We're the bait aren't we? You have set elaborate traps and we have no escape route. So you are very sure of this aren't you?"

"It'll work. Now I should show you something with that new shotgun."

"Okay if we get dressed first?"

After Lyle had his clothes back on he removed the plastic plug from the magazine. "What is that?"

"This shotgun will hold five shells without this plug. But when you hunt waterfowl it is illegal to hunt with a shotgun capable of holding more than three rounds—so, the plug." He put it back together.

"We'll go outside to load it."

He showed her how to slide the shells in and, "Then pull the bolt back and the shell pops up. Then let the bolt slide forward and it will slide the shell into the chamber. See?"

"No problem."

He unloaded it and handed the shotgun to April and said, "You do it just like I did."

He watched as she slid each shell into the magazine and then racked the bolt and the round slid into the chamber.

"Perfect, now you're ready to fire it. This is your safety. Push this tab forward and you are ready to shoot. Slide it back and the safety is on and can't be fired.

"See that white spot on the ledge?"

"Yeah."

"Aim at that and squeeze the trigger."

She did and dust blew away from the ledge. "Okay put the safely on and we'll go look at it."

"See, this has a wide pattern, about a third of the pellets hit the white rock while the others are scattered around it. The further back you are the wider the pattern. You okay so far?"

"Kicks like hell."

"Yeah a .12 gauge does. Do you need to shoot it anymore for practice?"

"Not really."

"Okay, you realize the bolt ejected the empty shell and loaded a full round. It is ready to shoot again. All you have to do is pull the trigger. When you fire all five shells, you'll have to reload again. Okay?"

"Okay."

"Okay, slide another shell in the chamber and we'll put the guns inside the camp." Lyle made sure they all were fully loaded and one in the chamber.

"I know I have asked this before, but do you think there is any chance they'll attack at night?" April was real concerned, and Lyle could hear it in her voice.

"Not knowing the area at all I don't think they would even attempt it in the dark, from the path or the lake. If they were to try the lake, believe me when I say the loons will wake us. If they try to come in from the point the wire trap will definitely snare them. So, no I don't think they'll come during the night. But I intend to sleep light."

"Do you have enough rope to string a clothes line for me?"

"I think so. If not there is a coil of telephone wire."

"Give me your clothes. I'll wash them while I'm washing my own. Then I'm going to wash up and wash my hair." She took her clothes off and Lyle handed her his clothes.

She carried their clothes down to the lake, while whistling and humming. Lyle stood and watched her walk to the shore. He was so happy to see April so happy as she whistled and hummed. He smiled, even with no clothes or shoes on her feet she had that little twitch to her butt.

April was happy, perhaps the happiest she had ever been in her life. Ten days ago she couldn't have imagined she would be washing out clothes by hand in the lake or scrubbing her body clean. Something had turned her world as she had known upside down now. Where she could see much clearer and understand and appreciate someone else more than herself. Yes something had happened to change them both for this moment and she had vowed to do whatever she could not to lose it. This new feeling she was experiencing was like seeing everything differently now; a new and higher consciousness.

She soaped her clothes and rubbed them together working the dirt and sweat out. When they were rinsed she squeezed the water out and laid them on the wharf. Then she soaped herself and her hair and then dove under the water to rinse the soap out. Then she did it all over again.

By now Lyle had joined her. "I'll soap your clothes then you can have it. I'll do your back if you'll do mine."

"Gladly."

With their clothes now scrubbed clean and their backs washed, it was time to get out. "We'd better hang these clothes up now." There were no clothes pins so she laid them over the wire. They'd be okay unless a wind blew in.

They finished drying off inside and dressed.

April was busy fixing a tuna salad with garlic flavored bread and wine. While she was busy with supper Lyle cut new wicks for the kerosene lanterns and washed the globes and replaced the torn gas light mantels and washed those globes also. No candles, lanterns will have to do. April was using a gas light in the kitchen and Lyle lit two lanterns and put one on the table in place of a candle. "That's the best I can do."

"Looks fine to me. Everything is ready." She filled two plates with salad and bread. Lyle poured the wine. Then April turned the gas light off.

"There; just enough light to be romantic."

Lyle took her in his arms then and hugged and kissed her. "Every day I'm loving you more, sweetheart."

April squeezed him as hard as she could, "I love you, Lyle. But we'd better eat."

"I never knew tuna fish could taste so good."

"Are there any fish in this cove?"

"Along the ledges on the right you can sometimes hook onto a salmon or togue."

"What's a togue?"

"Lake trout. In Maine we call them togue. If the sun isn't bright tomorrow we can go fishing."

They ate until they couldn't eat anymore. If you take the rest of the salad to the root cellar, it should stay good for tomorrow." She began laughing then.

"What's so funny?" Lyle asked.

"Oh, I was just laughing at myself. I was thinking how we are living out here at camp. No running water, an old outhouse instead of a flush toilet, gas and kerosene lights and a root cellar instead of a refrigerator to keep food from spoiling. I would never imagine living like this could be so enjoyable. You, my love, have introduced me to a whole new world. One that I like."

"I'm glad."

"Go on now, take the salad out while I clean the kitchen." When she had finished she went into the bathroom and took her slacks off, her bra and put her blouse back on but didn't button it up. Lyle came back. "Take your clothes off lover, except for your shorts and I'll pour us some more wine. I don't suppose you have any music do you?"

"There is an old transistor radio in the window seat."

She found it. "What is this wire?"

"You hook it to the radio battery."

She did and turned the knob to on, and surprisingly it worked. She slowly went through frequency settings and found a public network that was playing slow country and western music. "Oh, this is good. You undressed yet?"

"I'm coming!" he picked up the glasses of wine and set them on the side stand by the end of the couch. He sat down and she cuddled up in his lap and put her arms around his neck and kissed him. They stayed like that for a long time, their lips gently touching each other.

"Never in all my life while in the jungles of southeast Asia could I have imagined my life would be like this."

"I often think the same," and they kissed passionately. Their full glasses of wine sat untouched on the stand. They were too enraptured with each other to waste time for the wine.

April broke away from his arms and squirmed her way off his lap and went into the bedroom for a blanket and a pillow. When Lyle started to move the blanket April said, "No, not yet. Sit back and enjoy."

A melody was playing now on the radio and April began a seductive dance in rhythm with the music. Little by little the blouse slid off her shoulders to the floor. She was smiling and seemed to be enjoying this as much as Lyle was.

"God, April, you have a beautiful body."

She put a finger to her lips and,"Ssh." She was moving her hips in ways that were both seductive and beautiful. He wasn't aware how she was doing it, but her panties seemed to be sliding off her hips by themselves and down her legs. When they were at her ankles she kicked them off, still dancing to the melody. And then as the melody was ending she lowered herself to the blanket as if butter were melting into it.

She lay her head on the pillow and the melody finished Lyle joined her. Very gently he laid on top of April and they kissed for a long moment. Then at copulation April experienced a joyous moment of extreme ecstasy and warmth. She moaned and sighed and Lyle smiled down at her. "Slowly" she urged.

As their physical bodies and emotions were rising with the tempo as soul, now. Their light bodies intertwined and swirled together just above their physical bodies. As their physical bodies were experiencing a joyous union and copulations their light bodies now rose through the camp roof, high above the lake so they could see everything around them. There was no more darkness; everything was now all light. Their light bodies still intertwining and swirling together now as one conscious light.

They could look down through the camp roof and see them both copulating on the blanket. Faster and faster now with more urgency than before until that final single moment of total bliss and total awareness of each other. It seemed to the two of them that this blissful moment was lasting forever. They each were actually now in total full consciousness of the other. April looked into his eyes and saw this understanding and love and again Lyle was aware of her and the new discovery of each other.

Exhausted Lyle slid down and rested his head on her stomach. She began stroking his hair and caressing his face. "We were actually above the lake weren't we Lyle."

All he could say was, "Yes." And then he added, "It was a beautiful moment. It seemed to last for much longer than it did."

"I'll never forget that experience," April said.

"I don't think we could ever forget."

They lay like that for some time, just enjoying the moment. Then April rolled Lyle on his back and sat on him moving her hips in rhythm with a faster cadence with the music. Then just before April reached that special heightened moment a screech owl landed on the peak of the camp roof and screeched.

April screamed and in her shock she jumped forward until she was sitting on Lyle's face, "Holy shit! What in hell was that! That was no loon!"

She looked down to see Lyle's face under her and she began laughing and backed off and sat on his chest. "What was that?" Her heart rate still high.

"That was a screech owl. It's surprising how much noise it can make considering it is so small."

"Damn it anyhow. It spoiled a good moment."

"Sure did."

Chapter 15

"Hello, is this Avilla?"

"Yes, who is this?"

"This is Tomas Hernando and I wish to speak to Pietro."

"One moment please. Pietro, come to the phone."

"Hello."

"Pietro, this is Tomas. I have found a crew to help me with this target. One of them, Pedro, has an airplane and pilot's license. He and I are flying to Driftwood Lake tomorrow to fly over the target area. I want to see this first hand before sending anymore of my men in. I will be accompanying them this time. Four of us. I want to see these two key entry points to come up with a plan.

"Airplanes are not cheap, Pietro. I will need half of the diamonds as down payment. We will refuel at Houlton's International airport and I will call you from there and give you our ETA to Trenton airfield near you. Have the diamonds, Pietro, or you go after this guy yourself."

"Okay, Avilla will meet you in Trenton. When will you make the flyover?"

"Weather good, tomorrow. Should be back in Trenton mid-afternoon sometime."

"Sounds good, Tomas. I knew I could rely on you."

The next day Boston was socked in with low hanging clouds.

Lyle and April were awakened at sunrise by the friendly loon. "That loon is like an alarm clock. But what if we wanted to sleep in some morning?"

They laid there in bed for some time, listening to the loon and the stillness. "Last night, Lyle, was special. The sex was out of this world, but what we experienced while soul soaring above our bodies while we were making love and being so much aware of ourselves as one entity, was so divine."

"I think you have it right, April. Divine."

"Lyle, will you marry me?" There it was out in the open and it came out of her mouth so natural-like.

"Yes. I'll marry you, but not until this is all over."

The loon stopped calling and they rolled out of bed. "This looks like it'll be a good day to fish."

While April fixed breakfast Lyle brought the fishing equipment from the shed. He would have April troll for salmon, while he trolled deeper for togue. He put the equipment and net in the boat and went back to eat breakfast. April had never been fishing before and she was excited.

Lyle climbed in and April pushed them away from the wharf. Lyle helped April get her line out with a blue and white smelt streamer and then he let his line out but much deeper. He set the motor to trolling speed.

"Lyle, aren't we supposed to have a fishing license or something?"

"Yeah, we should, but we don't."

They motored out beyond the mouth of the cove and made a wide turn and started back. They did this two more passes and all of a sudden the tip of April's rod began bouncing. "Lyle!" she hollered, "Lyle, look at my fish pole!" she said excitedly.

"You have a fish on."

She picked up the rod and she could feel the fish fighting. She set the hook like she had seen fishermen on TV do. The fish really began fighting then. She started bringing it in slowly. Lyle stopped the motor and started reeling his line in so they would not get tangled.

It was a big salmon and it jumped clear out of the water

trying to free itself from the hook. April kept reeling it in. It took a long time to bring it in close enough to the boat so Lyle could net it.

When he had the hook out he held it up by the gills and said, "This is a beauty. I'd say about twenty-four inches and between four and five pounds."

April was smiling so happily. "My first fish ever and it's a beauty."

The clouds overhead were threatening rain and Lyle said, "Maybe we should go back to camp. The clouds look like rain."

It began to drizzle before they were back. An hour later it began to rain.

They spent the day sipping coffee and talking. "When you were with Pietro, did you ever use drugs?"

"I have never used or tried drugs of any kind. I could never see any sense in getting high to feel normal. What about you?"

"No. I had plenty of opportunity, but I always walked away."

"Have you ever gotten drunk?"

"Once. Then it took two days to get over it. I like wine and a beer when I'm thirsty."

"I like a lite beer also.

"After this is all over what do we do then Lyle?"

"Go back to the farm, I guess. Would you like that? I mean you have as much say in this as I do."

"I'd love to live at the farm. But you sold off the stock."

"Yeah, dairy farming was my granddad's and dad's dream. Not mine. I would like to turn it into a beef farm. We have the equipment, the barn and fields. There is also 300 acres in timber. Would you like to raise beef cattle?"

"I'd love to. What about children?"

"One boy, one girl. And not right away. I would like you and I to have some fun living together first. I figure we'll know when the time is right."

"That sounds good to me also."

* * *

The next day was clear and Tomas Hernando and pilot Pedro left the Haverhill, Massachusetts small airfield at daylight in Pedro's new Cessna 185. Then a stop at Augusta, Maine to refuel and then non-stop from there to Driftwood Lake. It was a beautiful day for flying and they had made excellent time. At 11:10 am they flew over the public boat landing and headed straight across the lake. They were high enough so they could see Deep Cove, the long peninsula that stretched from the end of Deep Cove east back to the lower arm of the lake. "There!" Tomas said, " Drop down and make a flyover."

Lyle and April both were outside and Lyle saw the plane fly across the lake. At first he didn't think too much about it. But he heard the plane circling and dropping altitude. "April!" he yelled, "April, run for the root cellar! Hurry!"

She didn't stop to ask why until they were safely inside. Then she too could hear the approaching plane. "It is after us isn't it?"

"Yes, but it may only be for reconnaissance, to see what they are up against. I doubt if they would risk trying to strafe the camp with only 9mm guns and flying that fast. It would only attract attention to them."

"Looks like they're circling around and going to make another pass. Come outside, hurry."

The plane was coming up the cove, but too high to strafe them, "Wave at them." They both waved as if seeing a friend.

"Look at that Pedro, they're waving to us. And a woman too. So he is not here alone. Waggle your wing Pedro to say hello. Then we go refuel at the airport.

"They're dipping the wing to us," April said. "Now tell me why we came out to wave at them?"

"I doubt that is Pietro or Avilla, but they will report back

257

to them. They'll tell them how we stood there waving to them as if there was nothing going on. This should make Pietro and Avilla mad. And a mad enemy can't think straight. They'll lash out and make mistakes. That's what I'm counting on. When they come at us next time they will intend to hit us hard and fast."

"But we'll be ready for them, right."

"Right."

"Let's go up and check out the wire snare and make sure it's okay."

"Will we have to do anything different then we have been doing?" April asked.

"We know they'll make another run at us. And we're almost sure those in the plane were scoping us out. They'll hit us again and soon. We just don't know when. Not in the rain, I don't think. So we'll have to be more vigilant. One of us will always have to be awake. We can take turns doing that." He could hear the worry and concern in her voice and he stopped and put his arms around her and hugged her and held her like that for a long time. "We'll be okay, April, I promise."

Everything seemed to be okay with the barbwire snare. There were no sticks or other debris lying on the wires. The gas bottle buoys were still in place. "Everything is okay April."

"I'm just beginning to understand some of what you went through in Vietnam, you did three tours living on the edge all the time and being pursued by the enemy. Over there you had whole army's after you and your team. This is nothing I guess compared to that. Maybe I can understand a little better now why you don't seem to be as worried as I am."

* * *

Pedro and Tomas landed at the international airport in Houlton and topped off the fuel tanks and paid with cash, so there'd be no paper trail. While Pedro was refueling Tomas went inside to call Pietro.

"Yes, we are leaving now, should be in Trenton in an hour and a half. If we're not there when you arrive wait. We won't be long."

"Pietro, that was Tomas. He saw what he needed and I'm to meet him in Trenton in an hour and a half."

"How did he sound? Can he do it?" Pietro asked.

"He sounded sure of himself. He didn't give me any particulars. I'll know more after I talk with him."

"Good. If anyone can get that bastard, it'll be Tomas. He's a good man."

It didn't take an hour and a half to fly down from Houlton, so they refueled the plane while they waited for Avilla.

Fifteen minutes later and right on time Avilla arrived at the small airfield. "Well what do you think, Tomas?"

"There was a woman with him and they had their arms around each other and waving. I had Pedro dip a wing to them. You are right, there are only two ways to get in. By boat and a path coming in from the lake. I'll send two men in on the path and Pedro and I will go in by boat. There is no escape. He'll be in a box."

"Are you sure, Tomas?"

"This should be a cinch to pull off. He sure wasn't acting nervous. No siree, not with that beautiful woman. I bet they even sleep in late. I know I would if I had me a woman who looked like she does."

All this talk about April was getting Avilla angrier and angrier. Tomas saw her mood change.

"The diamonds, lady. We are supposed to get half now and the rest after the job is done."

Avilla handed him a small valise. When Tomas opened it and saw all of the diamonds, he was speechless.

"When can we expect you to complete your end of the job?"

"Day after tomorrow, Friday morning if, that is, it ain't raining tomorrow. I have to equip the boat."

259

"With what?"

"We have to make it look like four men are just going fishing. So I need to pick up the necessary gear, to make everything look good."

"Okay, call us as soon as you can after the job is done."

"Will do, Ma'am."

During the drive back to the condo Avilla was so sick of hearing about April, that beautiful woman with the target.

"Well, did you meet with Hernando?" Pietro asked.

"Yes, and I gave him the diamonds."

"Well, what did he say?"

"He said there was a beautiful woman there and they had their arms around each other and waving at them as they flew overhead."

"That bitch went to him! What about the job?"

"He seemed to think the target, because of the woman, was not very cautious. He said he had himself boxed in without any escape. He's taking three other men besides himself and will attack from both directions at the same time. He seemed to think it will be a piece of cake."

"When does he plan on doing it?"

"Friday morning, unless the weather is rainy."

* * *

There wasn't much for Lyle and April to do until the next attackers came. Other than keeping a watchful eye on both entrances from the lake. At no time was either of them off by themselves. They had to keep watch for each other. The same as Lyle and the Mekong Devils had for three tours. All of that training was now quite necessary if the two were to survive this. Perhaps that's the only reason for him doing three tours in hell. It was preparing him for this one event, where it wasn't the lives of his team that was at stake, but now it was the woman who he had come to love. He understood this now as he stood watching while

April was sleeping on the couch. Soon it would be his turn to sleep and April to stand watch. And he had every confidence with her.

* * *

"When Tomas has completed the job, Pietro, Lyle will not be able to testify in grand jury against you. If you were caught, I don't know if the law could still arrest and hold you without anyone to testify."

"What are you saying, Avilla? Stop mincing words."

"I say as soon as we hear from Tomas that Lyle is dead we leave here. We don't know how much April has told the authorities about you and the drug cartel. So I don't think it would be safe for you to travel even when Lyle is dead."

"What are you saying?" Pietro demanded.

"Those two old ladies next door have never seen you, only April and I when I was kissing her. We dress you up to look like April and then if anyone, those two old ladies, see us they will only see April and me leaving. You and April are about the same height. I think you could fit in her clothes. Go try them on. If they don't fit I'll buy some new ones and a wig. Hair like hers. Now go try on her clothes."

A few minutes later he came back wearing April's clothes. "Turn around. They're too tight. You bulge where you shouldn't. Now for your face."

"What about my face?"

"How many women have you ever seen with a goatee. Honestly Pietro I'll never understand why you insist on wearing such an ugly thing. You look like a goat. All there is is a few long shaggily hairs. Lay down on the bed. On your back." Avilla sat on his chest to keep him from squirming and started plucking out the hairs with a pair of tweezers. Each time she pulled a hair Pietro screamed. "You're such a wussy, Pietro. It's a good thing you don't have a beard." Then she began plucking his eyebrows.

When she had finished she was satisfied. "With a wig on and some makeup you'll pass for a woman."

"Before I drive up to Ellsworth try my slacks on; and she slid her slacks off and handed them to Pietro.

He pulled them on and said, "There is more room in them. Won't you have to go to Ellsworth anyhow to find a wig?"

"Yes, I forgot myself."

"Let me have a look. Turn around. Those will do. Take them off and give 'em back to me."

* * *

Lyle let April sleep until it was time to fix something to eat. "I'll bake that salmon. While that is baking, I need some things from the root cellar."

"I'll go with you," he picked up the rifle and the two of them went out. He stood outside by the door on watch until she was ready to go back.

The joyous atmosphere was gone, for now. Lyle's senses and April's too, were on full alert. Watching and listening for the next attack.

When supper was ready they ate out on the porch. They could see and listen easier. "I wish they would just come and attack and get it over with. I don't like this waiting," April said.

"In a situation like this waiting is always the most difficult."

"I can't see these guys, particularly where they are from the city, attacking in the dark," April said.

"That's when the Mekong Devils were at our best. In the dark, when most of the enemy are afraid of the dark. We did our best work then. But as you said these guys will be from the city and probably without any military experience. They might be good street fighters, but when they come I think they'll have quite a surprise waiting for them."

After supper it was Lyle's turn to rest and April stood

watch. After Lyle was asleep she picked up the auto shotgun and walked back and forth in the camp.

The more she thought about their situation the angrier she became. Not so much that she knew they were going to be attacked, but that she had wasted this part of her life. When Pietro had found her, she was waiting tables. He came in and ordered an expensive meal and left a $100.00 bill for a tip. This impressed her and he had several drinks, until she was through work and later she had taken him back to her apartment. At the time he seemed like an alright guy who had plenty of money. Something April had never had too much of.

She was now hating herself for ever being taken in by Pietro. Tears were running down her cheeks. She looked at Lyle resting so peacefully and thought to herself, *I will not let them have you. Even if I must die.*

Then she could hear Lyle inside her head telling her that if none of this had ever happened, they would never have met. Lyle was always looking at things differently than most people and he could see the good even in this mess.

These thoughts helped to cheer her some and then she began thinking about their love making on the living room floor when the two had risen in consciousness together and their awareness had expanded. And remembering their love making then made her smile now.

In only a few short days she now understood how much her understanding and consciousness had traveled.

She waited until 11 pm before she awoke Lyle. "I made some hot coffee for you. I haven't heard anything unusual."

"I'll wait until you're asleep and then I'm going to take a look around outside. I won't be far away and I won't stay out long."

"Okay. I'm glad you said something about it. If I woke up and you were not here I would be worried."

She was tired, more so than she had thought. When she laid down, she was asleep before Lyle came back with his coffee.

He sat down and finished his coffee and then stood up and quietly went outside. A sliver of a moon was just coming over the south ledge wall. This little illumination would certainly aid anyone on foot. He just had a difficult time thinking these morons would be that astute.

He went down to the shore and standing in the shadows and scanned the cove. There was nothing out there. He listened for the sound of a motor boat. All was quiet except for tree frogs and crickets. He circled behind the camp to the path where lay the barbwire trap. All was quiet there also. He went back inside to watch over April.

* * *

On Tuesday before Tomas and Pedro made their flight over Driftwood Lake in Houlton, Maine the chief of police in Chihuahua, Mexico telephoned the Director of the FBI in Washington.

"Mr. Director, this is Chief of Police Hugo Emanual in Chihuahua, Mexico. One of our leading citizens has recently died and while I was going through some business reports I have discovered some very important information I believe your agency and the DEA will be extremely interested with. I was hoping you might send two agents here to review the information I have uncovered."

Hugo went on to briefly describe what he had discovered concerning the Flores Cartel. The FBI Director then telephoned Special Agent Henry Jones and told him, with the DEA Agent Hurley McRandall, to hop a flight to Chihuahua, Mexico as soon as possible.

At 6 pm that Tuesday evening Jones and McRandall were met by Chief of Police Hugo Emanual. They immediately drove out to the Flores coffee plantation.

"After I talked with your Director, Mr. Jones, I have found more information, which I believe you will be interested with Mr. McRandall. A list of the narcotic outlets in the United States. When Enrico Flores died everyone assumed his son Pietro would take control, but no one seems to know where he is. So the cartel has collapsed. The furniture business, the coffee plantation and the factory in El Paso where the coffee beans were ground and distributed, all has collapsed.

"I found equipment for forging their own passports and identification papers. Apparently Señor Flores was a master forger.

"I have everything I have found laid out on tables in the larger dining room. I have made reservations for you at the Roberto Fierro National Hotel. I will take you back now and in the morning I will provide you with a vehicle and driver."

Just like Chief Emanual had said, early the next morning a vehicle and driver, policeman, arrived at the hotel to take Jones and McRandall back to the plantation.

There was so much information to look through. They could photo documents and make notes, but Chief Emanual would not permit them to remove any documents.

They found many different passports supposedly issued for different countries and all to the same person with the same personal information. "This guy was a master at being able to move freely in any country," Jones said.

"We have always known drugs were being smuggled across the border and now we know how. The collapse of the Flores Cartel will slow the narcotic business for a while. That is until another cartel finds another way to smuggle large amounts of drugs. And we know where to go now in the U.S. and shut down the businesses that were part of the cartel. These documents really answer many questions we have had for a long time. Some of this we knew but never had any proof. Now we do."

Agent Jones was hoping to find some document that would link Enrico Flores back to Nazi Germany. But the closest that they found was a passport issued to Juan Esteban. Esteban's passport was stamped in leaving Spain, entering France and a day later entering Germany. There was nothing found to prove concretely that Juan Esteban was actually Hans Grubber. But there was enough circumstantial evidence that would suggest that when Hans Grubber's paper trail stopped in Germany, he had actually become Juan Esteban. And that this Juan Esteban had traveled with Admiral Wilhelm Canaris to Spain to talk with Francisco Franco just prior to the beginning of WWII.

There were documents how many guns had been smuggled across the border to Flores' furniture business in San Diego, but no name who received them, nor where the guns were distributed.

There were documents to connect Juan Philipe and Pietro Flores as the same person. But no marriage certificate that Pietro was ever married.

"This is all finally coming together Henry," McRandall said. "The cartel has collapsed and I'm not sure now if we can do anything about the traffickers along the Flores pipeline or not. But this is all good information."

"Have you heard anything from Sheriff Fye about Lyle Kingsley's plan to capture Philipe?" McRandall asked.

"Philipe or one of his lieutenants sent two gunmen after Lyle. He shot one in the stomach and the other one in the knee. He will need a prosthetic and the other one developed an infection in his stomach. They are both under guard in the local hospital and they both have lawyered up."

"From Sheriff Fye, he said Lyle is expecting another attack soon," Jones said.

They had been at the plantation all day without taking a break. "Are we done here, Henry? I have all the information I need."

"Yeah, I think we can wrap this up."

"This guy Enrico Flores was a clever bastard. Let's hope his son Pietro isn't as clever."

Chief Hugo Emanual joined them for supper that night.

"Did you find what you were hoping would be there?" Hugo asked.

"Mostly, we still have to put a lot of pieces together. What can you tell me about Enrico's daughter Avilla? She went to France but we couldn't find anything beyond that."

"I do not know. I know Señor Flores had a daughter that went to France and I think she stayed there for quite some time. When she returned to Chihuahua she did not stay for long. She and her brother Pietro seemed to have left about the same time."

"We would like to thank you, Chief Emanual, for notifying us about this and for the help you have given. Once we have transcribed our photos and if we discover anything you need to know I'll be in touch with you. Again I want to thank you."

* * *

At 3 am Thursday morning Lyle was needing some sleep so he knelt down by April's side and gently shook her shoulders until she started to moan. He kissed her and said, " I need some sleep, April. There's hot coffee on the stove."

"Okay," and she got up and only by the light of the moon she found a cup and poured some coffee. Lyle was already asleep. She took her coffee out on the porch and started pacing back forth. Listening with each footstep for any sound that was not supposed to be there.

At first daylight she began frying bacon, eggs, toast and a new pot of coffee. Lyle was awakened by the aroma. He went out on the porch to listen for any sounds. Particularly that of an approaching motor boat. Everything was quiet, except for the loon that saw Lyle on the porch and it started calling. Lyle cupped his hands and answered back. After a while, and tired of the game, the loon swam off.

They ate their breakfast on the porch and drank coffee until the pot was empty. When the next attack came Lyle was expecting it about this time in the morning.

"What are you thinking Lyle? You're so quiet."

"Just that when the next attack comes it will probably be early in the morning. About now."

"You are expecting them tomorrow morning aren't you?" she asked.

"Yes. And I think it'll come from both directions this time."

"Are you worried?"

"When you wait for an attack that you know is coming there is a lot that goes through your mind. You ask yourself, 'Have I done enough, will my plans work.' I have gone over a hundred times this scenario in my mind and I'm confident there is nothing more we can do but wait. And I'm confident our traps will work."

"Why don't you get some rest now? I'll stand watch and wake you at noon," he said.

* * *

Thursday morning Avilla drove to Ellsworth to a ladies shop on Main Street. During the ride over, she had a strong urge to keep driving. She could get out of the state even if Pietro couldn't. She'd take a jet from Boston to Paris, France using her old passport, Belle Saucier. But she had given her word to her father that she would look after her brother.

She found what she would need for makeup and she also found a dark brown wig that looked very similar to April's hair. She also bought a pant suit and a blouse for herself.

Back at the condo, "Come here, Pietro, let me put this wig on you so I can see how it looks."

He sat down in the chair. Avilla put the wig on him but did not secure it. She backed off looking at him. "You know I think with a little makeup we can transform you from a man to a woman. At least in appearance. Anywhere we go though, you'll have to let me do the talking. Yes siree, with a little makeup I think you'll look pretty good."

"I hope this plan of yours works. I'll feel awful silly dressed up like a woman."

* * *

After they had eaten Lyle said, "If you're still sleepy, go back to sleep. I'm alright."

"I would like a little more sleep. Maybe I'll lie down out here in the fresh air."

"Okay, I'm going to walk around and just double check on things again." He took his rifle with him just in case.

The two propane bottles were where they were supposed to be and the half buried one on shore was okay also. He then checked the blind to the left and set a few flat rocks on top to give him more cover.

At the barbwire trap he walked off the path to the sides to check the deadfall and trigger, and everything was okay. He checked the coils and they would be pulled across the road without catching on anything.

They had done everything they could. Now they had to wait. He went back inside the camp and made another pot of coffee, quietly. He didn't know what they would do if they ran out of coffee. He took his cup and went back out on the porch. He sat in the rocking chair sipping his coffee, keeping an eye on the cove and watching April sleeping peacefully.

As he watched April, he was not aware how much time was passing, until April stirred and opened her eyes. Lyle sat down beside her. "Hi."

She smiled at him and said, "Hi," back.

"Are you hungry? It's noon."

"I don't know. Let me get up and walk around and I'll see." She stood up and stretched. "Oh, I'll walk out to the outhouse. I have to pee."

Lyle went to the root cellar to get the fixings for making

ham and cheese sandwiches with tomatoes and lettuce.

Back inside the kitchen, "What are you making?"

"Sandwiches. We're going on a picnic."

"Okay."

"Can you get a bottle of wine from the cellar. My hands were full." Then he went out to the shed and brought back one of the larger fish baskets.

When April was back and saw the fish basket she looked questioningly at Lyle.

"Picnic basket."

"Oh, just where are we going?"

"I'd forgotten all about it before, but years ago my father built a wooden bench from cedar so it wouldn't rot as soon, on the point on top of the ledge wall on the left. It is not as high as the right side and there used to be a path leading to the top."

"You take the shotgun and wine." He put the binoculars around his neck and picked up his rifle and the fish basket.

Way over to the left of the grassy area and behind some bushes that had grown up was a path leading up to the top. The top was covered with a thick bed of moss and a scattering of jack pine trees. "It is beautiful up here, Lyle."

The bench was at the end of the point of the ledge and it was still intact. Weathered but still sturdy.

"There's a nice cool breeze up here." Lyle leaned the rifle and shotgun up against a tree and they both sat on the bench. April poured them each some wine and Lyle handed her a sandwich. All while they ate lunch they both kept scanning the lake for any boat traffic. There wasn't a single boat on the lake. "This is potato harvest time and everybody is probably busy in the potato fields."

They finished eating and April said, "I can tell you are sleepy, Lyle. I'll stand watch if you want to lay back and get some sleep."

"That's a good idea. This is apt to be a long night ahead of us."

"You think they'll come in the morning don't you?"

"Yes." He laid down on the thick moss and was soon asleep.

April was so happy to be there, regardless of the impending attack that Lyle was sure was coming in the morning. She was happy, but she was not letting her guard down. She kept scanning the lake from end to end with the binoculars.

She began walking back and forth along the top of the ledge wall. She sat on a rock buttress enjoying the beauty and peace in this little corner of the world. "Lyle's world and now mine too." Yes this was a tranquil place, but tomorrow for those who would be coming to kill them this peaceful place will turn into a blazing hell for them.

She let Lyle sleep as long as he needed. She knew he would be up most of the night on watch. Yes she was tired and sleepy, but now her whole world, her life was sleeping peacefully on the moss.

There were times, as she sat there watching Lyle, that she wanted to blame herself for bringing this trouble to him. Then she would remember what he had said 'There is a reason why everything has to happen,' then she would feel better. But this she knew, if it comes down to it she knew in her heart, that she'd give her life to protect him.

She looked at him again and smiled.

It was getting too dark to stay on the ledge any longer. She woke Lyle and said, "Come on Lyle, we'd better climb down off this rock while we still have a little light to see by."

"Why didn't you wake me sooner?" he asked.

"You needed your sleep. I figure you will probably be up all night."

They went slowly down off the ledge and by the time they were at the camp it was complete dark. The moon would be out a little later. April lit one kerosene lantern in the kitchen so she could make more sandwiches and a steaming pot of coffee.

* * *

Tomas and Pedro had the rented boat loaded with fishing equipment and four uzi machine pistols and extra clips already in the Ford sedan. Also rented. Tomas figured it would take about eight hours from Boston to Houlton. They left Boston at 10pm Thursday night. They would call Pietro from Bangor once the job was done, to pick up the rest of the rough diamonds.

Eduardo and Jorge slept most of the trip and Tomas and Pedro took turns driving. "Pedro, you and I are the only ones that have seen the layout of this cove, camp and lake. You take Eduardo and go along the path and I'll take Jorge in the boat for a frontal attack. If Pietro is correct they will not have any idea we'll be coming."

"This will be a piece of cake, Tomas," Pedro said.

"I sure would like to know what happened with the first two men I sent up. Emilio and Carlos. I haven't heard anything further than they were arrested," Tomas said.

"They did not call you from jail after they were arrested?" Pedro asked.

"I haven't heard a word. Anyhow when we flew over I didn't see anything much to worry about."

* * *

April stayed awake until midnight talking with Lyle. He was a quiet man, but she also found him so easy to talk with. "You'd better get some sleep now, sweetheart. I'll wake you long before daylight so we can have a little to eat and some hot coffee." There was no arguing. She stretched out on the couch. When Lyle was sure she was asleep he went outside and sat on the porch steps listening. There were the usual night sounds and a screech owl somewhere out back in the swamp. There were a few lightning bugs, most were gone now.

He started thinking about the future and not what was

coming in a few hours. As soon as this was over, he and April would marry, and buy several Hereford calves to start their beef herd. There was still enough of last year's hay left in the barn so he doubted if they would have to buy any . During the winter he figured he would selectively cut some of the huge pine and spruce trees.

He tried to figure out how much money he had. It will all depend when the will clears probate. The only thing that wasn't in his name already were his folks personal accounts. But even without that there was already over $155,000.00 in his account.

After a while he went back inside and poured himself another cup of hot black coffee. Then he went back on the porch steps. The trouble with drinking so much it made him have to pee often.

When his cup was empty he rested is rifle across his legs and scanned the cove with the binoculars. He could see a ripple almost to the mouth of the cove. It was too small to be of any threat. Probably a beaver or otter.

He walked down to the shore and walked out on the wharf and listened. Then he walked out to the path and stopped where the barbwire trigger crossed the path. The only sounds there were tree frogs. Satisfied he went back to the porch steps.

He checked on April and she was sleeping comfortably. Her hands were still clasped across her stomach.

Very quietly he started a fire in the wood cook stove and with the lantern he went out to the root cellar for some ham, bread and butter. He sliced off some ham and put that in a fry pan and he stood four slices of bread up in the stove stop toaster. And then he made another pot of coffee.

The smell of ham cooking made April wake up. "Is it time, Lyle?" no worry in her voice now.

"I thought we'd better eat something before they get here. The food will give us needed energy."

When the toast was done April buttered it and Lyle put a slice of ham on each plate and poured them some coffee.

It isn't easy to talk cheerfully when you wait for battle to begin. So they ate in silence. April broke the silence when she asked, "Is this how it was before each battle in Vietnam?"

"Actually, this is a cake walk. But yes, we were always quiet. Each of us going over and over in our heads what he had to do." He stood up then and went over behind April and hugged her, to reassure her "Everything will be okay sweetheart. As I think about it all now, I think I did those three tours to prepare me for this morning."

"You didn't eat very much, Lyle," April said.

"No, it isn't a good idea to eat too much when you know you are going into battle. But coffee will help us be more alert," and he filled their cups again. April had never drank so much coffee in her life.

The dishes were put in the sink to do later. And Lyle put wood in the stove. When April looked questioning at him he said, "Smoke in the chimney will give them the illusion that we are inside and not concentrating on our real positions."

April turned the lantern down and blew the flame out. It was almost breaking daylight.

* * *

As Lyle and April were finishing their breakfast Tomas and his crew were launching the boat off the trailer. "Don't forget the fish rods and tackle boxes." The 9mm uzis were in the tackle boxes out of sight from prying eyes. They boarded the boat and Jorge pushed them off. The lake surface was so calm it looked much like a mirror. Calm before the storm. The sun was rising fast, so Tomas navigated the boat to the point where the path began. Pedro and Eduardo got out with their uzi machine pistols. "I'll be glad when this is over, I'm hungry, Pedro," Eduardo said.

"Yes, me too."

"We should be at the camp about the same time you are. Don't wait for us if you get there first," Tomas said and turned the boat away from shore and pushed the throttle forward.

"Listen!" Lyle said, "Do you hear that?"

"Sounds like a boat."

"They're coming. I'll go out to the cellar with you until I see the boat at the mouth of the cove. Are you okay, April?"

"Yes, Lyle, I'll be okay."

They had gone over what to do so many times, there was no need to now. For some strange reason he knew he could rely on April and she would be okay. They lost the sound of the motorboat momentarily and then "There it is, sweetheart. I'm gone."

She took his hand and stopped him and then kissed him. "See ya when this is over."

"You bet."

Lyle hurried behind the camp down to his wood and stone blind.

April stepped into the root cellar and closed both doors behind her. Then she removed the piece of sod from the end giving her a small window to see the trap and to shoot through. "I knew I shouldn't have had that last cup of coffee, I need to pee now." That would have to wait.

Pedro and Eduardo stopped short of the trip wire. Pedro pointed to the smoke in the chimney and then to the outhouse. Eduardo understood.

Pedro's next step missed the first trip wire. He turned and leveled his gun at the outhouse and while pulling the trigger he hit the second trip wire just as Eduardo hit the first one releasing all of the coils of barbwire around them. Eduardo tripped and as he was falling he accidentally pulled the trigger. One shot hit Pedro in the back, one round went through the back kitchen door and one hit sod next to April's little window spraying dirt in her face. She was okay though.

The trap worked. She didn't know yet that Eduardo had shot his partner, but both of them were so entangled in barbwire and wouldn't be able to get out without help.

Just as Pedro was firing his gun, Tomas had cut the throttle and was now resting real close to the innermost propane tank. He and Jorge picked up their guns and began riddling the camp with bullets. Lyle shot Jorge in the shoulder knocking him overboard. Tomas turned his attention to Lyle and sprayed his blind with bullets. One bullet hit rock and Lyle was hit in the lower right arm by a piece of rock. Nothing bad. "This is enough of this foolishness." He sighted in on the propane tank and pulled the trigger.

There was a huge explosion and a fireball mushroom rose in the sky. The boat—well, the back end was almost totally blown away. Lyle could see Tomas lying face down in the lake.

Jorge was trying to swim away. Lyle ran over and hollered, "Hey you! Stop" When he didn't Lyle put a bullet in the water next to Jorge's face. "I said stop and come in!"

"Okay, okay mister! Don't shoot no more, I come in. Just don't shoot no more!"

Lyle hollered, "April! April are you okay?"

"Yes, are you?"

"Yes, I can't come up yet. I have a body to drag in."

He jumped in the water then and waded out to Tomas. He turned him over and saw a piece of fiberglass sticking out of his chest, but he was still alive. He dragged Tomas to shore all while watching the other guy.

"Come here and sit down next to your friend."

Tomas opened his eyes and looking around saw Lyle standing over him. "Who, who are you?" he was barely audible.

"You know who we are or you wouldn't be here."

"We never had a chance did we?"

"No you didn't. Who hired you?"

"Philipe—Philipe, he'll come after you." These were Tomas' last words as he died.

"What's your name?" he said to the wounded companion.

"Jorge."

Lyle ripped Tomas' t-shirt off and balled it up and said, "Hold this on the wound. It'll stop the bleeding."

While Lyle was finding a piece of rope in his boat to tie Jorge up April stepped out of the root cellar and walked close enough to look at the two men. They were still holding their guns.

"Throw your guns to the side of you." When they didn't move she said, "Now!"

Pedro started to bring his up to point at her and she let loose one shot in front of him and said, "Not a good idea. The next shot I take your head off."

"Okay lady, but I have a hard time moving."

"You'll manage. Now you in the back—"

Before she could finish Eduardo had brought his gun up and pointing it at April. But before he could pull the trigger she shot him in mid-section. He was dead.

"April, are you okay?" Lyle hollered.

"I am now. I have one dead and one alive."

When Lyle had Jorge tied securely, he said, "If you don't move around the bleeding will stop. Do I need to say more?"

"I understand, mister."

Lyle ran up to see April. "The one in back tripped and shot his friend in the back. Then he brought his gun up and pointed it at me. That's when I shot him. Now I have to go to the outhouse to pee," and she ran off.

"What's your name?"

"Pedro, are you going to get me out of this, mister?"

"In due time."

When April came back she saw blood dripping from Lyle's arm. "Lyle you're hurt. Let me see your arm."

"Oh, it ain't nothing, one of their bullets shattered one of the rocks and a chip hit me in the arm, I'll be okay, April. I'll have to telephone the Sheriff. There's one down by the wharf that's wounded. He's tied up, but you might want to check on him. This guy isn't going anywhere."

The dispatcher answered, "Sheriff Fye, please."

"Who may I say is calling?"

"Lyle Kingsley."

"Yes Sir, One moment."

"Hello, Sheriff Fye."

"Jim, Lyle. What is going on out there, Lyle? I've been taking complaints for a half hour now about a fiery mushroom cloud in the sky coming from Deep Cove."

"They attacked at daylight Jim. Going to need an M.E. and an EMT"

"Are you and April okay?"

"Yes, we're fine, Jim."

"Was one of them Philipe?"

"No, just four guys he hired. You'd better hurry."

"I think there's a warden plane in the area, I'll see if the pilot will fly an EMT in for you. Then I'll come with the M.E. and two deputies."

He hung up and went to the tool shed for a pair of wire cutters and a pair of gloves.

April was just coming back from checking on Jorge tied up near shore.

"While I cut away some of this barbwire you keep your shotgun pointed at Pedro here."

He began cutting and it was a lot of work. He had to be careful when he cut a strand that the other end didn't spring towards him. While he worked away April asked, "Which two of you flew over here in a plane?"

"Tomas and me. How is Tomas?"

"He's dead."

"Jorge?"

"Wounded, but he'll be okay."

"We were told you wouldn't have any guns. That you would be an easy target," Pedro said.

"What do you think now, Pedro?" April asked.

"I think I should have stayed in Boston."

Lyle came down to the last strand and before cutting it he said, "This is the last strand, Pedro. If you try anything April will shoot you. Do you understand this?"

"Yes, I saw what she did to Eduardo."

The wire was off Pedro now and Lyle ripped his shirt up so he could see the wound. "This is too close to your backbone, Pedro, for us to move you. The bleeding has stopped and the EMTs will be here soon." Just then a plane flew low overhead and dipped its wing.

"If you'll stay here April I'll go meet the plane."

"Sure."

Lyle watched as the plane touched down and taxied up to the wharf, or the pilot tried to before he saw the damaged boat. Lyle waded out and pulled the plane in on the sandy shore.

A deputy and two EMTs climbed out and the pilot. "Wow, what happened here?"

"This one was shot in the shoulder and that one," he pointed to Tomas, "caught a piece of fiberglass in his chest. Up behind the camp is another one, his partner shot him in the back."

One EMT went out back to look after Pedro and the other one tended Jorge with the shoulder wound.

The pilot, Gary Dumond, looked at Lyle and said, "Don't I know you? You're Lyle, or Sergeant Kingsley, if I'm not mistaken."

Lyle looked at Gary and now he recognized him. "Yes you flew us out of Cambodia a few times."

"You were with the Mekong Devils right?"

"Yes."

"What happened here?" Gary asked.

"These four were hired to shoot us."

"What happened to the boat?"

"They were spraying me with bullets so I shot a propane gas tank that I had set out there."

"Holy cow, that'll do it."

"There's another tank out there so be careful you don't hit it," and Lyle pointed.

The EMT untied Jorge and was cleaning his wound. "Deputy if you'll stay here with the EMT we'll go behind the camp."

When Gary saw April, a beautiful woman holding an automatic .12 gauge shotgun over the man in the barbwire trap, he was full of questions.

When Gary saw the barbwire he said, "A Mekong Devil's mouse trap. If I hadn't recognized you, Lyle, I would have recognized this and would have known you were part of the Devils."

"How is he?" Lyle asked, "We didn't dare move him when I saw the wound so close to the backbone."

"That was a good move. He'll be alright with some therapy. The bullet just missed his spine."

"Who shot this one!?" Gary asked.

April answered, "That one there. When he fell he pulled the trigger. He hit the camp, a near miss at me and him."

"Can he sit up to be flown out of here?" Gary asked.

"No, he'll have to lay on his stomach.

"Maybe we can rig something up in one of the boats."

"If you can't, I can take the back seat out and then you can lay him on the floor," Gary said. "If we do that I can only ferry him to the boat landing."

"Why don't we do that while we wait for the Sheriff," the deputy said. "I'll call dispatch and have an ambulance meet you at the boat landing."

Gary had the seat out and Pedro lying face down in the plane and one of the EMTs accompanied Gary to the landing.

The other EMT had Jorge patched up "And he is ready to transport anytime."

"Okay, we'll have to wait for the Sheriff."

It was another hour before Jim and the M.E. arrived. The medical examiner had to finish up another case.

"Deputy Watson."

"Yes Sir."

"You take this other injured man in the boat to the hospital. Call dispatch to send another deputy to guard him. Then come back here."

"Yes Sheriff."

The other EMT rode out with the deputy.

"Were any of the these four Philipe?" Jim asked.

"No. But this one, Tomas Hernando, said Philipe hired him to kill us. I know you have many questions. Maybe when Dr. Ryan is through we can all sit inside and we'll tell you everything."

"Yeah, this one is certainly dead," Dr. Ryan said, "It would be my guess this piece of fiberglass punctured his liver, lungs and diaphragm, causing him to ultimately bleed to death. You said there is another body, Sheriff?" Dr. Ryan asked.

"Yes, to the side of the camp. Follow me," Lyle said. April walked beside him.

Dr. Ryan took one look at Eduardo and said, "He died of a shotgun blast to his left side of his chest. Killing him instantly."

"Before we go inside, I want to start right here. Who shot this man?"

April spoke up, "I did Sheriff. When I told them both to throw their guns Pedro did. Eduardo brought his around and pointed it at me. I shot him fearing he was going to shoot me."

"Okay, I can buy that. Who shot Pedro in the back?"

"Eduardo did," again April answered. "When he tripped on the wire he pulled the trigger on his gun. One bullet hit Pedro, another into the kitchen back door and another towards me in the root cellar. The bullet kicked up some dirt into my face."

Jim took pictures of the barbwire trap. The root cellar where the bullet had hit and the kitchen door and the bullet lodged in a log in the living room. Jim dug that out and put it in an evidence envelope.

While April was busying making a pot of coffee, Lyle

told the Sheriff and Dr. Ryan what had happened there this morning. Being careful not to leave anything out.

When he had finished Dr. Ryan said, "Poor bastards never had a chance."

"As I understand it Philipe is still out there wanting you two dead. How much longer are you going to play it like this, Lyle?"

"Well, it's keeping innocent bystanders from being involved or shot. Philipe has lost six men now and he must think you are coming in on him. He'll get desperate and make a mistake. You've got to rattle his cage, Jim."

"And how do you suppose I do that? We don't know where he is," Jim said.

"You give the full story to the media. Make sure it is on every channel on this evening news. Make sure you identify Tomas Hernando from Boston who was hired by Philipe to kill us and before Tomas died he did a lot of talking. I guarantee this will unhinge him and he'll start making mistakes."

"I'd say his first mistake, Lyle, was coming after you. Damn! Lyle you two make a two man army. Excuse me, April, man and woman make an army." Then Dr. Ryan began to laugh.

"I take it Lyle that these booby traps of yours, you learned while a member of the Mekong Devils?"

"We used them both quite often."

Gary was landing out front again. "I hope he doesn't hit that other gas bottle. I told him about it."

Gary came and sat down with them and April poured him a cup of coffee. April was enjoying listening to the men talking and including her about what had happened here today.

"I've got something to say to you, Lyle, and all of you should probably hear it. By now I'm sure you know Lyle was a member of the Mekong Devils in Vietnam. But what none of you know, even Lyle, is that the Devils were the most feared unit in all of Southeast Asia. I've helicoptered them across the border into Cambodia and Laos and brought 'em back. I did this many times with other units and all of the other units would talk about the Mekong Devils. They all did three tours and the most serious injury, Russ Jones, was bitten by a damn big snake. No other unit in Southeast Asia can say that. I came back just before you, Lyle."

"Do you need help ferrying these bodies to the landing? I mean if you only have one boat coming back, you'll have to make two trips."

"That would help us, Gary."

"I'll ride over with Gary and we can put both bodies in my vehicle."

Both bodies were put into body bags and loaded into Gary's plane. "I'll have to come back for the seat."

As he was taxing out of the cove the deputy was returning with the boat. "Write this up Lyle and I'll get a news release for this evening news.

"You two take care of yourselves. Jesus, I'm glad you're on our side." As he walked down to his boat he was laughing, shaking his head and kept saying, "Jesus, Jesus, Jesus."

"I'd better go out and get that other bottle." He was still wet so he waded out with his clothes on and untied the rope and brought the propane bottle ashore. Then he picked up the one half buried in the sand.

"What are we going to do with the remains of that boat?" April asked.

"We'll have to get a set of come-alongs and winch it up on shore where we can burn it. The motor I think exploded with the gas bottle. I haven't seen it anywhere."

April put her arms around Lyle and began crying. They had been through so much. And it wasn't over yet, either. When she stopped crying she said, "When I shot that man, Lyle, I had no misgivings about taking his life. Does that make me a bad person?"

"No sweetheart. You did what you had to do to survive. If not him it would have been you. You did what you had to do. That does not make you a bad person."

Gary came back and Lyle helped him bolt the back seat in. "Thank you, Gary."

After Gary had left, April asked, "Do you think Pietro will still come after us?"

"Yes. Unless he can find a way to escape back to Mexico. And I don't think he can. You and I are the only witnesses against him and his cartel."

"So what do we do now?"

"If he does decide to come after us I don't think it will happen soon. He has lost six people that he has sent against us. He must be out of his mind by now and I would expect him to do something really stupid. And I think we must be prepared. But right now I have a window to fix in the kitchen door. But I have an idea. I don't think there'll be any threat from Pietro for a few days. We are both hungry and I think it would be good if we got away from here for a night."

"What are you suggesting?"

"We put on our best clothes and we go out to eat tonight and sleep at the farm tonight. Even if he was to come looking for us tonight he would never guess we'd be at the farm."

It was 4 pm before they left camp. All either one had had to eat all day was toast and a slice of ham. April now understood what Lyle had said about not going into battle on a full stomach. Her emotions were still on edge and she wanted to cry again but she would not let go.

They drove into Becky's Diner about 4:45pm. Ahead of most of the supper crowd. When Becky saw them come in she rushed over and hugged April and then Lyle. "Oh, I heard what went on at camp. I was so worried you two might have been hurt. What's going on, Lyle?" she said it all in one breath.

"It has to do with that drug related homicide."

They sat at Lyle's usual table, so they could see who was entering and no one could sit behind them.

"What would you two like to eat? The special for the day is pork roast?"

Lyle looked at April, "That sounds good to me."

"Make it two Becky. And Becky neither of us has eaten anything all day."

"Gotcha."

She came back a few minutes later with two heaping platters of roast pork, potato and gravy, beets and applesauce. "Wow!" April said, "If I eat all of this I'll look pregnant."

"That would look good on you too, Hon," Becky said.

"Do you mind if I turn the overhead TV on. It's almost time for the local news."

Becky saw Lyle and April look at each other and they both shrugged their shoulders. "Go ahead, Becky."

"Oh man, this pork is so good."

"It sure is and this gravy is homemade, not instant gravy from a foil package."

"Do you like to cook?" Lyle asked.

"Actually I'm a pretty good cook." Then she added, "I can prepare more than just a tuna fish salad."

"Well that was sure good."

The local news was on now.

"This is WAGM in Presque Isle and the saga of the drug related homicide continues in Houlton this morning. At sunrise four men hired by Juan Philipe, the shooter in the drug related homicide, to shoot and kill Lyle Kingsley and April Bianca—they failed. In fact, two are now dead and two remain in intensive care in the hospital. The leader of this gang, a Tomas Hernando from Boston, before he died told the authorities that they were hired by Juan Philipe to kill both subjects. Tomas also gave the authorities more information concerning Philipe. It would seem to this commentator that Philipe should not have come to Maine. Stay tuned to WAGM for more details as they unfold in this drug related homicide. From Sheriff Fye, Mr. Philipe, he wanted me to advise you. He will find you eventually."

Becky for the first time in her life was speechless. She just stood behind the counter looking at April and Lyle.

"Lyle, Hon, what are you into?" Becky asked.

"We can't tell you anymore, Becky, than what was just on the TV." Lyle said."

"This Philipe guy, he was up here, wasn't he?"

"Yeah."

"He's a real bad ass, isn't he?"

"Yes he is," April replied.

"Why does this guy want you dead, April?"

"I was with Lyle when the first two attacked."

"They couldn't kill me, Becky, and leave a witness," Lyle added.

"I suppose not."

"Not to change the subject, Becky, but I have asked Lyle to marry me and he said yes."

Becky jumped up all excited and talking a mile a minute. "I'm so happy for you both."

"Becky, would you stand up with me at the wedding?"

"Of course I will, sweetheart. See Lyle, I told you all you needed was a good woman."

"When is this going to happen?"

"Not until this is all over," Lyle said.

"I can't eat anymore, Lyle. I'll explode if I do."

"I can't finish mine either."

"Let's go home, Lyle. Take a hot bath and snuggle."

"I'll go for that."

* * *

"Damn Tomas!" Pietro yelled. "Why hasn't he called?"

"I don't know, Pietro, unless something went wrong. Do you suppose he took the diamonds without ever planning to complete the job?"

"It's possible, but he knew I'd come after him," Pietro said.

"Just how are you going to do that when you can't leave the house?"

"He wouldn't hire Pedro to fly him from Boston to Houlton to survey things unless he was going to do the job. I wish he'd call, damn it."

Avilla put some food on the table for supper and Pietro turned the TV on, and then sat back at the table. "Soup and sandwich, soup sandwiches, is that all you know how to fix?"

"If you don't like it, you fix something," she went into the living room and sat down. She was too apprehensive about not hearing from Tomas to eat anything.

All of a sudden Pietro started screaming and hollering and he threw the soup bowl against the cupboard. Avilla came running out. "What in hell is wrong with you now, Pietro? Have you finally gone crazy?"

He pointed to the TV and said, "Look! Look damn it! That son of a bitch killed Tomas and Eduardo and the other two are in the hospital!"

The same news broadcast was now on every local station throughout the state. Only in Aroostook County, their news came early.

Pietro was hysterical and Avilla had to slap his face several times to calm him down.

"How could he do that? We send four good men against him and he kills two and puts two more in the hospital. Who is this guy, Avilla? You knew him. What is he? What can we do now?"

He kept going on and on. Whenever he started to become hysterical again she would slap him, until he stopped his yelling and screaming. If she hadn't promised her father, she would leave him here.

Pietro was crying now, "What are we going to do, Avilla? All I want is to go home."

"I don't know, Pietro. We'll have to wait to see if there is anything else on the news in the morning. We may have to risk it and try leaving."

That night after Pietro had shut himself in his room. Avilla laid awake for a long time thinking about Lyle Kingsley and how to bring him down and get even with him.

She had stopped venting her anger towards April. It was now all about Lyle, ruining their life.

* * *

As the local news was broadcasting the update about the drug related homicide and the attack that morning on Lyle Kingsley and April Bianca, Sheriff Fye placed a call to FBI agent Henry Jones. "Special Agent Henry Jones, how can I help you?"

"Agent Jones, Sheriff Fye."

"Oh, hello Sheriff, I was just going to call you when my phone rang. What's up?"

"Philipe hired a crew of four to go after Lyle. Two are now in the hospital and two are dead. The leader of the group Tomas Hernando said Philipe had hired them."

Agent Jones let Sheriff Fye finish telling him about the attack before he advised the sheriff about what he had discovered.

"Sheriff, your boy may not have to worry about Philipe. The Chief of Police, Hugo Emanual from Chihuahua, Mexico called a few days ago that Enrico Flores had died and he had discovered many documents he thought the FBI and DEA would be interested in. Myself and McRandall flew down. Emanual would not let us remove any documents but we photographed everything and today our specialists finished transcribing everything.

"We didn't find concrete evidence that Enrico Flores was Hans Grubber, but we did find that he was smuggling guns across the border into San Diego to be given to Nazi sympathizers to attack the U.S. from within.

"Juan Philipe is actually Pietro Flores, son, and Belle Saucier is actually Avilla Flores, daughter. There were documents linking the Flores Cartel to homicides, a coffee grinding factory in El Paso, and a spider network for their narcotics."

"And listen to this. The family had equipment for forging fake passports. They all had many aliases. They could travel practically anywhere in the world using these forged passports. The Flores Cartel has collapsed totally and if Pietro or Avilla return to Mexico there are already warrants for their arrest. All airports have been notified to watch for Pietro and Avilla."

"Would you do me one favor Jones?"

"What's that?"

"Don't release this information to the news media until early tomorrow morning," Sheriff Fye asked.

"It is set to be released at 6 am tomorrow morning. Will that work?"

"That'll be fine and thank you."

Sheriff Fye hung the phone up. "Finally some good news," he said aloud.

His wife and kids were gone for the night and he was hungry so he went to Becky's Diner for supper. "Hello Jim. You just missed Lyle and April. They came out for the special."

"What is the special, Becky?"

"Roast pork."

"That sounds good."

While he ate his supper he kept thinking whether he should tell Lyle and April. By the time he had finished eating he decided to wait. It would be on the news come morning and he really didn't think Pietro would be a threat anytime soon. He would probably be more interested in trying to leave the country.

* * *

Lyle backed the pickup into the empty barn and closed the doors. He had turned the electric hot water heater off and it took some time now before there was any hot water.

When the water was ready April filled the tub and sat down at one end. "Lyle, this is big enough for two people. Come on and take a hot bath with me."

289

He got in the other end and sat down. "Wow, the water is hot."

"You'll get used to it."

They stretched out so they each were laying with their feet up on the edge of the tub. They stayed like that until the water was only luke warm. "I have to admit I feel better now. That hot water actually relaxed my muscles," Lyle said.

They were both tired after the long day and they went to bed.

The next morning they went back to the diner for breakfast. The house was practically empty of food. It was 7 am before they were up, and the diner was only about half full.

They sat at their usual table and Becky brought some coffee. The TV was on and the local commentator broke in.

"Excuse me for breaking in, but this news alert just came in. The Flores Cartel from Mexico has recently collapsed with the death of the founder Enrico Flores. His son Pietro Flores, also known as Juan Philipe, is wanted in connection with the drug related homicide that occurred earlier in Houlton, Maine. We will keep you informed as this story unfolds."

Everyone in the diner turned to look at Lyle and April.
"Everyone is looking at us, Lyle."
His only answer was, "It's a small town."

* * *

Avilla was preparing breakfast when the news report came on. She couldn't see or hear the TV but Pietro was watching it in the living room and he started screaming hysterically. Avilla dropped what she was doing literally and ran into the living room. "What is it, Pietro?"

"It's Papa, Avilla. He's dead! And our cartel has collapsed

and now the whole country knows my true identity!" He was sobbing now.

Avilla stood in the doorway staring at the TV. "Someone or some agency must have raided the plantation and found Papa's papers. There's no question now, Pietro, we must leave the country. Now while you are dressing up as a woman, I'll put a few things together."

After Pietro was dressed Avilla applied makeup to his face and put the wig on and secured it and brushed the hair. "You can't wear your own shoes, Pietro, wear a pair of mine." The one thing she had forgotten was a purse for Pietro. But it was too late for that now.

She finished dressing, filled her small traveling bag and went to Pietro's room. He was crying again and tears were washing the makeup off. She didn't know what she was going to do with him. In desperation she brought out her gun from her purse and shot her brother in the forehead.

She had what she needed and she left the condo. Outside the two old ladies had been walking towards their car when they heard the shot. And now they had turned around and were walking back to their own condo. Avilla saw the two women walking away, but there was no time to deal or worry about them. She got in her car and left. The two old ladies turned to watch her drive off. Then they went inside and called 911.

"911 dispatcher, what is your emergency?"

"My friend and I just heard a gunshot next door and then the woman drove off. There has been two women living there, but only one left."

"I'll send an officer right over."

Two Hancock deputies arrived twenty minutes later and the two old women were waiting for them at their car.

Betty explained they called 911 only a few minutes after hearing the gunshot. "We were standing right here deputy. Then we started to walk back to our condo and this woman came out of this one and got in her car and left. We only saw the other woman once. The two of them were leaning against their car kissing. We never saw a man here."

There was no answer when they knocked on the front door and it wasn't locked. They entered and one of them hollered, "Hello, Hancock Sheriff department! Anyone here!"

No answer. "Greg, in here. The body is still warm. She hasn't been dead for long."

The M.E. was called and it was an hour and a half before Dr. Haelow arrived.

"In here, Dr. Haelow."

"This isn't a woman, deputies. This is a wig," and he pulled it off. "He has been crying also. Look how the makeup started to run with the tears."

Greg found the sales agreement and recognized the buyer's name.

"Holy shit! You know who we have here Bill?"

"No idea."

"This is Philipe, wanted for murder in Houlton. His real name is Pietro Flores of the Flores Cartel in Mexico. He has been all over the news. I'd better call Sheriff Fye in Houlton."

"Aroostook County Sheriff Department."

"I'd like to speak with Sheriff Fye. This is Deputy Sheriff Greg Hanscomb."

"Sheriff Fye here."

"Sheriff this is Deputy Greg Hanscomb. I'm at the scene of a homicide that occurred only two hours ago. We have found the sales agreement papers and this guy is your Philipe or Pietro Flores. He was shot by a woman who left."

"Well I'll be damned," Jim said. "I didn't think it would end like this."

Deputy Hanscomb told Sheriff Fye everything he could about the scene. "I'll have to bring a witness down to identify the body. Where will it be?"

"It'll be at the County Morgue in Ellsworth. Dr. Haelow said it will be there for five days."

"Thank you, Deputy. You have made my day. I'll be in touch."

Jim wrote on the office blackboard. Philipe a.k.a Pietro Flores is dead.

Jim left his office, and drove up to see Lyle at the farm. Lyle's truck was sitting in the driveway.

April and Lyle were on the porch. "You're just in time for a cup of coffee, Jim," April said and went inside for a cup.

"That was some revelation about the Flores Cartel and the old man wasn't it?" Jim said.

April came back and handed Jim a hot cup. "What brings you out here on a Saturday, Jim" April asked.

"You don't have to worry about Pietro anymore," and he took a sip of coffee.

Lyle and April waiting patiently for Jim to explain. "This morning two Hancock deputies responded to a gunshot heard in a condo in Bar Harbor. Seems as though two old ladies were getting into their car and heard a shot and reported it. They also saw one woman drive off. When the deputies entered the condo they found Pietro Flores shot in the head. He was dressed up like a woman." Jim could hear both Lyle and April breathe a sigh of relief.

"These two old ladies said they had never seen a man there, only two women who they saw kissing each other one day leaning against their car." April choked on her coffee and spit some up.

"Excuse me, coffee went down the wrong way."

"Are you okay April?" Lyle asked.

She coughed a couple of times and said, "I'll be fine."

"So that's the end of your threat. The end of the Flores Cartel. Can you drive to Ellsworth with me Monday morning to identify the body?" Jim asked.

"Yeah, I can ride down with you."

"Me too, Jim. I'm not leaving his side," April insisted.

"Belle shot her own brother. I just don't understand it," Lyle said.

"Avilla shot her brother," Jim corrected. "I don't know

293

what was going on inside that condo, but it looks like the two of them had lost any hold on reality. Be at my office at 6 am Monday morning, okay?"

"Okay."

"Now you wouldn't believe the amount of paperwork I have to do on this case."

"Ah, Jim, one more thing, April and I are getting married next Wednesday, and I'd like you to stand up with me."

"I'd be happy to. Oh, I have one more thing also. Have you given any thought about what you are going to do for work, now that you sold off your dairy herd?"

"April and I talked about raising beef cattle and selective cutting the woodland."

"Oh."

"What's on your mind, Jim?"

"Have you ever thought about becoming a deputy sheriff? You would still have time for your beef cattle. Hell, it wouldn't be long before you'd have my job. Think about it. I'm hiring three new deputies next February and sending them to the academy."

"I'll think on it, Jim. It would be a good job alright and we wouldn't have to move."

"What about you, April?" Jim asked.

"I would like to go back to school. I would like to be a nurse."

"We have a college right here in Houlton. The Ricker College."

"I'll look into it, Jim. Thanks."

Jim left.

"I don't believe he'll have any questions for you now. I think he has all the answers he needs. And it'll only be a matter of time before the authorities locate Avilla."

* * *

Avilla had no remorse about shooting her brother. He had

lost all control and composure. He had caused all these problems and he couldn't or wouldn't take responsibility for it. He had let Lyle Kingsley outwit him. He toyed with him driving him crazy. And she didn't know if April had decided to turn against them before Pietro had slapped her or not. But when she left, that helped to push him over the edge.

As she drove south on I-95 there were no tears for Pietro. Only for her father who died by himself.

She had to keep reminding herself not to speed and draw attention. If only she could get to Logan Airport in Boston all would fall in step then; she was once again Belle Saucier from Paris and Belle Saucier she would remain for the rest of her life.

The more distance she was putting behind her the safer she began to feel. She had stopped thinking about Lyle, April, her father and having just killed her brother. She could only think about herself. And how she was going to get herself out of this. "I should have just left days ago. I would have, damn it, if Papa had not asked me to look after Pietro." Well, Pietro and her father were gone. She was alive and she would do whatever was necessary to survive. Everything now was about her.

As Belle Saucier, she knew she could pick up her life in Paris. She felt safe as she closed in on the Maine-New Hampshire border. No one was looking for a white Mercedes with Massachusetts plates.

When she stopped at the Kittery toll booth she handed the money to the attendant without looking directly at her. She would soon be in Boston. The anxiety of the last few weeks was gone now and she was feeling relaxed and hungry. But she would wait to eat once she was onboard the jet.

As she pulled into an empty parking slot at the airport she breathed a sigh of relief. But before leaving the car she made sure no one was watching and she wiped down the interior of her fingerprints. The vehicle was rented under the name of Juan Philipe so there shouldn't be any way the authorities here could connect it with her. Not for a few days at least.

She removed her small gun from her purse to her light jacket pocket and put all of the cash she had taken from the condo into her purse. She took a deep breath and exhaled, got out, put the keys on the seat, locked and closed the door.

She went directly to Air France, "I'd like a first class seat, please, on your next departure for Paris."

"You are in luck today, first class is only half booked. Departure will be in twenty minutes."

When Avilla handed the attendant her passport and cash for the ticket, the attendant thought the passport looked a little off. Without saying a word she pressed an airport security alert button and finished making out the boarding pass and ticket. "Have a nice flight, Miss Saucier."

"Thank you."

Avilla headed for C-4, the departure exit for Air France. Five minutes later two security police arrived at the ticket attendant's desk. "A woman using the name Belle Saucier has a passport that I don't think is real. I think it is a false passport." She gave the two officers a description of Belle Saucier. "She went straight to the departure area in C-4."

"Thank you."

"They will be boarding in only a few minutes."

No sooner had Avilla sat down and she saw two security officers walking towards her. They walked straight towards her. Avilla knew her entire world was beginning to crumble now.

"Miss, there seems to be a question with your passport. May we examine it?"

Avilla stood up and reached into her purse and handed her passport to one of the officers. Her heart rate was off the scale and she could feel blood draining from her face. She was thinking, *How in hell did they find me so quick?* If arrested, she would be charged with murder and when her background was investigated her entire past would be revealed. She had decided in that moment that she was not going to let the officers arrest her.

When the officer took her passport she put her hand into her jacket pocket and gripped the gun.

"Miss Saucier, there seems to be a problem with your passport. You will have to come with us." The other officer who was watching Avilla's facial expression change had his hand on his gun. Avilla pulled her gun out and before she could even point it at the officer standing directly in front of her the other officer shot her in the chest. People everywhere were screaming and running out of the departure area.

Avilla was dead before she hit the floor.

* * *

"April, are you hungry?"

"I could eat; what are you thinking?"

"Let's go eat at the diner then go shopping at the IGA to restock the house."

"Okay, but before we leave, there is something I must do."

"What is that?" Lyle asked.

"You wait here and I'll be right back." April disappeared in their bedroom and came out with a handful of $100.00 bills. "I don't feel right keeping this and I don't know what to do with it. When I decided to leave Pietro I took this money. Now considering where it came from, I would rather not keep it."

"Just a minute; I'll be right back," he disappeared and came back and gave April a small pouch. She opened the pouch and poured the uncut diamonds in her hand. She looked at Lyle with a questioning look.

"I have always felt guilty of keeping these. When I returned from my last mission, Belle had already left. No note or word of any kind; only these. And like the money I don't know what to do with them."

"We could give an anonymous donation to some local charity," April suggested.

"That would work. There's a Goodwill food kitchen that

297

helps to feed the needy."

"Let's do it. We can put them both in a small package and mail it. Do you have any stamps here, so we wouldn't have to go to the post office?"

"I'll check." In the top drawer of his father's desk were two rolls of stamps.

"What about a small box?"

"That would be upstairs. My mother never threw away an empty box if she thought she might need it someday."

Upstairs in his mother's sewing room they found just what they were looking for, a small stationery box.

Before they wrapped the box in brown paper, April very carefully wiped all of the fingerprints off. Lyle put $3.00 worth of stamps on it

"Your mother must have some white gloves. They probably would be in the bureau she used."

By now Lyle understood the reason for the gloves. "Are we ready?"

"I think so."

On the way to the postal box April asked, "How much do you think the diamonds are worth?"

"I wouldn't dare to guess; maybe between $10,000.00 and $30,000.00. How much cash was there?"

"I never counted it, but I'd say $2,000.00 to $3,000.00. This will buy a lot of food."

They didn't have to drive into the business section of town before they found a drop off box.

"Now I'm hungry," April said.

While they were eating Jim Fye came in and sat down at their table. "Becky," he said.

"What?"

"Would you turn the TV on please?"

"Okay."

"Before I forget it I won't be able to leave Monday until 10 am."

"That'll be okay, "Lyle said. "What's this with the TV, Jim?"

"It's coming on now. I thought you might appreciate hearing this. Here it comes now." April and Lyle just looked at each other.

"This is WAGM news with a special broadcast concerning the saga of the Houlton drug-related murder. The woman who was seen leaving the condo in Bar Harbor shortly after the two women reported hearing a gunshot has been shot by Logan International Airport Security Police Officers. Apparently there was a problem with her passport and when the officers asked to see it, she pulled out a handgun and leveled it at the officers. One officer shot her in the chest. Her passport was issued to Belle Saucier. But the police officers said it was a good forgery. In her purse was another passport issued to Avilla Flores with the same date of birth and physical description. The death of Avilla Flores is the last of the Flores family and the Flores Cartel."

"So that ends it. There are questions about Saigon that I know will never be answered," Lyle said.

"She was about ten minutes from boarding an Air France jet for Paris. She was trying to skip the country."

"Everything wrapped up in a neat package. You know the only people who were injured or killed were those involved with the Flores Cartel.

Becky broke in, "Looking forward to Wednesday."

"Ah, we had to move it to Thursday at 11 am. The minister had to be out of town on Wednesday," April said.

"Jim, Becky is standing up with April. Becky, Jim is with me. This is going to be at the farm," Lyle said.

"See you at 10 am Monday morning," Jim said.

After Jim left, April said, "Now it is all over and I feel safe." Lyle didn't say anything. He just hugged her.

* * *

They got up later than usual Sunday morning and then they went back to the camp to clean up the mess around the camp. He also brought along a come-along and enough chain to wench the damaged boat up on shore. "What will we do with this now?" April asked.

"This winter sometime we'll come up ice fishing and we'll burn it on the ice."

The evenings were turning seasonally cooler and at sunset they had to move from the porch inside.

That night they snuggled close together all night. The next morning at 10 am they were at Jim's office. "You ready?" he asked.

"Let's go."

As they were crossing the bridge over the Penobscot River in Medway Jim said, "Oh, I almost forgot. The damnedest thing happened this morning. I received a phone call from the Goodwill Food Kitchen on Bangor Street. Someone had sent them a large donation," he left it at that for the moment.

"That's good," April said, "helping to feed those who need it."

"What's so strange, it was an anonymous donation."

"What's so strange with that, Jim?"

"It was the amount."

"Okay," that's all April said.

"Yeah, there was $2,800.00 in one hundred dollar bills, and probably $50,000.00 in uncut diamonds."

"Holy cow, Jim, are you serious?"

"Sure am. That will feed a lot of people. "

If it hadn't been for the uncut diamonds Sheriff Fye would not have suspected these two at all. But neither one had let slip that they knew anything about it. He also suspected that somehow these two knew more about this whole fracas than either one was letting on. Not that they were involved or protecting someone, but he suspected they each knew something. But for all intents and purposes the case would be officially closed, the moment Lyle identified the body. He grinned to himself, and thinking he sure would like to know the rest of the story.

"The weather forecast this morning was predicting snow squalls tonight after midnight."

"Snow!" April said. "Already? The leaves are still green. We went swimming last week."

"It probably won't amount to anything. The ground is still too warm," Jim assured her.

"I think tomorrow we'll go shopping. You need a whole wardrobe and a car. With all we have to do I'm glad the minister couldn't marry us until Thursday."

"Remember Lyle, nothing happens by coincidence. You told me that," April said.

At 1 pm they drove into the parking lot at the Hancock County Morgue. "We've been expecting you, Sheriff Fye. Follow me."

Downstairs and at the end of a long corridor they found the morgue and Dr. Haelow, M.E.

"You must be Sheriff Fye. Come in. I'll pull out the body."

Lyle took April's hand in his. Haelow pulled the roller tray out and pulled the plastic covering back. Lyle moved closer for a look.

April squeezed his hand. "That's Philipe, alright, or Pietro Flores. He looks so different than that day when he shot Newcomb. He had a measly looking goatee then, but there's no doubt who he is."

"He might look a little different because he had makeup on before he started crying and the tears washed through some of it. Are you absolutely sure?"

"Yes, absolutely."

"Good, I'll need your signature on this form. And yours also, Sheriff Fye."

Back in the cruiser and heading home Lyle said, "I don't know if I'd recognize him dressed like a woman."

"I'm hungry," April said.

"If you can wait until we're back in Bangor, I'll treat you to a dinner at the Governor's Restaurant. Call it an early wedding gift."

* * *

A wardrobe for April was purchased: so, too, were wedding rings and a diamond. And she cried when Lyle slid it on her finger. April liked the looks of the Ford Mustang, but decided her owning a sports car would not be very practical in the winter. So she settled for a Ford XLT Bronco, red and silver like the pickup truck.

Everyone arrived early at the farm for the wedding. Becky and her husband Fred, Jim and his wife Selena and even the minister, Ralph Jones, was early. Becky cried all during the ceremony. As everyone was leaving Jim shook Lyle's hand and said, "Someday I'd like to hear the rest of the story. Congratulations to you both."

"Thank you for coming, Jim."

"Think about becoming a deputy?"

"I will."

It was an Indian summer day and Lyle said, "I would like you to walk with me, sweetheart, to the top of the knoll where I spread my Mom and Dad's ashes."

"I would love to."

They followed the road through the fields to the apple trees on the knoll. The second growth grass was so green it looked like velvet carpeting. "I know my folks are not here in their physical bodies, but I know they are in spirit. This was their most favorite place on the entire farm for them both. When we were kids, my sister and I built this seat for them." And they sat down.

He took April's hand in his and said, "Mom and Dad, I'd like you to meet April. My wife."

"Hello, Mom and Dad," April said. Just then wind rattled the tops of the apple trees and then it was gone.

"I think they heard us, my husband.

"Pinch me, Lyle."

"Why?"

"Because I want to know that this is all real and that I won't just wake up from a happy dream."

"OUCH!"

About the Author

Randall Probert lived and was raised in Strong, a small town in the western mountains of Maine. Six months after graduating from high school, he left the small town behind for Baltimore, Maryland, and a Marine Engineering school, situated downtown near what was then called "The Block". Because of bad weather, the flight from Portland to New York was canceled and this made him late for the connecting flight to Baltimore. A young kid, alone, from the backwoods of Maine, finally found his way to Washington, D.C., and boarded a bus from there to Baltimore. After leaving the Merchant Marines, he went to an aviation school in Lexington, Massachusetts.

During his interview for Maine Game Warden, he was asked, "You have gone from the high seas to the air. . .are you sure you want to be a game warden?"

Mr. Probert retired from Warden Service in 1997 and started writing historical novels about the history in the areas where he patrolled as a game warden, with his own experiences as a game warden as those of the wardens in his books. Mr. Probert has since expanded his purview and has written two science fiction books, *Paradigm* and *Paradigm II*, and has written two mystical adventures, *An Esoteric Journey*, and *Ekani's Journey*.